CRUISE CONTROL

Aidan de Vries

CRUISE CONTROL

Erser & Pond

Cover design by Doug Porter

Printed in Canada by Erser & Pond Publishers, Ltd.
1096 Queen St., Suite 225, Halifax, N.S., Canada B3H 2R9

Library and Archives Canada Cataloguing in Publication

De Vries, Aidan
    Cruise control / Aidan de Vries.

ISBN 978-0-9781761-1-2

    I. Title.

PS8607.E975C78 2006   C813'.6   C2006-905926-8

10 9 8 7 6 5 4 3 2

This book is dedicated to my wife and children,
and to their children down through the ages.
May they appreciate their blessings always,
and may they continue to flourish
in the land of the free.

If you're not a liberal when you're young,
you have no heart.
If you're not a conservative when you're old,
you have no brain.

attributed to Winston Churchill

CHAPTER ONE

C aptain Nikolas Constantine had just received notification from his employer, the *Neptune Cruise Line*, that he had been selected to command the largest ship in the fleet. The news had come directly from the fleet captain, so there was no question of its authenticity. The new ship was due to be launched in three months, and sea trials were scheduled to begin in France as soon as possible after the launching ceremony.

Constantine had been at sea for thirty years, but had only commanded cruise ships for twelve of those years. There were other captains employed by the same company who had more seniority than he did. Several of them were at least as qualified as Captain Niko, as everyone called him, but the deciding factor in choosing who was to command the new vessel had little to do with management competency or seamanship. Every one of the candidates for this command were able, but Niko was chosen because he was the most affable. He could be counted upon to come up with a *bon mot* at the appropriate times. What's more, the passengers adored him. When his deep, cheery voice spoke English over the ship's loudspeaker system, the passengers were amused by his accent and comforted by his relaxed tone.

The decision to put Captain Niko at the helm was really a no-brainer. Although the ship that was nearing completion was the largest ever constructed and the most expensive to build, there was little difference between the new vessel and her smaller sisters in the way they handled. Adding another 150 feet in length and ten feet more draft did not change the basics involved in maneuvering a huge ship through the seas of the world and into its ports.

Members of an expanding middle class were vacationing on cruise ships more than ever, and cruise lines were competing fiercely with one another to attract the growing number of passengers. Part of the challenge for the Neptune Line was to get new business. That was up to the sales and promotion people. The most profitable part of the cruise business, however, was the repeat customers. If the passengers could be kept happy, they would faithfully return for additional cruises. Pleasing an existing customer is a better business tactic than finding a new one, because it costs less to keep a customer than to replace one. Captain Niko's performance was unparalleled in this respect. His statistics for repeat cruising customers were far and away the best of all the company's ship captains. He had a following, and people actually would request a cabin on his ship, sometimes without regard to the cruise destination. Putting an additional 500 guests aboard Niko's ship for each cruise would go a long way to pay for the new vessel.

The captain of a cruise ship is something of a celebrity. It is an honor to sit at his dinner table, and Niko's table was always a hot ticket item. Those who made the cut and ate at the captain's table were regaled with humorous sea stories and the occasional racy tidbit from his seafaring experiences. Naturally the majority of guests at his table came from the upper deck cabin suites – the luxurious and expensive ones. Niko was doing his duty by coddling the passengers who had paid heavily for the elegant quarters they occupied. In his heart he didn't really prefer the company of the rich and famous, but he knew how to handle them. To the extent that his schedule permitted, he could be found all over the ship participating in the activities. He usually worked out in the gym and swam in the pool when the ship was in port and most of the passengers were ashore, and occasionally he attended the movies and live entertainment performances.

Passengers anywhere on the cruise ship could encounter the peripatetic Captain Niko, night or day, fore or aft. He seemed to be everywhere at once, always greeting his customers with a big smile and a hearty hello. He would gladly pose with anyone who asked. He often claimed that his photograph was in more family photo albums than anyone except Mickey Mouse.

He lived exclusively aboard his ship ever since his divorce fifteen years before. His Greek wife had detested the long separations when he was at sea, but she hadn't liked it much better when he was ashore. Now, with her divorce settlement and the support she received for the children, she was able to live quite comfortably in Athens without having to work. The two children were now teenagers and took after their mother in the ambivalent attitude they showed to Niko. They accepted the financial benefits that accrued from having a father with a comfortable income, but they rejected the notion that they owed him any filial obligation of a personal sort. It amazed him how much more disrespect he accepted from his ungrateful children than he would take from any of his crew members.

The truth was that he received no disrespect from his crew, nor would he have stood for any had it been offered. He came from the old school of seamanship that accorded the captain sovereignty aboard the ship. Captain Constantine thought of the ship as his own, in the same way that his namesake, Constantine the Great, regarded Rome as his domain. Within the rigid hierarchy of command, he displayed admirable equanimity, and he was well liked by those who served under him. His bridge officers were collegial, his engineering staff was cooperative, his cadets were appreciative of his experience, and his food, entertainment, and housekeeping staff performed admirably under their supervisors, who ultimately reported to him.

As soon as the announcement of his new appointment was publicly released, there would be considerable staff shuffling. He would recommend Giorgio, his first officer, to take over command of their present ship, but the final decision would come from the head office. Niko hoped that Giorgio, in fact, would *not* be selected to be the captain of the old ship. He would love to have him continue to be his first officer on the new ship. As seamen from Mediterranean countries, their souls were similar in character. Both men had good senses of humor. Both were committed to their careers at sea. Giorgio's Italian wife, however, had stuck it out with him, and they had reached a détente that passed as a good marriage under the circumstances. Niko was more ebullient, but Giorgio was not far behind. He was a highly qualified seaman and he deserved to be a captain, and that caused mixed emotions on Niko's part.

Niko was 49 years old, six feet tall, and had a full head of steel grey hair. He had worked hard to keep the fat off, and with the constant availability of shipboard cooking, that was no small accomplishment. He owned practically no clothes other than his uniforms, but when he walked about his ship he was the best-dressed man aboard. His tailored, open-necked white shirts had shoulder boards emblazoned with four golden stripes, revealing his Captain's rank. His dark navy or black trousers were always perfectly pressed, and his immaculate black shoes were also tended to by his cabin steward. His dress uniform was elegant, and outshone even the most tailored tuxedos present at the formal affairs. He was the living image of the perfect cruise ship captain.

Niko liked life in general, but he especially loved his life at sea. He was born to command, so the enormous responsibilities of a huge vessel of great value and the lives of nearly 3,000 passengers and crew rested easily upon him. He was saving money to buy a small house in the port of Piraeus when he retired. He planned to watch the busy port traffic come and go from his terrace while he drank ouzo or coffee. His new job would tax him a little until he got used to it, but he didn't worry about such things. He would receive a generous salary increase and other benefits to compensate him for whatever additional duties came along with his new command, and it would assure the fulfillment of his retirement dream.

One day, a couple of years before, Niko had decided to have his meal in his quarters. A Chilean waitress who worked aboard the ship delivered his tray. Her name was Mercedes. She was a small, shapely woman with dark eyes and black, luxuriant hair. She was twenty-five and really quite beautiful. Niko, engaging as always, had begun talking to her as he ate. One thing led to another, and Mercedes stayed with him until it was time for her shift to begin in the morning. She supported a husband and a young son who lived in an Andean village in Chile. Niko never asked her personal questions about her situation, and she never volunteered any information about her life ashore. They had fun together, laughed, and had sex. They learned to meet each other's needs, but there was no serious talk about their relationship.

Occasionally he would ask her to visit his cabin. She would never refuse, and never once indicated that she was jealous. She never asked when they would meet again or made any demands of him. The sign-up list to have a mistress like this would be long indeed. As far as he could tell she seemed to enjoy being with him, but she certainly was behaving outside the norms of his considerable experience with women.

There seems to be something particularly attractive to women about men in uniform, especially high-ranking officers. Perhaps it's because his importance is immediately recognizable by the stars, stripes, and chevrons that clearly mark a uniformed man's position among his fellow men. Successful civilian men don't have such clearly marked signs of importance. To identify a powerful man in business or politics, a woman has to find out something about his circumstances, and that can take time. Wealth and possessions are not obvious on a cruise ship, so the captain is the unrivalled alpha bull in attendance. A captain who is unmarried has an additional advantage, of course, when it comes to the women in his orbit. When Nikolas Constantine acquired his fourth stripe, he became all but irresistible to certain female passengers. His position and his uniform, combined with the sexually liberating effect that cruises seem to have on many passengers, turned him into an unexpected buccaneer of the bedroom.

Naturally the cruise line frowned on fraternization with the passengers. Nevertheless, occasionally things did happen, but a blind eye was turned on these peccadilloes as long as standards of propriety were not entirely ignored. As could be expected, young people who were working far away from home for extended periods of time violated many marital promises.

Niko's crew was composed of people from fifty-three nations. The bubbling hormonal stew of some 700 crew members, mostly people in their twenties and thirties, was a formidable problem. The crew was a veritable United Nations, but under his command the cohesive results achieved were far better than the UN's.

Niko had personally refused an incredible number of sexual overtures. He did not respect the women who made aggressive attempts to catch his attention by the use of crass language or inappropriate touching. He had had to develop several rejection techniques that he hoped were not too damaging to female psyches. Mostly he kept things on a humorous and light-hearted level when interfacing with the opposite sex. Occasionally he would succumb when he was in the mood or came across a woman who was particularly attractive to him, but never until he had done some background checking in the purser's passenger files. He was not about to engage in any messy entanglements with irate, jealous male companions. Nor was he willing to risk his job for the sake of a fling. If Niko knew that a woman of interest to him was traveling alone or with a female friend, he might consent to a one night stand as long as it was understood that there could be no chance that it would lead to anything more.

Captain Constantine was amazed at how many candidates accepted his terms. In fact, on most cruises he could have had a different woman, mostly Americans, in his cabin every night. Now that he was approaching 50 he couldn't help wondering where the plethora of willing women had been hiding during his 20s. When he was a poor cadet on merchant ships, things had been very different. Even when he was a junior officer aboard cruise liners, his services were not in such high demand. The ironies of life were abundantly clear to Niko. Now that he was a very experienced lover his sexual capacity was declining. He was still functioning well, but his libido had fallen far from what it was when he was 20. These days he had to ration his amorous encounters.

In the cruise ship business Niko had learned how to provide the services that please the vacationing customers. In his middle age he had also learned how to provide satisfaction to the women of his choice. He chuckled to himself about how he had become a one-man service industry. He loved the female body, though he seldom loved the women who inhabited them. He devoted himself to the pleasure of his companions, only satisfying himself at an appropriate time after he was sure his guest would go away happy. One of the compensations of growing older was the concomitant growth of his patience quotient. His lady friends tended to be much younger than he was. For them he was to be their first captain, but they were not to be his first young women. The advantages were all his, and though the game got a bit tiresome at times, he had to admit that it was mostly very pleasant.

Captain Niko was popular with the male passengers as well. He would gladly repeat the facts about the ship to the "guys" who asked questions.

"How fast is the boat going?"

"Sir, the ship is making 22 knots, which is cruising speed for this *ship*." The emphasis on the word "ship" was to differentiate it from the lifeboats that hung from their davits amidships.

"How much fuel does the ship consume?"

"The ship consumes 1,000 tons per hour of very expensive fuel at cruising speed, which is why cruises cost so much."

"How do we manage to carry enough water to supply the needs of so many people?"

"We start every cruise with full tanks that we fill at our port of embarkation. From that point on we make our own water, using two desalinization plants that convert seawater into very good quality potable water. These two systems produce 1,000 gallons of drinking water per hour, 24/7."

One of the statistics that always provided a hush was that the fee for this vessel to transit the Panama Canal is U.S. $267,000, paid for by the captain before transiting the canal.

Niko always added a comment about how this would make the passengers feel better about paying highway tolls.

Captain Niko had had four uninterrupted years of cruising with no major problems, and life was sweet. It should be said that he was not just an entertaining, make-believe captain. When it came time to lay his ship against a dock, he was as clever as the best captain anywhere at sea. Some men would have a heart attack if they had to command a docking exercise that includes the elements of wind, current, engine and thruster speeds, timing, orders to the crew, and a host of technical details too numerous to mention. He knew that it was at times like those that he was really earning his money.

The smell of roasted lamb permeated the cave. The men sitting around the fire spoke Arabic with a guttural inflection in their deep voices. The leader, a tall man with a full pepper-and-salt beard, was telling the others that Allah had not given them an easy task.

"If Allah had wanted us to accomplish small victories, he would have made the enemy weak. But the Almighty One sees fit to challenge us to defeat a great enemy – America, the right arm of Satan. Our victory on Allah's behalf will bring down the devil, and raise the only God, Allah, to his proper place on earth. Allah is eternal. His measurement of the sands of time is different than ours. Our victory may seem a long time in coming, but in his reckoning of time it is as the blinking of an eye. Therefore, brothers of the one true faith, we must be patient. We must plan far ahead. We must heed the word of Allah as it is recorded in the Qur'an by the Prophet Muhammad, peace be unto him, and death to all infidels."

His words were an introduction to a planning meeting being held by the leaders of a group of militant Islamist warriors known as the *Scythe of Allah*. The leader, who called himself Ali Bin Yemeni, was wearing the traditional floor-length aba, as were the six others seated on cushions in front of him.

Ali was experienced as an inspirational speaker. He had often made his audiences rise to their feet, shake their fists in anger, and pledge him allegiance to the death in the cause of Allah. In this case that would not be necessary, as these men were already his trusted lieutenants. All seven of them had been responsible for the deaths of many people, and could be trusted to be true to the holy cause.

"We have all spent much time recruiting and training young men to serve Allah well," he continued. "Using the wisdom of our beloved prophet Muhammad, peace be unto him, we must now find warriors for very important future missions. These recruits must be men of patience, capable of holding back their righteous anger towards the infidels until they are ordered to perform great tasks that will further our glorious cause and guarantee their entrance into paradise.

"I'd like to call your attention to the successful mission performed by our Chechen Muslim brothers in Grozny a few years ago," he continued. "During the building of the new stadium, three months prior to the installation of the Russian puppet president, a holy bomb was imbedded in the concrete of the dais. When the fool stood up for his investiture he was sent to his final destiny. The lesson to be learned here is that the planning had to be done long before the event. Allah requires that we, too, act the same way. We must anticipate what the Americans will do and react accordingly, but we must do so long in advance."

Bin Yemeni paced the floor of the cave, raising little puffs of dust with each step.

"Let us think positively, as Allah would have us do. We have already accomplished much to bring down the American fools. Think how much they spend to try to protect themselves. The billions of dollars spent in this fashion are diverted from increasing their military might, thus weakening them for the big battle that is to come.

"Allah requires that we bleed them in every way we can. We sap the strength of these immoral, perverted and depraved infidels every time we attack them. These attacks give weight to our threats. Every successful attack enables us to bleed them by only *threatening* to attack again. If we bleed the goat often enough it will grow weak and die."

The tall Arab swung his arm around the cave, pointing at the bare walls.

"The Americans and their Arab lackeys think we suffer because we live in caves. But we don't mind, because if Allah is pleased, we will live forever in palaces in paradise. We see our progress daily on the Devil's own television programs. The budget for the Department of Homeland Security is more than the combined military budgets of all the Arab nations, and it produces nothing but a false sense of security. The latest U.S. budget increased the amount allotted to this department by another 400 million dollars. Our attacks are responsible for this. And what does it cost us? Practically nothing. Our network of hand-to-hand financing, the hawalas, collect all the untraceable funding that we need. We bleed their economy every day. When their economy is weak enough, Allah will hand the carcass of the Devil to us for burial. The Devil's own internet will broadcast the requiem.

"The American Army is stretched thin in Afghanistan and Iraq. The debauched democratic nations are divided about how to combat Islam. Half of them think they can negotiate a peace that will allow them to continue their morally depraved ways, while the other half think they can subdue us by force of arms. But both are wrong. We are not divided; we are united by the great miracle, our beloved Qur'an. Neither sweet talk nor force will ever defeat the will of Allah that his one true faith must prevail.

"Our brothers in Hamas have played the infidels for fools and have arranged to be elected democratically in Palestine. Gaza has been returned to the Palestinians by Israel, and the West Bank and Jerusalem will be next. These weaklings will do anything for peace. We want victory, and nothing less will do. Syria and our Shi'ah brothers in Iran support us because our fight is theirs also. Listen to me, brothers. Step by step Islam is on the march, and nothing can stop the will of Allah."

Ali looked down at his fellows and smiled.

"Now let me hear from you the ideas you have brought me. I am not so much interested in today's targets as those that could be hit six months to ten years from now. We'll discuss them together, concentrating on the propaganda value and the relative difficulties of the missions involved."

Ali sat on a pillow, and the plotters formed in a circle to begin their discussion. Each of the men presented their short list of targets. Ali noted them down on a large pad that rested against the wall of the cave.

In the end there were twenty-six possibilities. Ali decided to break down the list into those attacks that could be mounted in three months to three years time, and those that would take up to ten years to accomplish. The men all agreed that the targets presented carried significant risks, but if successfully attacked each would deal a strong blow to the prestige of the infidel Americans.

Missions were doled out to each of the six terrorist field commanders. Ali Bin Yemeni would act as coordinator, but each commander was to have total autonomy in planning and executing the missions he had been assigned. It was possible that these men would not see each other again alive, and probably it would be years from then, if at all.

"Allah's will be done," they all said in unison.

The horrendous attack by the Americans on the caliph headquarters beneath the Ka'bah itself in Mecca had shocked the religious leaders of the Arab world. The pride of fundamentalist Muslims had been badly damaged by this attack, but they were forced to hold their fury in check in order to cover their embarrassment, and because their governmental leaders were in cahoots with the American devils. The average Arab in the street had not read *Council of Caliphs,* the account of the raid in Mecca that had been written by the cowardly novelist Aidan de Vries, writing under a pseudonym to protect his worthless hide from the righteous vengeance of Allah. But a few of the cognoscenti suspected that the author was dealing with facts, not fiction, and had accurately described the events just as they had happened.

There was no shortage of candidates claiming the right to be caliphs, so Islam did not lack potential political religious leaders. The inner sanctum of clerics had been maintaining records to substantiate claims of this sort since the Prophet had walked the earth, and they were still hard at work on it. Ironically, the assassinations in Mecca had been true to the traditional way that usurpers came to power in Islam, so the successors could claim their ascension even though the credit was actually due to the American Seals, an arcane twist that would please the new successors to the Islamic hierarchy.

On a practical level, the most serious problem for activist groups such as the *Scythe of Allah* was the disruption of the communications system caused by the American raid on Mecca. The secret code contained in the imams' copies of the Qur'an was broken. The American devils had completely destroyed the communications center that unified the efforts of all Muslims involved in the fight to see Islam achieve its rightful place as the one true faith for the world. The secrets of Islam had been thrown open to the unrighteous eyes of the infidels. This one act had been a stab in the heart of Islam, and those responsible would pay dearly. These men and their cohorts in the SOA had pledged their lives to see to it that Allah was avenged.

They had risen to their feet to begin the ritual cheek-kissing used by Arab men when parting from one another, when suddenly they were interrupted by the sound of several heavy, earth-shuddering thuds coming from the direction of the cave entrance. They all ran immediately toward the noise. At the entrance to the cave they met several dust-covered Arab fighters who reported that they had been attacked by guided missiles.

"We have suffered some casualties," they told their leaders. "You must all leave at once by the escape route we arranged in case of just such an emergency. Obviously our location has been discovered. Please go now. For a time we will fight any troops who may follow in the wake of the missile attack, and then we will slip away with the help of Allah and the local tribesmen, as we always do."

In the Situation Room at the White House Ivan Welland was pacing the floor, awaiting the results of the missile raid the President had ordered on Ivan's advice. The electronic and photographic report on the effectiveness of the attack was unclear. Special Forces would have to be sent in via helicopter to verify what was going on in that remote location in the mountains on the Pakistan/Afghani border. The attack had been triggered by an electronic device that reported the use of a satellite navigation instrument in a place where none should exist. To avoid a friendly fire incident, all U.S. and allied troops in the area had been contacted to make sure they had not used such equipment in the past twenty-four hours.

Ivan had discussed the proposed attack with the Chairman of the Joint Chiefs of Staff and the Director of the CIA. None of them could account for the use of this kind of equipment by tribesmen in the area. They would not have had access to such a sophisticated instrument, nor would they have known how to use it even if it had somehow fallen into their hands. Only a trained terrorist fighter of some importance would be so equipped. The hunt for Osama bin Laden was still on, so the possibility of attacking him or some other high-level jihadist operatives could not be missed.

In the age of real-time communications everybody expected swift results, including the military. Impatient staff officers were standing over their junior officers waiting for information, as if simply being there could hurry things along. Ivan Welland had to admit that he was no less anxious. He was the one who had cracked the code of the caliphs, and the one who had planned the incursion in Mecca. If that information had become known among the jihadists, he would have become a prime target for the *Scythe of Allah* and a fatwah on his life would have been issued in a Meccan minute.

When the previous president's second term was over and Ivan's boss, the Secretary of State, had retired, Ivan's services as coordinator of intergovernmental international security affairs had also came to an end. Within the hallowed halls of the White House, however, Ivan's reputation was such that the incoming president offered him the position of National Security Advisor. This was a big job for such a young man, but Ivan was no ordinary man. At 6 feet 7 inches he was the Shaquille O'Neal of the White House staff. His discovery of the existence of the caliphs, their location, and their method of controlling worldwide Islamist terrorism, had altered history. He had become the national security team's franchise player on the strength of that performance.

The emphasis of Middle Eastern politics had shifted toward sanity ever since the terrorist organization had been decapitated. Without the leaders who had died beneath the Ka'bah building, the murderous attacks came to an abrupt end. Citizens of many nations were again enjoying security. Nevertheless, many of the killers were still at large, licking their wounds and hoping to recreate the cells that had caused mayhem and misery for so many innocent people. Many of the terrorist leaders had avoided being captured or killed, so Ivan still had more work to do. The outlaw nations such as Syria, Iran, Sudan, and North Korea continued to pose large potential problems for Ivan and his colleagues. But for the moment, the diplomats were handling these troubled areas.

On the personal front, Ivan's home life was going extremely well. His wife, Marina, had finished her teaching contract with Harvard and had moved to Washington to be with him. She was carrying their first child, and was in her third trimester. They didn't yet know the sex of the baby, since they had not wanted the ultra-sound technician to give them this information. Ivan thought it was a boy, but Marina felt quite sure it was a girl. Whichever it was, Ivan, like most men, was astounded by the size of his wife's belly. He had never seen a pregnant woman's body before, and now, because they slept in the buff, he saw one every night. He had awkwardly put his foot in his mouth and said she looked like a little Buddha. Marina was not amused.

CHAPTER TWO

Ali Bin Yemeni and his six co-conspirators left the cave by the small exit that led to the next valley. They quickly broke up into small groups and went in different directions. A few hours of walking in the rough mountainous terrain with the friendly tribesmen as guides, and Ali would vanish into thin air.

He was proud to be the leader of this group of stalwart Muslim men. Ali was only really comfortable in two places on earth: mosques and deserts. He was glad, however, that two of his brothers in arms were from port cities, two others from very large cities, and two more men with a Bedouin background like his own. They were a diverse group in nationality, education and experience, and Ali was certain that together they were going to accomplish great things for Islam.

Desert nomads have a special metabolism. Centuries of walking long distances in hot conditions have given them lean bodies and effortless gaits. As he walked alongside the camels, Ali was thinking that obese, lazy, weak people like Americans could never live a single day on the Arabian Peninsula. He plied the old Arab caravan routes just the same way as his people before him. And like his forebears, he carried smuggled goods in his camel bags. The preferred items to transport these days were explosives to be used in IEDs, Katusha rockets, and RPG launchers and ammunition. These materials were heavy, so Ali spared his camels by walking instead of riding. He didn't mind, because he did his planning during these long, solitary walks.

At the end of the day he and his caravan mates would unload the camels, hobble them, and rest in the relatively cool evening air before the cold dessert night set in. The caretakers of the oases always welcomed Ali, and the Arab custom of showing hospitality was still going strong in the desert. Not to show hospitality to Ali was known to be a dangerous oversight, and all the Arabs along the trade routes were aware of it. Heroic Bedouin sheikhs existed and were still revered in this part of the world, even if they had been consigned to the fiction of the *Arabian Nights* elsewhere. Ali reclined on his bed of sand, closed his eyes, and recalled his days in Texas.

Commanded by his father to go to America to study the infidels and their ways, Ali had obediently attended the University of Houston. Most of the Arabs in Texas were studying petroleum engineering for obvious reasons. Ali's interest was more specifically in explosives, so he had majored in chemical engineering. The contacts he made with the scions of other important Arab families had lasted him his whole life.

Following his father's orders to learn about the culture, Ali focused on the religion of the Americans. He attended a Baptist church, where he became an immediate celebrity since so few Muslims had ever shown an interest in Christianity. He was invited to Christian homes for meals. He attended Bible studies and was taught the principles of Protestantism. But in private, and in his heart, he always prayed to Allah to assure him that he was only associating with Christians in order to know the enemy. He felt sure that Allah had approved of his plan to learn what he could about their faith so that he could attack its false doctrines when the time came. He even got a scholarship in his last year at the university. He gloated over the fact that the Americans had paid to teach him how to blow them up.

He thought the religion of the infidels was weak in many ways. It was based on the hearsay of men, whereas the Qur'an came directly from Allah. Although there were a great many similarities in the origins, philosophies, and ethics of the two religions, the irreconcilable disparities were revealed in the lack of disciplined religious practice. Christianity lacked the powerful authority of Allah as revealed in the Great Miracle of the Qur'an, the Five Pillars of the faith, and the necessary reality of submission to God's will. Ali felt American Christians were weak in their fear of God. They seemed to believe they could do anything they wished, and God would forgive them. That was why they were so blatantly immoral. Young women were wearing clothing that exposed every inch of skin that could be revealed short of nudity. The way the girls moved their hips in their skimpy skirts, the way they danced in such a provocative manner, the liberties they took with men they hardly knew – all these things brought home to him the moral laxity for which Allah would punish them.

The girls he met in church acted demure and holy, but once outside the church they behaved like prostitutes. Ali was tall, handsome, and interesting to Christian girls because he was different. One night one of the girls in the Bible study said she would give him a ride home in her car. Ali, who had walked incredible distances all his life, thought it was funny to be driven home such a short distance, perhaps only four miles. The girl was pretty much average in general appearance. She spoke with a southern drawl that made it difficult for Ali to completely understand her.

"I know a place we can go," she said.

Ali thought he had a place to go, and it was home, but he said nothing.

She drove to a deserted back road, stopped the car and took off her glasses. Before he knew what was happening she had taken his hand and placed it on her breast. Ali had no idea how far this was going to go. If she were a Muslim girl he could be killed for what he was doing.

She led his hand down and under her skirt. He had never expected to be this close to a woman who wasn't his wife. It was exciting for him, but he promised himself that he would not fornicate with this infidel harlot. He would touch her only for educational purposes, so that he could learn about the female anatomy and be able to please his wives when he married.

The experience turned out to be a disappointment for him. He found it tawdry and disgusting. The girl had used him for her own pleasure, and then had left him frustrated. Not only that, she had mocked him for his ignorance and incompetence.

"What do you guys *do* back in your own country?" she had asked him petulantly afterward. "Don't you know *anything?*"

She had put her glasses back on, adjusted her clothing, and driven him home without saying another word.

He was deeply embarrassed, and the last thing he could tolerate was embarrassment. He nearly flew out of the car when they stopped. He would try never to see this girl again. The loss of his dignity that night would plague him all his life, and would contribute to his deep hatred of American women.

Ali's ego was bruised again when he was bested by the smartest girl in one of his classes. She would usually beat him on the exams by a few percentage points. Although he tried to hide his anger about being outdone by a female, he was inwardly furious. His pride would not allow him to be less intelligent than a woman. He comforted himself with the thought that he was not less intelligent, just less educated. The Texan woman had attended a fine high school in Dallas and was better prepared for university courses. The classes were given in English, too, which was her native language. Nevertheless, Ali was devastated by losing out to her,

Soon afterward another co-ed crossed his path. She had noticed him on campus, and when she saw him at a mixer, she made it her business to talk to him. She asked him a few questions about his country and seemed genuinely interested in his answers. They spoke quietly together for most of the evening, and didn't mix as the party hosts had intended. When the party ended the co-ed suggested that he walk her home. Ali liked walking, so he agreed. She took his hand and held it as they strolled along in the humid, warm air of the Texas night.

"In my country holding hands with an unmarried girl is forbidden," Ali said.

The girl gave him a sidelong glance. "In America," she told him, "people live together and even have children without marrying. It's just the modern way."

When they got to her place she invited him in for a drink.

"I don't drink alcohol," Ali said. "It's against my religion."
"Well how about tea? You can drink tea, can't you?
"Yes," he said. "I drink tea. I can show you how Arabs make tea, if you like."
"That would be nice," the girl said. She opened the door and went inside, with Ali following behind. "Would you like to take off your jacket? You must be very warm in this heat."
"I'll take off my coat, but compared to my country, this is like Iceland. The desert goes up to 130 degrees sometimes." He removed his jacket and handed it to her.
"Well, it seems hot to me," she said, as she hung his coat in the closet. "I'd like to change into something more comfortable now that I'm home."
She went to the other room, leaving the door open just enough for Ali to see her undressing. She kept an eye on him in her mirror, to make sure he was watching her. He looked away when she caught him taking a peek. At that point she was down to her bra and panties.
"Do you want me to keep undressing?" she asked. She removed her bra without waiting for his answer. She knew from experience that her full breasts were highly regarded.
"Why don't you get comfortable, too?"
She lowered her panties and stepped out of them. She walked over to him, put her arms around his neck, and leaned against him.
"Let's start with this nasty thing," she said flirtatiously, undoing his necktie.
Ali had never before been close to a naked woman. His religious beliefs were in direct opposition to the requirements of his manhood. These forward American women were always tempting him to defile himself.
She sensed his reticence. She wasn't sure if it was timidity, surprise, or prudishness. She had already made it perfectly clear by her actions that she was willing. Usually it took less than this to have a man tearing off his clothes to jump into bed with her. Having gone this far, she didn't want to be rebuffed. She was already opening his pants before he could stop her.

She put her thumbs in the waistband of his shorts and jerked them down, stripping him to the knees in one fast move. "You've seen what a naked American woman looks like. Now I want to see what a naked *Arab* man looks like." She stepped back and took a good long look. "You're circumcised! Are you a Jew?" To be taken for a Jew was too much for him to bear. He quickly pulled up his pants, fastened his belt, grabbed his jacket and started for the door. "Don't leave. I'm sorry. I was only joking." "I don't tolerate jokes like that, you harlot!"

Ali was glad that he would soon be returning to his country. He would ask his father to find him a bride. Now that he was a university graduate it was time for him to be with a decent Arab woman. His father had agreed.

Now, ten years later, he had four good, well-chosen Arab wives, and no domestic or sexual problems. Ali wondered why these thoughts of those American whores had come back to haunt him after all these years. He hadn't learned much about Western women except that they were all tramps. But he had learned chemistry while he was in the U.S., and he had enough explosives in his caravan to make a lot of them into widows.

Dr. Ivan Welland, National Security Advisor, was on the list of government officials to be called into the Situation Room as soon as news about the missile attack was received. He was in bed when the call came. He put down the phone and bolted for the bathroom, leaving his wife, Marina, still half asleep.

He remembered how wonderfully surprised he had been the first time he had uncovered Marina's superb female body. Now her incredibly swollen belly distorted that perfect image. As he soaped himself in the shower he thought how amazing it was that his outfit had delivered the "Lovin' Spoonful" that had caused such a transformation in Marina's body. It was truly a miracle, and no less of a miracle for his wife.

Marina had heard the phone ring, looked at the clock, and saw that it was only 4:30 AM. She tried to go back to sleep, but she couldn't. She felt her belly. She was delighted by the feelings that were stirring in her protuberant abdomen. She had never had to pay particular attention to keeping her body trim. A sensible diet and lots of walking had been enough to maintain what genetics had given her. She wondered what she would have to do to recapture her svelte form. Whatever it took, she would do it for Ivan's sake as well as her own.

Marina had initiated the idea of having a child as soon as possible because of her age. She always felt secretly guilty that her desire to quickly have a child had cut short the honeymoon period of their marriage. She missed the sexual contact that this latest stage of pregnancy had imposed upon them. She knew Ivan missed it too, but she had the baby inside her to keep her company, whereas Ivan was cut off.

"Is no problem," she thought. "When baby comes he will be with me again. I know he will be good father in spite of his huge responsibilities to his country."

Ivan came out of the bathroom and found Marina struggling to put on her housecoat. He wanted to laugh, but thought better of it.

"I have only gained average amount of weight for woman my size during pregnancy," she commented, "and yet my breasts and belly are enormous. How big will be this baby?" She looked at Ivan as if his large size was the cause of hers.

"You didn't have to get up," Ivan said, wanting to turn the subject away from the sensitive issue of her weight.

Marina knew all about his change-the-subject ploy, but she allowed him to think he had managed to avoid the responsibility he had for her present physical condition.

"I know, but I am awake now. I make you breakfast?"

"No, don't bother. I've got to get going right away. I'll get something at work. What are you going to do today?"

"I work on my book. I consult often with my assistant these days," she remarked, patting the top of the round shelf that was her assistant's home. "She has given me some good ideas."

Ivan was ready to go out the door. He slid his hand under Marina's robe to rub her belly.

"I'm rubbing the all-wise Buddha's stomach so that I, too, may have the benefit of his wisdom."

"Buddha says if you are wise you will not mention his name again," Marina said with a smile. She gave him a quick kiss and pushed him out the door.

He got into their van and drove off. They had bought a Dodge Caravan because Ivan's NBA proportions fit more easily into that style of vehicle.

It may have been a good decision for other reasons, too. His conservation-minded mom and dad had marshaled all the folks from their church in Dallas to dig up their old baby gear for shipment to Ivan and Marina. Ivan's mom had labeled each item with the name of the donor so that thank-you notes could be sent and credit given to the giver. It looked to Ivan as if he would need a van to accommodate all this equipment, and that was another reason he was glad to have such an ample vehicle. Being a government employee he felt he should buy American, so he had purchased the Dodge Caravan.

Ironically Daimler Benz, the German car builder, had acquired control of Chrysler, so Ivan wasn't sure he was helping the United States economy as he had intended. He wondered if this meant that the profits from Chrysler were now being sent to Germany, leaving the U.S. with only a few blue-collar jobs. The association of the word *caravan* with the hunt for terrorist leaders brought his mind back to business as he passed through the security procedures at the White House.

It was 5:10 AM, and the Situation Room was already busy enough to convince the American taxpayers that they were getting their money's worth. Ivan walked up to the Director of Communications, who was sort of the *maitre d'* of events for this most important room in the U.S.

"What's going on, Dick?" he asked.

"Well, Dr. Welland, there's been a fierce battle out there in the area where the missiles hit. The strength and the ferocity of the fighting would seem to indicate that the targets were there, all right. We've got something like a hundred Special Forces and Airborne units on the ground. Enemy fire has lessened, and in the last hour we've been able to advance on a cave that seems to be in the middle of things."

"Which means in the middle of nowhere, I expect."

"Something like that," Dick said. "Anyway, it's not clear as yet whether we're making inroads or the enemy is stealing away to fight another day. In either case we have to proceed slowly and carefully. We expect the usual booby traps with improvised explosive devices to be left for our boys to work around. I'm guessing we've had another close miss, sir."

"Thanks Dick, it sounds as though you're right."

The affair beneath the Ka'bah in Mecca had dealt a severe blow to the terrorists. There was no doubt about that, but the problem was a long way from being solved permanently. The root of the problem was that the Arab man in the street didn't identify with the American cause, and given the choice he would side with the terrorists.

Ivan didn't believe that forcing free elections on Arabs would automatically improve the terrorist situation. The election of Hamas in Palestine was a case in point. A free election had taken place there, and the people had chosen to put the terrorists in power.

The clerics, who should have been applying a healing balm to the widespread wounds of the Middle East, were in fact exacerbating the situation with hate rhetoric. These men were the opinion formers of their nations. Through their sermons in the mosques they had the power to calm or foment their captive audiences. It was clear to Ivan which tactic they had chosen by their rejection of any sort of reinterpretation of Islamic principles in the light of current situations. Those who proposed a peaceful reform of Islam were threatened with religiously-sponsored assassination, called a fatwah. It seemed to Ivan that the extremist wing of Islam understood the solution to all problems to be a jihad leading to the death of all those who didn't agree with them.

Ivan's first task as National Security Advisor to the President was to advise him of any potential or actual dangers threatening citizens, property, or the national interests of the United States. At the moment nearly all the blips on his danger radar screen were coming from Islamist terrorists who had not been arrested or killed in the Mecca raid and its aftermath.

Ivan had had an idea that morning while he was taking a shower. It was based on his feeling that violence is the number one enemy of the world. Americans believed in freedom of religion, therefore Americans did not have any arguments with those who practiced the religion of Islam. They had no problems with Buddhists, Hindus, or any other religious practitioners as long as they did not practice or support violence against other faiths. They could not, however, stand idly by and allow violent actions to be perpetrated against Americans at home or overseas, no matter what the circumstances. Murder was never justified, and any religion that preached murder had to be changed.

That was the precise moment that he had hit upon his plan to stamp out violence in the Middle East and elsewhere. Any issue was negotiable, but violence would not be tolerated under any conditions. Curbing violence meant curbing weapons. It wasn't weapons of mass destruction that were killing people in these times, it was the masses of destructive weapons. Ivan would put his mind to work to relieve the Middle East of its conventional weapons as well as the nuclear ones. Gunmen without guns are a whole lot easier to deal with.

He decided to reconvene the group that had assisted him with breaking the code of the caliphs and put them to work on this problem. He instructed his secretary, Brooklyn, to call the men and ask them to come to his office the next day.

"Tell them it's an emergency meeting," he added.

CHAPTER THREE

Captain Niko was gathering up his personal effects, preparing to transfer to his new command. The news of his promotion had now been released, and he was glad not to have to keep it a secret any longer. The ship was in its berth in Tampa, Florida. He would take a cab to the airport and fly to Paris that evening, continuing by train to Toulon the next morning. His new ship had been built there, and was now awaiting her captain in order to begin her sea trials.

The modest little knock on his cabin door had become familiar to him. He knew it was Mercedes León.

"Come in. The door is open," he called out.

She slipped in quietly, closed the cabin door behind her, and locked it.

"How are you, my dear?" Niko said.

"I feel sad that you must leave," Mercedes said softly. "I hoped to accompany you in the new ship."

"I can't take you with me. I'm so sorry. For the next few months I'll be doing sea trials and there'll be no passengers, so there won't be any service staff aboard."

"And after the trials?"

"I don't know. The Department of Human Resources assigns the crew members to the ship. I don't have anything to do with that. I'm in charge only after the crew is on board. It would be quite irregular for a captain to request that a particular waitress be assigned to his ship. Unfortunately, I can't do that. It might ruin both our reputations. You understand, I'm sure."

"Yes. I understand, but it does not please me. It may be that this is the last opportunity that we are together."

Mercedes was off for shore leave, but had chosen to stay aboard so she could say good-bye to Niko. He realized that, and knew she had given up her day off to be with him for a few hours. She was not required to be in uniform when she was not working, so she had worn her favorite skirt and a tailored white blouse styled like his dress shirt.

"You look very nice in civilian clothes. I don't think I've ever seen you out of uniform. Of course, I've seen you out of *your* uniform. Well, you know what I mean."

"Yes, Niko, I know what you mean, and what you need."

"And I know what you need too, little one, don't I?"

He unfastened his belt and let his trousers fall. She helped him get his feet clear of the rumpled pants around his ankles. She conjectured that the captain must have been very close to exceeding his sexual capacity these days, but she didn't care about the other women. Her relationship with Niko had no jealousy component. She knew exactly what he liked, and she gave it to him. She asked nothing in return, and for this reason he gave her what mattered most to her: she was his favorite. The wealthy dowagers could scheme, the married women could secretly fantasize, the beautiful young nymphets could flirt, but she, Mercedes, was the one Captain Niko wanted most. None of them knew it, nor would they ever have guessed it, because in their minds she was only there to serve them. Mercedes liked it that way. Her warm secret filled her with a happy, friendly spirit that brought her more tips than anyone else.

Niko stroked her hair. "Human Resources be damned," he grunted. "I'll find a way. I'll get you on board the new ship. Just leave it to me."

Ali was the man most responsible for the emphasis the Islamist fighters had begun to put on improvised explosive devices. He had taught many of the Prophet's warriors to make the lethal IEDs, and they had in turn trained others. His position was that until Islam conquered the world for Allah, it was essential that young men know weapons more than wisdom.

"The Qur'an and the Prophet Muhammad, peace be unto him, teach us all we need to know," Ali used to say.

His training courses were similar to the seminars he had attended during his time in America, with handouts containing simplified instructions for using the various types of chemical explosives. His job was to source and deliver the materials to the fighters and martyrs, and their job was to learn the lessons he was teaching them about how to make and successfully use IEDs. The bombs were not innovative in and of themselves, for the chemistry he was teaching them was not new or original. The innovative part had to do with where, when, and how the bombs were placed. Those Muslims who had heard of "The Terminator" referred to Ali as "The Detonator."

Up to this point Ali had flown under the American radar screen. He was in the transportation business, and had no permanent residence. His family ran a scrupulously honest business, emulating El Ameen. His sons and nephews knew nothing of Ali's real business, and he kept that information secret for their protection and his own. His four wives lived quietly with his tribal nomad people, moving here and there with their sheep and goats.

His family didn't know that he maintained small business offices in the larger, more troubled centers of the Arab world. Explosives, weapons and chemicals were shipped with false documentation. The original manufacturers of the materials were also kept in the dark about the purposes and the eventual destination of their products. Although they may have suspected that the goods were being sold to and used by terrorists, they either didn't care, or in any event the documents covered their butts. Ali's system of trans-shipping the explosives and weapons was as intricate as a spider's web.

Money and personnel were no problem in his business – an envious position to be in for most businessmen. Ali, however, was an idealist. He could have made a huge personal fortune, but he saw to it that things ran on a stable, self-sustaining profit basis, and that was all he would allow. The money to finance his operations was supplied in cash from sources even he didn't know. His labor pool came from the millions of disaffected young Muslim men from all over the world – fanatical young fighters aching to do something for Islam.

Madrasa schools, many thousands of them located in all parts of the Middle East, were the minor leagues for terrorist candidates. The scouts were the teachers in these schools, and the names of any physically fit, idealistic young men who could be guerilla fighters or suicide bombers would be passed along to the cells for tryouts in the big league. Ali's transportation outfit was a conduit for these young men, along with the weapons he was smuggling. Cannon fodder and workers in unending supply were thus provided at no cost to Ali and the cause.

In the aftermath of the Meccan incident large numbers of weapons and explosive devices had been destroyed or impounded. Ali's company was under heavy pressure to help restock the cells with arms and personnel, and his suppliers were salivating at the prospect of a lot of new business. The original source of the guns used by the terrorists was well known to the security people of every nation concerned with the politics of the Middle East. What became of them after they were made was not the concern of the original manufacturers, or so they said. Most of the small arms, pistols, rifles, rocket-propelled grenades, mortars, shoulder-fired missiles, scuds, katusha rockets and other ammunition were manufactured in Russia, China, Iran and North Korea. Getting them from their country of origin into the hands of the terrorists was Ali's forté. He was doing his best to see to it that anyone willing to fight the Americans had a gun and ammunition to use in the battle against the enemies of Allah.

The Americans and their Arab lackeys had improved their surveillance techniques and committed billions of dollars in the effort to find Bin Laden, the figurehead and inspiration in Islam's fight to counteract the Americans' disgusting efforts at perverting the Muslim world. Yet they failed to convince any nations other than their dependent allies of the merits of their aggression against the Arabs. If the U.S. managed to capture or kill the leaders they had hunted unsuccessfully for years, these men would become martyrs of the One Faith, and others would immediately take their place.

"History reveals the will of Allah," Ali would often say. "These infidel devils will be defeated just as we vanquished the crusaders in the Middle Ages. But this time it will result in the universal installation of Islam as the religion of the one true God, Allah. Then, and only then, can we rest."

His hate-twisted mind dwelled continuously on the ironies of the Western adherents' positions in the conflict. The hypocrisy and naiveté of the Americans was a pitiful example of why Islam must grind them into the dust.

"They say they believe in free speech," Ali would tell his attentive acolytes, "but they speak with forked tongues and unclean lips. They elect leaders and then refuse to follow them or be loyal to them. They claim the hegemony of the individual is at the base of their politics and their religion. Can the fools not see that mankind must take its leadership from Allah? They have no unity in their positions because they have not heard Allah speak through the Prophet Muhammad, praise be unto him. The Qur'an tells mankind how it must be with men. Islam is united in its absolute belief that The Book is the final word, and those who don't believe must perish."

The crowd of adoring listeners would cheer madly.

"The American fools tell us every day what their plans are, via the never-ceasing din of their free speech media," Ali would remind them, encouraged by their rousing cheers. "They will still be screaming diatribes of political correctness at each other while we cut them to ribbons. When they install their precious democracy over the will of the people, as in Iraq and Palestine, we will vote to elect the followers of Allah.

"We have been to their schools and we know how they think. We have seen the depraved lechery of their men and women. They want to convert us to their perverted way. Ha! Their women do not submit to their men, and their men do not submit to their God. Why would we wish to be like them? Hollywood can produce smut and paint it with gold, but anyone can see the false morality."

Ali was absolutely certain that he was acting in accordance with Allah as he and his men planned their 26 detonations on behalf of their one true God.

Ivan Welland called his staff meeting to order.

"Gentlemen," he began, "We must have a new approach to fighting terrorism. I'm going to propose a new program for the future, and I'd like you to examine it and tell me if you think it can work. So I'll begin by asking you a question. What's the primary action that identifies someone as a terrorist?"

"They commit violent crimes," said David Feingold, his second in command.

"What do they use to commit these crimes?" Ivan asked.

"Weapons and explosives."

"And if we could disarm them, would violence end?"

"Probably," David said.

"Okay. Then let's make sure they have no more weapons."

"But how can we stop all the armament manufacturers from selling weapons to anyone who wants them?" asked Damian.

"Well, suppose *we* bought all the weapons?"

Abdul, Damian, and David looked puzzled.

"Who's *we?*" asked Damian.

"We the people," Ivan said. We're spending billions in taxes anyway, and our brave young men are losing their lives to defend us from terrorist violence. Wouldn't it be cheaper to just buy all the weapons and munitions from these arms dealers so they can never fall into the wrong hands? In this case we'd at least have all the weapons to show for the money spent."

"How can we determine who the weapons dealers are?" Damian wanted to know.

"I'm not sure," Ivan said, "but I'm putting you in charge of finding the answer for the rest of us. It seems to me that we've captured enough weapons in our operations to know which companies are making them. Maybe we could go directly to the manufacturers and cut out the middlemen, in this case the arms dealers. Or we could deal with the governments directly. If we pay them more, will they sell to us instead of to the criminals?"

"How much can we afford to pay?" David asked. "Please find out what our military expenditures are for our operations in the Middle East. David, you can dig into the economic side. What I'm trying to accomplish here is the initial preparation of a plan, supported by facts and evidence, that will put an end to the bloodshed of jihadist terrorism, and which I can submit to the President for his approval. We'll divide the work into four parts and each of us will report back later for a progress assessment meeting. I'll take care of diplomacy and international consular affairs. David, you do the research and prepare the economic data. Damian, you locate and research the hardware manufacturers. Abdul, your part in this project is to investigate the weapons dealers and distributors, and also to serve as our Arabic resource person. It may be that my concept is faulty. Maybe the whole thing is naive, but part of the idea stems from influences in my childhood. My mother used to confiscate all my dangerous toys. Everything pointy, swords, spears, and knives magically disappeared. All guns that fired were banned. Her actions were judicious, unilateral, and clearly unpopular in some quarters, but the results contributed greatly to the safety of the children in the neighborhood."

Damian suggested that the gun makers didn't have to be involved at all. If the U.S. could concentrate on the ammunition makers and not the gun makers, the weapons could be rendered useless by cutting off the supply of ammunition at the source.

"Excellent," Ivan said. "Now take that idea and develop it into a plan that includes every aspect of the why, how, who, when and what, and I'll be meeting with the Commander-in-Chief before you know it."

The meeting broke up some time later, and the four men returned to their offices. Ivan realized that until they had a plan and new policies to follow, he would have to return to the game of hide-and-go-seek that he was playing with the terrorists all over the world, but particularly in the Middle East. For some reason his mind of late had been particularly concerned with the logistics of the terrorists. Who was transporting the weapons to the jihadists, and how was it being done?

Ivan had been aware for some time that the Islamist fighters had been manufacturing bombs in neighborhood businesses in Baghdad. Backyard forges and metal working shops were to be found all over the Middle East. Little chemistry labs were making explosives in the kitchens of many homes. But who was supplying the know-how? Who trained these people to be bomb makers? Ivan once heard a story about an Iraqi young man who was not a terrorist, and who had gone to the U.S. to study chemistry. When he returned he was taken hostage and forced at gunpoint to make bombs for the suicide bombers. Ivan didn't miss the irony that the U.S. had trained terrorists to make the bombs they were now using against us.

He called Brooklyn, his long-time assistant, into his office and explained to her what was on his mind.

"I'd like you to get a list," he said, "of all the Arab students who received a degree in chemistry or chemical engineering, and then returned to the Middle East."

Brooklyn had already figured out that this list might be a place to start a suspect identification investigation. She knew that the universities sent out literature on a regular basis to their alumni, so they might be expected to have addresses for these people. Brooklyn's fertile brain was off and running.

Ivan never had to worry about any assignment he gave her. She did them right, and she did them fast.

"So what do you say, Brooklyn? Are we racial profilers?"

Brooklyn shrugged. "When Hamas bombs people in Israel, or Hezbollah takes hostages, isn't that racial profiling? Or when they blew up the U.S.S. Cole in Yemen, or brought down the World Trade Center, weren't they targeting Americans? I say to hell 'em. I'm just trying to stay alive here in this world, and that's not easy for a Jew. We've been profiled for thousands of years, so Jews can't afford *not* to profile their enemies. Still, some people haven't learned this lesson, and they're the ones who can get me killed. If they want to die, that's up to them, but I want to be the last one standing at the O.K. Kibbutz."

CHAPTER FOUR

Three months had gone by quickly for Captain Niko. He was ensconced in his new ship, the *Controller of the Oceans*, and was permanently moved into his cabin aboard. He had spent long hours in training sessions with engineers from the various companies, testing and learning to utilize the capacities of their equipment. He was fascinated by the new methods of training that had been developed since he had been a cadet. He had been put into a simulator that exactly paralleled the instrumentation on the bridge of the *Controller of the Oceans*.

For several days he was tested in the simulator to see how he would react in a variety of circumstances that could arise during a cruise. His ability to command had been subjected to a wide range of weather conditions, maritime law, navigation, electronics, communication, rules of the road, docking, general maneuvering, and the executive management of a huge floating city that represented an investment in the hundreds of millions of dollars. The company had wanted to be sure that their selection of Captain Niko was justified, and that he was the best man for the job. Niko was proud to have passed all the tests with flying colors, but he was glad to have all the testing over with so he could get back into the line command function that he enjoyed so much.

The schedule of cruises for the new vessel had been decided, and over the next twelve months the agenda called for the ship to visit 103 ports around the world. The full panoply of Captain Niko's maritime skills would be called upon to manage the maiden voyage of this magnificent ship. Few can imagine the level of detail involved in such an enterprise. Meetings with his department heads took up most of his time in the latter days as he prepared to set sail. The engineering department was faced with some big changes that required upgrading their skills so they could handle the latest equipment.

Replacing the inefficient propulsion systems with gas turbines had made huge savings, but very few of the ship's engineers had previous experience with the new motors, so there had been a floating engineering classroom below decks for three months. Niko's old ship had had a number of upgrades and renovations throughout its long life to keep it up with modern technology, but nothing to compare with this new vessel, which contained the latest equipment, all of which was brand new. It was the next thing to an aircraft carrier in complexity.

Even the housekeeping department of the ship had to undergo new training. The very large on-board laundry had been upgraded, and a central vacuuming system had been installed. Passengers would no longer have to dodge past vacuum cleaners in the corridors. Industrial engineers had worked long and hard to develop efficient ergonomic procedures that would enable fewer people to do more work with less effort.

In theory everything had been thought of, but in practice it all had to be tested under the actual conditions. The company knew that the people on the maiden voyage would be asked about the cruise, and the company wanted them to have a fantastic trip and say only good things about their time at sea. This meant that everything had to be ironed out before the ship's first cruise, and the crew could not use the first passengers as guinea pigs.

Sales, promotions, and public relations departments had been operating at full throttle for months. People all over the world had witnessed on their TV's the *Controller of the Oceans* slide into the water at her launching in Toulon. They had been told how this largest of cruise ships was the monarch of the seas. The emphasis of all the sales promotions had been on the luxurious decadence of the vessel that was built to provide every passenger with the most pampered experience of his or her life. The hyperbole about the ship's opulence hit the media of the world like a tsunami. Captain Niko and his crew were going to have a hard time providing the incredibly hedonistic interlude that everyone who boarded the ship would expect after reading the brochures and the publicity.

The ship did have elegant appointments that would take the breath away from the most discerning travelers. The naval architects had done an incredible design job. The entire top deck was devoted to swimming. There were three large pools. The center pool had perpetual surf for those who preferred to swim in a simulated sea. The dining and cabin areas had huge glass windows to provide the passengers with ocean vistas no matter where they were in the ship.

Every detail of the vessel proclaimed her to be the queen of the sea. The maiden voyage passages had been offered to customers who had taken previous cruises with the company as a way of saying thank you. The value of repeat business had been demonstrated again, as the maiden voyage was 85% booked by cruisers who had sailed with the company before.

Ali Bin Yemeni had read in the Arabic newspapers about the launching of this newest of the West's licentious obscenities. His list of twenty-six targets had included the destruction of a large vessel at sea. There was nothing like the sinking of such a ship to get the attention of the world. The sinking of the *Titanic* was still making big news, and it had happened before World War I. The sinking of the *Controller of the Oceans* would make even bigger news for the cause of Allah than the glorious 9/11 achievement. He began at once to search the internet for every mention of the new liner. He paid special attention to the plans and diagrams that the free American press so generously and reliably provided. Most of his successful work had been accomplished with the incomparable aid of the journalists from the West.

Ali was the last thing from a fool, and he knew that security for the new vessel would be tight, but the image of this icon of

Western decadence sinking into the sea was very tempting to him. He would create a clever plan, and meanwhile he would carefully evaluate the risks involved in such an attack. He felt that everything having to do with a first voyage for a ship of that size would be surrounded with confusion. Confusion, he knew, was the opportunity that Allah provided to his righteous fighters so that they could accomplish great things in his name. He would study the sites, the circumstances, and the ways that confusion could be provoked in order to increase the chances of a successful attack.

When Mercedes' contract expired, she went back to Chile to visit her son and her parents, and to give herself time to consider whether she should sign up for another contract with the cruise line. Mercedes had been home for seven days when her husband, Diego León, heard about it. Diego did not suffer from lack of self-esteem. In fact, he had far more esteem for himself than was justified by anyone's measure except his own. San Bernardo Rancagua had become a bustling small city, and Diego had moved there because there were more things to do, and also more people to do there. Everyone, in his and Mercedes' village nearby, were on to him, so he had to either move or work hard to make his way. He chose to move. When an acquaintance told him that he had seen Mercedes in the village the day before, the light bulb of opportunity lit up in his dim head. He decided to find his wife and get some money, or sex, and possibly both, if things went well. She was his wife when he wanted something; otherwise she was nothing to him. He decided to catch the bus and pay her a visit.

Eduardo and Maria Villanueva were very happy to have their only child at home for a few months. Nothing much had changed in their lives except that they had grown noticeably older. Maria worked at the rectory, and Eduardo was occupied with his small vicuna herd. He kept his animals in a fenced-in area in the back of the house, and fed them hay at the times when the snow and cold weather kept the grazing land in poor condition. Mercedes slept in her tiny room as she always did when she was home. Her parents occupied a small bedroom on the other side of the house. During the time she was staying at home with them her parents let her sleep until she awoke naturally. One morning, after her mother had gone to the rectory and her father had gone to the hills to check the pasturage, Mercedes was suddenly awakened when the door burst open and slammed against the wall.

There stood her husband Diego, looking down at her with a lascivious glint in his eye. He had decided he would get Mercedes pregnant again. Having only one child, in the culture of the village, was taken as a blot on a man's macho escutcheon. Besides, he knew that the supercilious slut thought she was too good for him and didn't want to have more children with him, which was reason enough in his mind to give her one.

As soon as Mercedes realized that she was facing a life of sexual submission to her cad of a husband, she had secretly decided to begin using birth control. In a small Catholic village a married woman of Mercedes' age who was using birth control methods was anathema to Church and society. She would have to find her way to the city to acquire what she needed. She only hoped it was not too late already.

Diego was brutish, but not stupid. He suspected that she would try to interfere with his desire to inseminate her. He searched her room and her purse looking for pills. He was bound and determined to control her. She was his wife, after all.

Since in Diego's warped mind all women were whores except for the Virgin Mary, he believed he had carte blanche to rape them at will. He had utter disdain for his partners. They existed only to satisfy his primitive desires. His aim was to gain power over them and to fecundate them with or without their consent. He had always been that way, but in the early days of his marriage to Mercedes he had played unsuccessfully at being a lover. Now there was no more need for pretense. He did as he liked with her, and believed she should be honored that she had a husband at all.

Diego had no redeeming qualities as a man. He would simply order Mercedes to strip and lie on the bed, then he would throw himself on top of her and force himself on her. He didn't care how she felt. He liked it that she was dry and tight. When she cried out in pain or shed a tear, he felt it was a compliment to his manhood.

Now Mercedes knew she was about to undergo a woman's worst nightmare – she would be raped by her own husband and possibly have to bear the child of a hated enemy. Having another child by him was unthinkable. It would give him control over her body for many years to come. Juan was eight now and halfway grown.

She just couldn't face another spate of years with Diego in her life. Every night she prayed that God would keep her from getting pregnant, or from needing to get a church-prohibited abortion. If she went back to sea she could get away from him for a time. He couldn't follow her or bother her when she was out of the country, but she knew she could never leave permanently. Juan was with her parents, and she loved these three people more than anyone or anything in the world.

Diego would come to the house and demand money on a regular basis, whether Mercedes was there or not. He would threaten to take Juan away with him if his in-laws didn't give him what he wanted, so they always forked over what little they had saved since his previous visit.

His demands for money were eating into Mercedes' savings too, and were driving her to sign another contract with the cruise line. She had to get away from him, but she didn't want to risk making him so angry that he would make life more hellish for her parents and her son than it already was. If she continued to send money home maybe he would be satisfied with that, and not destroy the life of an innocent little boy. Mercedes thought he would realize that something was better than nothing. He could get his sex elsewhere, but who else would give him money?

Without his knowledge or consent, she signed another contract and mailed it to the company. In two months she would be in Santiago to take a flight to the port where her assigned ship would be waiting. The name of the vessel and the port, probably Tampa, Florida, would come in due time. She would enjoy a few months' respite from Diego, and she eagerly looked forward to this time of peace and security.

Mercedes had no way of knowing, at the time, how this bullying, ignorant peasant would reach out and touch her from a distance of thousands of miles, and in a world about which he knew nothing.

During their discussions in the long-range planning meeting, Ali Bin Yemeni and his lieutenants decided that one of their 26 targets against the West should include a raid to release Al Qaeda prisoners. In the discussion it had been agreed that the captives had already given themselves to Allah, so their lives were not a primary concern.

"Although it would be nice to rescue some brothers from the infidel prison," Ali told his men, "that would not be the reason for such a raid. Even if we released the prisoners, they have no doubt been photographed, finger-printed, blood-typed, and DNA-sampled. They would be too easily recognized by the foreign devils. Their families would be watched, and so they couldn't go home. They could never simply return to serve as they had before their capture. The real reason for such a liberation raid would be to show the world that the infidel dogs cannot hold Allah's heroes against his will."

Prisoners were being held in many countries, but average Muslims might not realize that most of the jails that held the Prophet's fighters were in Arab countries. Their jailers were sympathetic to the cause of Islam, but they were being paid by government flunkies to be guards. Ali regarded these as soft targets, worth attacking for their value as symbolic gestures to show the continued strength of the insurgency to the greater Arab world. Some of the larger prison camps such as Abu

Ghraib in Iraq and Guantanamo in Cuba, were guarded by Americans and more likely to be difficult to attack than those in other parts of the Islamic world. So Ali focused on camps in Saudi Arabia, Lebanon, Israel, and Jordan.

One of the men brought up a rumor that he had heard about an escape that was being planned in Yemen. The prisoners themselves were arranging the escape, and had purchased the cooperation of some of the guards. This might be an opportunity for the *Scythe of Allah* to assist these men in joining Osama Bin Laden and the other fugitives who had never been caught. The embarrassment factor to the Americans and their Arab lackeys would be great if a large number of prisoners escaped and could not be recaptured.

Ali viewed the opportunity with a sense of personal pride, as his heritage was in Yemen. It was decided that the SOA would assist in this jailbreak by making the detainees disappear after the escape. It was just the kind of action that Ali loved. It required a low-cost investment on his part, and promised a disproportionately expensive reaction on the part of the infidels. Even if some of the men were recaptured, their escape would still embarrass those in the government who were selling themselves to the infidels. He was practically licking his lips at the thought of the costs to the American Navy for patrolling the Red Sea and the Arabian Sea, trying to keep the escapees from leaving Yemen by boat. Each of those warships burns tons of fuel oil every hour, and the oil profits go into Arab coffers.

"I have no intention of taking our fighters out of Yemen by sea," Ali continued. "Why would I do that? I will not put all these men who have risked their lives for Allah into one boat and send it out into the water where the Americans have absolute control, sensitive shipboard radar, fighter planes, and electronic surveillance of every known type. If the Americans steam their ships all over the oceans looking for these men, they are beyond stupid. I will move them little by little over land as we have always done."

Thousands of years of tribal brigandage in the desert had resulted in Ali's evolution into a canny warrior. He had seen the effect of sand on the machinery of the enemy. Tanks, trucks and helicopters could be turned into junk by one sand storm, while he and his camels lived on to fight year after year. Air filters clog up, but the nose of a camel was designed perfectly to separate air from sand. Ali pointed his own nose in the direction of Saana. He would conduct the escapees to safety through the desert.

In Washington the two-party-system was functioning perfectly. As always, the party in power did not know what it was doing, and the party not in power had all the answers. Ivan Welland had his own ideas about political parties, and they were not very charitable, but he worked at the pleasure of the President who was in power, so he was properly sliced and diced by the opposition's political pundits, who, not being in power, had nothing else to do but criticize. By virtue of having spent some time in Washington, and by the nature of his job as the National Security Advisor, Welland was used to being labeled as the incompetent kid responsible for the fact that the entire nation was suffering sleep deprivation because of security worries. One wag on CNN wanted to know how it was that with all the electronic spying toys, both military and civilian, Congress found it necessary to add another 30 billion dollars to its budget of 560 billion dollars already allocated to the task of finding one six-foot-four-inch Muslim terrorist.

Ivan was under the impression that he was working for all the American people, not just the ones who were elected, or those who wanted to be elected. This seemed to be a novel thought that the two parties could not agree on, along with everything else.

In his moments of discouragement Ivan thought that there would never be unified policies until the citizens of his great land heard the muffled steps of camels on their front lawns. Even then, many might be more concerned about who was to do the poop scooping than anything else. Ivan clearly knew that the President needed a better Middle East strategy, one that would bring results and put an end to the senseless killing of innocent people by the terrorists.   He had challenged his little group of thinkers to come up with this most needed strategy, and they were hard at work.

David Feingold had charged ahead with the economic portion of the study.   He had dug up all the budgetary statistics for the previous ten years, organized the numbers so that any hare-brained politician could see the trend toward skyrocketing expenses and little or no improvement as far as results were concerned.   His work would be the underpinning of the policy paper that Ivan would eventually present to the President, pointing out that there were a number of intelligent, untried, and cost-effective plans that could be implemented to remove terrorism from the world's stage.

Damian Rutledge had already prepared a list of the producers of weapons found in the Middle East.   His list showed the locations of the factories that produced the weapons, the ownership of the manufacturing companies, and some notes estimating the volumes of weapons on hand, together with unit street prices and total production capabilities. His initial feeling was that no weapons should be sold to arms dealers, and that all weapons sales should be made directly from the manufacturer.

It would be even better if gun dealing were seen as a war crime.   All preliminary figures were being checked and rechecked for accuracy.   Damian expected to come up with a good picture of the players, volumes, kinds of weapons, and worth of the industry worldwide by the next meeting.   He hadn't had time to do research on the manufacturing and distribution of explosives, but he expected to have more on this by the next meeting.

Abdul al Sharif had been busy, too.   His job was a much more shadowy one.   Arms dealers and distributors keep a low profile.   Their sub-rosa dealings fly under the radar of most international security agencies.   His work was essentially investigative in nature.   Initially he felt that if and when their program was adopted, all the arms dealers should be arrested, brought in for questioning, and required to give the names of the weapons purchasers. Evidence of any illegal activities should be placed in the hands of prosecutors. The money trail would have to be followed in order to ascertain the source of the financing for weapons.

"Would you like me to get authorization for the release of intelligence information from the other governmental agencies?" Ivan asked Abdul.

"That would be nice. I'll send you a list of things that would be interesting to know. Then you can decide which sources to contact."

"Good. Consider it done," Abdul said.

Welland's part in the meeting was to chair it, formulate the findings and recommendations, and present them to the President. He would work out what the international consequences of implementing their strategic plan would be. He would try to negotiate a joint effort with other interested nations, but failing that he would have to evolve a plan of action that would encourage cooperation and deter interference.

The truth of the matter was that he had begun writing his part of the project before he had held the first meeting. Ivan liked to see things in writing. As a prolific speed-reader, he had a decided preference for written plans and documentation. Ivan always tried to be ahead of the wave, not behind it. When his team had the data prepared he would be ready with the philosophy, rationale, and the evidence-based sales pitch to convince POTUS to approve the strategy for implementation. If the evidence did not support his position paper, Ivan would shred it. No one had seen it yet, and no one would lay eyes on it until the team had finished its work. If he had jumped ahead and shown it to anyone it might have prejudiced the team's honest efforts, and he didn't want it to seem as if he had made up his mind before they did their end of the project.

Brooklyn, Ivan's competent assistant, had put together a small group of staffers who were following up on his suggestion that they prepare a list of all the chemists and chemical engineers who had come from Islamic nations and received degrees from American institutions of higher learning. Brooklyn immediately took the bit in her teeth. She had already warned Ivan that the list was going to be long. Perhaps there were many who were educated in the U.S. and were now training terrorists to make bombs, but it seemed to her that it was more likely to be one man who had started the knowledge pyramid.

CHAPTER FIVE

Niko's sea tests had turned up a few problems. *The Controller of the Oceans* was a huge vessel and the number of things that could go wrong was legion. But fortunately what did go wrong could be put right before the great ship's first day at sea. The builders, equipment manufacturers, and service suppliers had all signed contracts with the company to have the work completed a month before the first advertised sailing date. The last month was a sort of grace period, but failure to comply with the terms of the contract carried very high financial penalties, so the pressure aboard ship on the part of outside contractors in the harbor in Toulon was enormous.

The vessel was crawling with workmen, and the resulting confusion created the opportunity that the *Scythe of Allah* was looking for. There was no question of changing the sailing schedule, as the inaugural cruise was completely sold out. Any contractor who hadn't finished his work to the company's satisfaction by the appointed date was in serious financial trouble. Captain Niko and his staff officers were coordinating with those representatives who had not yet met their contract standards. It was a lot of work, but Niko still felt confident that embarkation for the final shakedown to LeHavre could take place as scheduled.

An Algerian marine engineer, fluent in French and Arabic, was working on the bridge, programming software for a piece of navigational equipment that had been balky during preliminary trials. Three weeks before that day, he had been in one of the many cafés frequented by North African Muslim immigrants to France. He had been sitting at a small table with a friend from his old neighborhood. They were enjoying their coffee and talking about generalities, when the friend happened to mention to the engineer that he would like to introduce him to someone. A man at the bar had evidently been watching them, and when he was given the high sign he quickly came over to their table. The friend introduced them, and the man sat down and faced the engineer.

"Allah has a job for you to do," he said.

The engineer looked at him with narrowed eyes. He was neither political nor religious, so he was immediately suspicious of the stranger.

"What job would that be?" he asked.

"We'd like you to reprogram the navigation computer on the new ship, the *Controller of the Oceans*."

"That can't be done," the engineer said firmly. "It's impossible. The shipboard computer is pre-programmed before it's installed on the ship so it's synchronized with the satellite signals. I can do nothing about that."

"I am sure you are right about that," said the man, who had been introduced to the engineer as Rashid. "But what happens during a severe electrical storm? Can the signals from the satellite not be interrupted?"

"The navigation systems have redundancies. There are backup systems," the engineer replied. "Ship officers still plot the course and position of their vessel on charts as a manual check on the Global Positioning System."

Rashid leaned forward.

"But let us presume, for example, that the skies are cloudy and the navigator cannot take any sights because the celestial bodies are not visible, what then?

"The crew would plot their estimated position on a course line," the engineer replied. "They'd do that until they could get a fix to establish the exact location of the ship along the line. As soon as the GPS was back in service they would revert back to the use of the electronic system that is accurate to within a few feet."

Rashid looked at the engineer with a hard, firm stare.

"If the electronic system is interrupted for any reason," he asked, "isn't there some sort of a default routine in the programming to reboot the system where it left off?"

"Yes, but it's on the hard drive in the computer itself."

"Look, Monsieur, you change the hard drive, or change the default, that is up to you. It is the same to me. But your wife, Yvonne – that is her name, is it not? She wants you to find a solution to comply with our request. You married a French woman, but you are still a Muslim first. And your children, Abdul, Mehta, and Maurice – they will want to be proud of the sand in their blood."

The engineer paled as Rashid continued to speak.

"Islam only requires one thing of you. You must arrange the system so that the *Controller of the Oceans* arrives at this exact latitude and longitude on the morning of its scheduled passage from Lisbon to Barcelona. This position is very close to the course it most likely will take anyway on its scheduled Mediterranean cruise."

Rashid passed the Engineer a slip of paper that read, *Lat 27 Degrees 11 min 18 sec N, Long 5 Degrees 30 min 41 sec E. April 17th AM.*

The engineer took the paper and examined it carefully. He knew that the position was somewhere in the Mediterranean Sea, north of Algeria. The date would be the same date that the ship was scheduled to pass through those waters anyway. He was thinking about what would be involved in programming this information into the Sat/Nav system, but when he looked up again Rashid had disappeared.

His friend just shrugged his shoulders.

It was not unusual that one engineer among the swarm of contractors on the bridge of the *Controller of the Oceans* was working on the navigation system. Nearly every electronic system on the ship was being tested during the period shortly before she cast off for her maiden voyage. Nearly all the personnel working aboard were men, so Niko was having a long-needed respite from the company of women.

He was surprised that he was able to move from feast to famine with so little effect. His work was absorbing every moment of his life during this period of testing and trials. Soon it would be over, and the ship would be cleared to make its first passage with him in command. He looked forward to giving the commands, *let go forward lines*, *let go spring lines*, and finally *let go all lines*.

He would soon be at the helm of the largest cruise ship in the world. He was at the acme of his career at sea. With the power of the enormous ship's engines throbbing below him, obeying his every command, and with the thousands of crew and passengers looking to him for their safety and well being, Niko was indeed about to be master of all he surveyed. He had no doubt that his new position would renew the supply of women to his bed. He could have no idea that there were those who wished the *Controller of the Oceans'* maiden voyage, and the voyage of the other maidens under Niko's control, to end prematurely.

Brooklyn's research team had produced a list of several thousand names of chemists and chemical engineers from Islamic countries educated in the United States. Nearly all were men. The team members had encountered several problems when they tried to get current addresses for these men. Snail mail in the Middle East was usually not returned to the sender if the intended recipient was no longer at the same address. Families in Arab cities tended to stay put, but over a fifteen to twenty year period the postal trail went cold for the majority of men on Brooklyn's list. Meanwhile the Internet had come into being between the present day and the time most of the students had been in the U.S. The degree to which the new electronic communications systems were being used by al Qaeda was amazing, and the various security agencies tapped into this source to monitor terrorist activities.

The results of this work turned up useful information about the recruiting of young people through chat rooms and cyber cafés. Cheap and efficient networking enabled the terrorists to plan and coordinate attacks, obtain financing, exchange bomb-making instructions, and receive 80% of the information they needed to conduct attacks from information provided free on the net. Brooklyn was forced to conclude that her research would have to involve a heavy electronic component in order to be effective. She wanted to chew over the parameters of the search with her boss before launching into a major project involving other agencies.

"Let me have a look at the snail trail before we blow this thing out of proportion," Ivan said, after he had read the papers Brooklyn had given him. "Let's superimpose two criteria over this list and see if we can reduce it to a more manageable size. Search the list for those graduates who took courses in the chemistry of explosives. Usually there's a cross-disciplinary course with mining engineering departments. Explosives are used as a quick method to blast rock walls to expose or retrieve a vein of minerals or gems. Petroleum explorers identify and chart promising geological formations using radar equipment to analyze ultra-high frequency radio wave signals after the blasts. Any people who did a chemistry major plus a mining explosive elective should be flagged."

"Okay, boss."

"Then those graduates who have never been back in touch with their alma maters should be selected out of that group. We are looking for someone who is very clever, someone who applied himself and probably did well in school. My guess is that we're looking for a guy who knew from early on that he didn't want to be traced. His name is probably changed now from his university days, and he would never have kept in touch with his professors or fellow students. When we get this narrowed down a bit we can consult with Abdul to see if he can correlate any of our selections with his list of arms dealers. The man we're looking for must also be a sort of genius in the field of logistics and transportation, as the terrorists never seem to run out of weapons, or bombs, or suicidal fanatics. We're constantly uncovering caches of weapons, but there are always more. So get busy applying these new criteria, and let me know how it goes."

Ivan was peeved. Not one of the escaped prisoners from the jail in Yemen had been recaptured. Not one. In his opinion there was no way this could happen without collusion from the Yemeni guards. Once on the loose, these men had to have received assistance to flee the country. That was where Ivan's "master of logistics" theory came in. Ivan's intuition indicated to him that some individual was in charge of distributing the weapons, and also distributing terrorist personnel around the Middle East.

Osama Bin Laden was the philosopher king of Al Qaeda, but the ruler had his minions. There was a Minister of the Exchequer, so-called, though no one in the West knew who he was. There was a Lord High Chamberlain, and probably a Lord of the Admiralty, all of them equally operating in the shadow of the king and the shadow of secrecy, but executing their powerful offices nevertheless.

How were a relatively few terrorist leaders able to hold sway over such a large part of the Islamic world? Ivan wrestled with this thought nearly every day of his recent working life. Applying horrible methods of duress in the places where these clandestine governors operated was certainly one way for them to maintain their power. There is nothing like the threat of decapitation to deter dissension. Ivan's usual method of rational examination of situations was not working in this case. He realized that he could be perfectly rational and not get anywhere with an enemy that had no mercy, no sense of humor, no wish for liberty, and no willingness to compromise.

The more he thought about it, the more Ivan came back to his plan to neutralize the terrorists by declawing them. If he could arrange to dry up their supply of weapons, their talons would be gone. The irony of the terrorists acquiring and using the weapons of the hated West against the inventors and producers of the weapons never eluded Ivan. Now they wanted to acquire or produce nuclear weapons to turn their war of hate into a total disaster for the world.

"They must be denied nukes," thought Ivan, "but we must go back a few steps and deny them the masses of destructive weapons first."

He was more resolved than ever to get his plan to the point where he could present it to the President. Ivan's fertile mind had been developing a second stage of his plan that would take the weapons of today and stack them next to the suits of armor, swords and shields of the Middle Ages in the museums of the world. He realized that he was a long way from being able to present Stage Two. First, of course, Stage One had to be successful in a hugely noticeable fashion. It was essential for everyone in the world to see the benefits of a no-death-by-guns policy. He was just beginning to think about how the criticisms of the cynics would be piled on him for his naiveté in thinking that all other countries could be made to agree, for they would never do it of their own free will. He came out of his idealistic reverie when his phone rang.

"Hello?"

"It's your wife, Dr. Welland, on line two," said a voice he didn't recognize.

"Hello, dear. How are you?"

"Ivan, I think I am in labor."

"You think? You're not sure?"

"It is hard to be certain for sure," said Marina, sounding rattled. "So many women have babies since world began, and still we are not certain when things start. I have very serious contractions at intervals of ten minutes."

"Have you called the doctor?"

"I will call him, but I think you must come home now."

"I'll be there before you know it."

He hung up and immediately called Brooklyn.

"Please order my car to be brought around at once. Marina is in labor and I'm going home."

He packed up his desk, picked up his presidential hot line phone as well as his own cell phone, and headed for the door.

"Good luck, boss," Brooklyn said, as he passed her desk. "I've cleared the rest of the day from your calendar. Call me later and let me know if you're going to be here tomorrow. Your driver should be out front in a minute."

The chauffeur sped out of the White House driveway and headed toward Ivan's apartment building. When they arrived, Ivan ran to the door, turned the key in the lock, and entered the apartment. There was Marina, sitting in a chair looking at her watch, with a small suitcase standing on the floor next to her.

"Was I too long?" Ivan asked, breathlessly.

"No, not at all. I time contractions, not you."

Ivan picked up the suitcase and held Marina by the arm as he closed the door behind them. In a minute they were being propelled toward the Washington Hospital Center on Irving Street. The hospital was an enormous facility, but fortunately the Wellands had taken a tour of the maternity ward a few weeks earlier, so when they arrived they knew what entrance to use. They went through the revolving door, stepped into an elevator, and got off on the fifth floor. In a minute or so Marina was being led away by a friendly nurse to a nearby room to be gowned and prepped.

Ivan sat down in the waiting area. After a few minutes the same nurse came looking for him.

"You may come with me to the labor room, Dr. Welland," she said.

Ivan felt a bit uncomfortable being called *doctor* in these surroundings, but he followed along in the wake of the efficient nurse. How did she know he was a doctor, anyway? He hoped that calling him by this title did not imply that she was expecting him to do any doctoring in the near future.

When they got to a door with the number 3 on it they went inside and found Marina sitting up in bed, already wearing one of those silly hospital gowns.

"You may keep your wife company until she's ready to deliver," said the nurse. "It won't be for some time yet, but the doctor is on her way."

Ivan took a seat next to the bed and held Marina's hand. Every once in a while she would grip it with all her strength as the contraction intervals became shorter.

"The nurse told me my cervix was open 4 centimeters. She also shaved me. I wonder how long it is before I look normal to you again."

He lifted the sheet and looked under it. "I'd say about five to six weeks will do it. Oh, and by the way, she missed a couple of spots."

Marina wanted to smack Ivan's hand in mock anger, but another contraction had just started, so she gripped it instead. The time between contractions was decreasing. Periodically the nurse would come in and check to see how far along she was. Ivan wondered why the measurement was in centimeters. The U.S. had had its chance to switch to the metric system and had decided against the idea, in spite of the fact that Canada and Mexico had chosen some time before to adopt the measuring system used everywhere else. Had it been up to him, the U.S. would have gone along with the simpler system in order to be in synch with the rest of the world. He felt the temporary pain of the changeover would have been worth the long-term gain.

Marina's forehead was beaded with sweat, and Ivan wiped it off with a cool, wet towel. She was in serious labor now. Suddenly the doctor swished into the room.

"Hello, Marina," she said in a hearty voice. "How are we feeling?"

"I do not know how you are feeling, but I am not feeling so good," said Marina.

"Nice quip," said the doctor. "She must be doing okay," she added, winking at Ivan, who wasn't in the mood for this kind of talk. Maybe the exchange of mundane, useless information was a reassuring thing for a woman teetering on the edge of motherhood.

"It'll soon be time," the doctor said, looking at her chart.

Marina, like so many brave women, had refused the offer of an epidural injection to lessen the pain. Ivan didn't argue with her, although his guilt about having put her in this position was at its zenith. She wanted natural childbirth, and he respected her decision.

"It's time now," said the doctor. "I'm going to break your water and move you into the delivery room."

Another deft doctoral penetration down below, and the amniotic fluid flowed from between Marina's legs.

"Let's get you gowned up now, Dr. Welland. You're going to be a father in a few minutes, and we don't want you to miss seeing your baby born, now do we?"

The nurse assisted Ivan into an asparagus green doctor's gown that was too small for him. He donned a surgeon's cap and mask and was shown into the next room. Marina was lying on her back with her feet in stirrups. The bed had been elevated so that her pelvis was at the doctor's eye level when she sat on a stool between the thighs of the mother-to-be. Ivan was standing at the head of the bed out of the way, but he was able to watch the proceedings with the aid of a large, strategically-placed mirror. When she was not giving Marina commands to push or not push, the doctor showed Ivan the various items of interest in the landscape, paying particular attention to a dark, wet mass of black hair located at its dead center.

"The baby's head is crowning," the doctor said. "A few more pushes and the Wellands will be a three-person family."

Ivan was well aware of the anatomy involved in the birth procedure, but nonetheless he felt he was witnessing a miracle like no other he had ever seen. It was simply incredible that a woman was able to deliver such a large item as a baby from a space barely large enough to contain the guilty instrument that caused the problem in the first place.

Marina was straining to pass this perfect little life into the world. Life that had been formed out of love nine months before was now taking on its own separate existence.

The doctor was exhorting Marina to push with all her might. Then with a huge, magnificent effort, accompanied by a primordial groan, Marina delivered the baby's head face down into the doctor's waiting hands. She turned the baby a quarter turn so that the shoulders could pass, and Marina pushed the child out with one last effort. It was not a pretty sight – blood, slime, and some cheesy material covering a slightly blue-toned infant.

"It's a girl," said the doctor. "Congratulations!"

She put the baby, still connected by the umbilical cord, on Marina's stomach. She tied a knot in the cord and handed Ivan the surgical scissors so that he could cut the cord just above the knot.

Once he had done this the pediatric nurse and the delivery nurse whisked the baby away. They suctioned the child's mouth, put drops in her eyes, wiped and dried her, saw that she had begun breathing, and noted the cyanotic blue color was turning to a normal flesh tone. They measured and weighed her, then wrapped her in a little white blanket and handed her to Ivan.

He looked into the face of his daughter for the first time and wept for joy. The couple had decided to call the baby *Julia,* after the Secretary of State who had hired Ivan and become Marina's best friend. Had the baby been a boy he would have been named Lincoln, after the President.

The nurse was making a much-relieved Marina more comfortable, washing her face and fluffing her pillow. When she had Marina settled she took the baby out of Ivan's arms and laid it on Marina's chest so that she could look at her child. The doctor was doing a little repair job down below, and seeing to it that the fundus was properly in place. She cast a couple of stitches to aid the healing of a slight tear that she claimed was perfectly normal.

Marina saw the tears of happiness in her husband's eyes, and shed a few herself. They both looked at the child in amazement. Although they had been expecting her for a long time, the actual appearance of the baby, its gender, and its little face were a new experience for the first-time parents.

Eventually the nurse placed the baby in a crib in the hospital room to which the family had been moved. Marina fell into an exhausted sleep, and slept for a couple of hours while Ivan sat with her. He and Marina had just brought their child into a very dangerous world. He vowed to do his best to make the world a safer place for his little Julia, and for children everywhere. After all, the family name, Welland, was the name of the chief armorer in Beowulf, so Ivan was determined to live up to his name and do everything in his power to shield his nation from its enemies.

CHAPTER SIX

Mercedes took the evening bus to Santiago. She hadn't told Diego that she was leaving on a new contract with the cruise line because he would have tried to prevent her from going. Her parents knew that she needed to support her son, and they had grown accustomed to her long periods away from them. They were also well aware that Diego would be livid when he learned that his wife, blackmail victim, and sexual slave had managed to make her escape. It was her father's hope that Diego would simply accept the money that his wife sent home and leave little Juan safely in their care.

Diego was indeed furious when he found out that Mercedes had gone back to her job at sea. He thought seriously about upsetting her parents by taking Juan away from them, but he knew that having a kid in his life would be a constant burden and an unwanted expense. In the end he decided to settle for whatever money he could pry out of his in-laws during the absence of his whore of a wife. He would wait until Mercedes came home to punish her for leaving without his permission.

Mercedes was not totally surprised when she received her posting to the *Controller of the Oceans*. The company could have assigned her to any of their ships, and therefore there was always the random possibility that she could be assigned to the Neptune Line's newest ocean liner. Whether it was fate, or the Captain's doing, or part of an unknown supreme plan, she was to be reunited with Captain Niko for the maiden voyage of his new command.

She had mixed emotions about being aboard his ship. On the one hand, Niko was a kind and gentle man, and although he didn't really understand her, he did his best to satisfy her needs. On the other hand, it's always awkward to rejuvenate sexual relationships that have been allowed to cool over extended periods of time. She didn't know how Niko would feel about seeing her again. He might be glad, or he could feel some sort of obligation to renew their liaison. She didn't want him to feel compelled by guilt to reawaken their affair. She knew only too well, from her recent sexual experiences with her husband, Diego, what an odious thing guilty, obligatory sex could be.

The plane tickets supplied by Neptune called for her to fly from Santiago to Buenos Aires, where she was to catch a flight to New York and change to a flight for Paris. In Paris she would take the train to Toulon to meet the cruise liner. This kind of long distance traveling, moving across three continents in twenty-four hours, was exhausting. After boarding the ship, Mercedes only slept for five hours before she was required to attend a long succession of training sessions, despite her extensive experience with the cruise line.

Each department head was focused on giving good service to the passengers by heading off any potential problems. Every aspect of good food service was discussed and demonstrated. Some of the basics had been taught to the new crew members during classes ashore before they boarded the ship. Each table had a primary server and an assistant server. The primary servers were trained to take the orders in the same way every time so that there were no questions to be asked of the diners when the dishes arrived. It was always to be clear which person ordered which meal. The assistant servers poured the water, served the other beverages, distributed the bread and butter, supplied the steak knives if required and generally made themselves useful to the primary servers. Mercedes had become a primary over time, and had learned the ingredients and dishes of many international cuisines.

Because she knew the recipes, had a good ability with the English language and a pleasant way with people, Mercedes had achieved a modicum of popularity with the dining room's headwaiters and the *maitre d'*. Everyone's tips depended on the friendliness of the serving staff, so good waitresses were highly appreciated in the small world that surrounded the galley of a cruise ship. The salaries of servers on ships are very low. The tips make up for the poor wages, along with the room and board provided. The "Suggested Tipping Schedule" that was not so subtly published in the literature distributed to the passengers, was an enormous help in leveling the earnings of those in the crew who depended upon the generosity of the passengers for their economic survival. Before the introduction of that schedule, earnings were far less stable for food servers, and they never knew what to expect at the end of each cruise. Now the big tippers could add something to the suggested amounts if they wished, but the real difference was that the stingy, or uninformed tippers, were now apprised of what was expected. Onboard computer accounting also helped because tips could be charged to the passenger's credit cards, and there was no longer a last minute passenger scramble for cash to leave for tips.

Mercedes' new assistant server was a streamlined woman from the Philippines. The crew was of many nationalities, and the Islands of the Philippines had provided their fair share of them. It was possible for a server to maintain only a nodding acquaintance with her assistant outside of working hours for the duration of an entire cruise, if they kept their socializing within their own ethnic or national grouping. Mercedes' onboard group of Chileans was much smaller, and she didn't know any of them. She would no doubt meet them and have a chance to speak Spanish occasionally, but she was not aware of any potential special friends among her countrymen.

In general Mercedes kept to herself. The loneliness factor was perhaps what made her strange alliance with Captain Niko possible. She was alone, and he was too. She could speak to no one on board about her affair with the Captain. If she had, she would most likely not be believed, or if believed, she would be envied and hated in the way the other students hate a teacher's pet in school. He could also not speak of their liaison with anyone because it was against company rules to fraternize with subordinates aboard ship. The secrets of the past were securely behind them. Neither Niko nor Mercedes were anxious to reopen their risky relationship. The odds were that they would meet each other at some time or other even on a ship the size of the *Controller of the Seas.* Mercedes did not know if Niko was aware that she was aboard, but she was not going to make any effort to be the first to make contact. Despite her pretension at self-control, however, she knew herself well enough to realize that if Niko invited her to his cabin again, she would accept.

Back in San Bernardo, Diego sat in a seedy tavern playing cards with his buddies. His family sinecure provided him with cash for gambling. His playing partners enjoyed Diego's source of revenue too, since he usually lost when he bet on cards. Diego thought winning card games was a matter of luck. The real gamblers didn't agree, and proved their point by separating him from his money nearly every time they had Diego at the table. Diego didn't prize common sense, and in any case he had very little of it. He was brash, but not brave. His will was strong, but his will power was weak. If he had abstained from gambling he could have saved his money, started a business, and lived a comfortable life, but he was dominated by his exaggerated self-image. He was sure of himself and never questioned his ethics or morals. He was certain that it was only because of bad luck that he had never achieved his proper place of respect and admiration in the world. He told himself that one day his luck would change and he would be the wealthy and important man that he was meant to be.

A couple of days after Mercedes had left the country; Diego was playing cards as usual in the rear room of the cantina that he frequented. The influx of his wife's money in his coffers had encouraged him to increase his wagers. But his judgment had not undergone any improvement, and he was falling into debt to the local small time hood. Finally, out of money and out of credit, Diego was forced to leave the table. He went to the bar and ordered beer. A stranger was standing next to him.

"I couldn't help noticing your temporary run of bad luck," the stranger said, in a nondescript foreign accent. "But next time you will do better, I am sure of this."

"Thanks," Diego said. "But I've exceeded my credit limit and I won't be able to recoup my losses till I settle my debt."

"Perhaps I can help you," said the stranger.

Interested now, Diego turned to listen to the man, expecting him to offer some sort of loan proposal.

"Why would you do that?"

"I'm not offering to *give* you money. I have a proposition to make. You could earn a great deal of money. What do you say?" He gestured at an empty table in the corner where they could discuss the deal.

Diego had nothing to lose by sitting down and listening to what the man had to say, so the two went over to the table, taking their beer with them.

"My name is Ricardo," said the man, extending his hand.

"Diego."

"I know your name," said Ricardo.

"Is that so? Why?"

"I know it because you're the husband of Mercedes de León, am I right?"

"Why do you know my wife?"

"I don't know her. I only know that she works for the Neptune Cruise Line. Don't worry, I do not want you to do anything illegal. I need her to perform a small errand aboard her ship, that's all. If you ask her to do it for me I'll pay you 5,000 American dollars. Half now, and half after she delivers a tiny object to someone on board. That's all. Can you assure me that your wife will follow your instructions?"

Relieved that it was nothing more than that, Diego quickly returned to his usual swaggering persona.

"Mercedes will do anything I tell her to do."

"Good, then do we have a deal?" Ricardo asked.

"Yes, but first show me the $2,500 you talked about."

Ricardo reached into his jacket pocket and fished out an envelope with Diego's name written on it, and passed it to him.

"Your wife will be contacted aboard the ship and told exactly what to do. You must warn her to be on the look-out for her instructions. You won't see me again. After Mercedes does what we ask of her you can go to the Banco de Chile branch here in San Bernardo. See the Manager, tell him your name, and he'll give you an envelope just like this one. Is that clear?"

Diego didn't have any questions. It never occurred to him to ask the stranger how he came to have an envelope with 2,500 dollars in it and with his name on it before they had even met. As with his card playing, he preferred to think of it as good luck, but he was wrong again. There was no luck involved.

"Just to make sure I've got this straight," Diego said, "I'm to call my wife and tell her to run an errand for someone on the ship who will contact her. And that's all you want from me?"

"That is correct. Can you assure me that she will do it?"

With the envelope containing the money in his hand, Diego's ego was at an all time high.

"She'll do it, or else." He made a throat-cutting gesture with his hand.

"That won't be necessary," Ricardo said. "Just make sure she does what I said."

Diego took the envelope into the back room and whispered into the ear of one of the mobsters who was sitting there. He passed him a small wad of bills, and the man acknowledged him with a nod. Then Diego resumed his seat at the card table and asked the guys to deal him in again. The mobster, who seemed to control the game, gave his tacit assent. With his credibility restored, Diego resumed the pursuit of his sportive lady luck. Ricardo, meanwhile, had left the cantina, hailed a taxi, and ordered the driver to take him to the Santiago Airport. He would fly from there to Buenos Aires, then to New York, and on to Paris, where he would catch a train for Toulon.

Ali was very busy. He had managed to smuggle the escaped prisoners out of Yemen, and they had dispersed to various cells that could both hide them and use their services. At the moment he was directing the repacking of a truckload of ice cream. Inside the heavily insulated freezer truck three men in sweaters were gingerly placing rectangular boxes of two-liter ice cream packages containing high-powered plastic explosives in among the genuine ice cream boxes. Ali had the ice cream sent from France to Beirut via ship in a refrigerated container. He arranged to sell just enough of the ice cream cargo in Syria to make space for the plastic explosives which he had transported via camel caravan from Yemen.

Months before, some Algerian Islamist sympathizers had supplied Ali with a pallet of new unused strawberry ice cream container packaging. He had been holding it for a special occasion, and this was it. The rest of the truckload was assorted flavors of ice cream, everything but strawberry. Ironically the containers read "Explosion de Fraises." It would be easy to separate the ice cream from the plastic explosives when they arrived at their destination in Algeria. The seeds of destruction were strawberry flavored; the rest would be donated to the Grand Mosque to be distributed to the children at the close of the Ramadan fasting period.

Transporting the explosives in a refrigerated truck had several benefits. Keeping the plastic cool was very helpful in avoiding unplanned detonation. Ali himself would drive the vehicle, and when he passed through the various customs points along the route he would just open up the back and offer the guards some ice cream. Who could be suspicious of a truckload of ice cream? No Muslim customs inspector would force him to unload ice cream bound for a children's Ramadan celebration, especially not in the burning North African sun. Ali would be accompanied by one of his sons who had been trained in the U.S. to be a certified repair mechanic on Thermo King mobile transport refrigeration units. Factory trained to use U.S. know-how to keep the cargo frozen... Ali liked the irony of that, just as he liked the fact that his knowledge of explosives had been taught to him by U.S. professors. It seemed like poetic justice.

Ali still remembered his sexual humiliations at the hands of those American whores who wanted to make him waste his time with them when he could have been at home making fine Muslim sons. Ali's third son, Amin, was not nearly as clever as his father, but he was a good mechanic and kept the equipment in good repair, and that was a valuable contribution in itself. He was not close enough to the succession of Ali's sheikhdom, or to taking over the command of the *Scythe of Allah*, to worry Ali. He was a good boy who followed his father's instructions and was loyal to the death, if need be. Ali was looking forward to the long drive with his son to deliver the ice cream, as he wanted to discuss finding a wife for him, and reprove him for a few slippages into non-Islamic thinking that he had noticed.

All was in readiness. Amin had checked the oil, coolant, diesel fuel, and tire pressure, and was satisfied that the truck could make the long trip from Syria to Algeria. The distance was roughly the equivalent of a trans-continental trip across the U.S. Ali had the way stations plotted on his map. They'd skirt Israel, though Ali would have liked to deliver some strawberry ice cream to the Knesset. The clever Jews had become so wary from the incessant bombings of the Palestinians, that it was difficult to trick them anymore. Ali regarded Israel as a festering pustule that Allah would lance in due time. The father-and-son team would pass through Jordan, head for Egypt, and follow the coastal roads West through North Africa to Algeria. The sun would be behind them most of the time. Ali was like a fighter pilot in that he always liked to be coming out of the direction of the sun. Amin would do most of the driving. Ali would use the long hours on the road to do some planning.

Ivan was becoming more and more convinced that there was a mastermind of terror at large in the Middle East. He had hoped that the violence would come to an end with the death of Imam Mansur and the other two caliphs. The fact that the violence was on the rise again was proof in itself that someone was behind the latest attacks. Ivan would have liked to devote a little more of his time to his personal life. He wanted to be at home with Marina and baby Julia, but conditions in the world were not cooperating with his desires. His morning briefing sessions with the President and his intelligence officers led him to the conclusion that something big was in the works. It was not so much what was actually happening that troubled him. It was a feeling in the pit of his stomach that kept gnawing at him, like the calm before a storm. He decided to check in with Brooklyn to see what progress she was making in her search for American-trained demolition experts.

She had narrowed the list down to around 300 possible suspects, using the criteria that Ivan had added at their last meeting. She had taken her list over to the CIA and used their algorithm to compare her list to their list of known terrorists. There were some correlative names. Brooklyn showed them to Ivan along with the information she had collated from the files. He was stroking his chin and deliberating when an unwelcome thought suddenly occurred to him.

"What if the algorithm was tampered with just slightly?"

"What do you mean?" Brooklyn asked.

"Well, somebody over at the CIA wrote the software to analyze the data. Suppose the programmer inserted a little coded sub-routine to skip a few names if they ever come up? Or perhaps he could have substituted the name of a sacrificial lamb. How often are these programs reviewed down to the level of each line of code?"

"Are you suggesting that the CIA files are corrupted?" Brooklyn caught her breath as she said this.

"No, I'm not suggesting anything, but I'd like to feel secure about the statistical tools we're using. After all, I'm the Security Advisor," Ivan said. "Get Grayson on the phone for me, will you please, Brooklyn. I want to ask him about his software review protocols."

Jim Grayson was the relatively new Director of the CIA, but he was an old-line political sort of guy who had been around government agencies in Washington most of his life. He was in the mold of previous directors in the sense that he spoke publicly as little as possible, and said nothing when he did speak. These guys treated the Agency's files as though they were their personal undershirts. Ivan did not expect to get much help from Grayson. The President appoints the Directors, and the Senate confirms the appointments, but once that's over the fiefdom is turned over to the appointee. It's at this point that the protective walls of the castle are buttressed against the likes of the President's staffers. Usually the only way to get anything out of the CIA is to have the President ask for it personally at his intelligence briefing sessions.

"When secrecy concerns are given as the reason for stupidity, America is in trouble," Ivan thought. He almost rescinded his request that Grayson be called. Ivan's tangle with the previous Director was well known in high circles, and any calls from him would put the Director on the defensive. Until his team finished their research on weapons curtailment he didn't want to have to speak to the President about a related matter lest he be forced to spill the details of his new proposal before he was ready. He would have to be cautious during his chat with Grayson, and just inquire about the protocols.

The Director took Ivan's call, and the result of the conversation was pretty much as Ivan expected. Jim Grayson would check out the procedures they used to update and vet the software the Agency used, and get back to him with the details. Ivan could tell that the Agency was all over the problem of hackers from outside, but he suspected that not much was being done to defend against internal systems tampering. This, in spite of the treasonous example of Deputy Director Richmond, whom Ivan had exposed when he discovered the traitor had sold out to the caliphs in Mecca. It was natural to trust your employees and your co-workers, Ivan supposed, but in the intelligence business it could be a fatal mistake. Granted it was a lot of mostly boring work for a programmer to go over the logic of another programmer's work, but if isn't done on matters of national security, what sort of intelligence service is being provided?

Ivan's intuition was working overtime. As many so-called facts as he had been taught, plus the number of theories he had been exposed to, and the number of assurances he had been given that turned out to be worthless, all these had only worked to make Ivan more reliant on his intuition.

"Please show me the list of people you turned up again," he said to Brooklyn.

She handed him her list.

"How many names were totally unknown to the CIA?"

"Four," she answered.

"Okay, so let's focus on them. Pull any information you have on those four and bring it to my office."

"Sure, boss." She used the title *Boss* whenever she felt Ivan was acting too officious.

Brooklyn's meaning was not lost on Ivan. He was like a bloodhound on the scent just now, and he didn't want to be called off the trail to receive a tiny social reprimand. On the other hand, he needed her to be at her best, and he really hadn't meant to command her to do something she would happily have done if only he'd said *please*.

He added "please" as an afterthought.

"You're welcome," Brooklyn said sweetly.

When she returned with the files, Ivan took them from her, thanked her, and opened them one by one. He pored over every detail. There was nothing unusual about any of them, at least none that he could see at first glance. They seemed to be like all the rest, young Arab men who studied chemistry or chemical engineering while in the U.S. They had attended different universities. All of them had done well in their coursework and had received good grades. They had all been born in the same decade. One was Egyptian; one was a Saudi, one from the Emirates, and the last from Iran. Why didn't the CIA have the names of these ordinary men in their files? Were they above suspicion? Was there something about these names that was unrecognizable to their computers? Were the names false? Could they have been deleted from the intelligence files intentionally? Ivan was doodling while he contemplated the files. He was a big time word game fan – one of those people who always completed the Sunday New York Times crossword puzzle, usually in jig time.

He was idly playing around with the letters in the name of the first man's file as though it were an anagram. Rusnam Thoufanili. Strange name, Ivan thought. It doesn't seem particularly Arabic. Maybe it's Persian? But this was not the Iranian man's file. This man was from Dubai, or at least he claimed to be. If he shifted them around, what names could be made out these letters? He tried the most obvious possibility first, backwards. *Mansur*, he spelled out. He sat up as though struck by lightning. *Mansur*, he had learned meant *victory*, and it was the name of his nemesis in the days when he had been in Chechnya. Mansur had been the Imam of the Mosque in Grozny, the man Ivan was sure he had shot to death, until a corpse with two healing bullet wounds showed up as one of the caliphs in Mecca. Mansur had told him that he had studied electrical engineering at M.I.T. This man Rusnam Thoufanili's file stated that he graduated from R.P.I. in Chemical Engineering. Probably it was a different person altogether. Mansur was a fairly common Arab name after all.

Ivan decided to see if the last name could be unscrambled into something meaningful. He tried several combinations using the letters T-H-O-U-F-A-N-I-L-I. When he got to ILFATIHOUN he knew he was onto something. Mansur il Fatihoun was the full name of the Imam in Grozny. Were they two different men with the same name? The Imam had told him he studied engineering first, and then theology, but he could have lied about the order in which he took his studies. It might make sense that he had done things in this latter order because a recent educational law in Jordan had been passed making it required of clerics in that country to take a degree in some other discipline before they studied religion.

Prior to this law no studies but religious studies had been required to qualify students to become an imam, and as a result the worst students became clerics. Of course, Ivan thought, this law was passed in Jordan, one of the most progressive of the Arab states, and it might not apply elsewhere. However, it might be the precursor of things to come in other lands, and it might signify a shortcoming in the education of clerics in

general. Wielding a mighty position in the social structure of a
nation with no knowledge other than that found in the Qur'an
could certainly account for some of the loose cannons that had
sprung up all over Islam. The Mansur that Ivan had known in
Chechnya was certainly not among the worst students, nor
would his pride allow anyone to think that for a minute, so he
might have taken a U.S. degree just to prove that he could do
the work and still be an imam. The anagram of the imam's
name was just too coincidental for Ivan to believe it had no
relevance, or that it pertained to a totally different man.

"Brooklyn, will you please check with M.I.T. and see if the
registrar has any record of a student named Mansur il Fatihoun,
or Rusnam Thoufanili? Find out everything you can about the
student, and have his transcript faxed to us. I'm going to work
on the other three files while you're doing that."

Ivan was very excited. He felt he was onto something big.
It was on a par with the tingling sensation he had experienced
when he first uncovered the code of the caliphs. Every synapse
in his brain was standing at attention as he opened the second
file. Ali bin Yemeni was the name on the file. This name did
not seem like an anagram to Ivan, but it didn't seem like a real
name either. In translation it would read, *Ali son of a man from
Yemen.* His home was listed as Riyadh, and his citizenship as
Saudi. His education was exactly as Ivan supposed it would be.
He had a degree in chemical engineering from the University of
Houston. His course work included every class that could be
helpful to someone planning to build bombs, or train others to
build them. Maybe this man was the elusive terrorist leader
who designed the suicide bomber jackets so widely in use by
Islamist fanatics. He could be the very man who taught the
terrorists how to build the IED devices that were now the most
lethal weapons in their arsenal. *Yemeni* – the name suggested
the bombing of the U.S.S. Cole in Saana, Yemen.

"Brooklyn, please put out an APB to every security agency
in the world to send us information about this man." He passed
the file to her. "You can file this third one permanently, as he is
deceased."

"Excuse me," she said, but how can you know that?"

"His name tells me so." Ivan replied.

Brooklyn looked at the file and said, "Ammad Humatta tells you he's dead?"

"Yes," Ivan answered. "Read it this way, *Muhammad Atta.*"

"The terrorist hijacker, the leader of the 9/11 attack?"

"The very same," said Ivan.

"We're onto something big, aren't we Dr. Welland?"

"I believe we are, Brooklyn. There's something funny about this fourth file, too. Let me work on it for a minute."

After a while Ivan looked up and said, "This fourth guy is a total fraud. He uses the name Sayyid Qutb. Nasser hanged the real Sayyid Qutb in Egypt in 1966. I think this guy means to imply that he would like to be Qutb, not that he *is* Qutb. Maybe he is a son of Qutb? We must look into that, Brooklyn. This man may well be the most dangerous of all terrorists, if he's anything like his namesake."

"I've never heard of anyone called Qutb," said Brooklyn.

"Most people in the West haven't, but he's sort of the Karl Marx of the caliphate. He wrote a commentary on the Qur'an that's 15 volumes long in the English translation. He wrote it during the forty years he was locked up in an Egyptian prison. His philosophy of the jihad is the origin of modern Islamist terrorism. In fact, his brother Muhammad, who escaped from Egypt and became a professor in Saudi Arabia, was one of Osama bin Laden's teachers. We must find this guy because he could be the keeper of the flame of the violent wing of Pan Arabism and the Islamic Brotherhood movements. Qutb went to school in Colorado and got a masters degree in education in the late 1940s. His biographer reports that the conduct of our American women with their sexual freedom was so traumatic for him that he ran back to Egypt, filled with hatred. So we've got to find out everything we can about this other man who uses the name of Qutb."

CHAPTER SEVEN

Mercedes was taken aback when she was paged to receive a ship-to-shore call. She was surprised first of all because the ship had not yet put out to sea, and secondly because the radio services were withheld from the crew except under unusual circumstances, such as emergencies. As she hurried to answer the page, she worried that something had happened to her son, or perhaps her parents.

She was astonished when she heard Diego's voice.

"Mercedes, I want you to do something for me. I'm very angry that you left Chile without my permission, and I've been making your son pay for your sins, but if you do something for me I'll ease up on the little weasel."

"What do you want from me, Diego?"

"It's very simple *chata*," he said sweetly.

Mercedes hated him when he was trying to get something out of her by pretending to be affectionate. She could sense the effluvium oozing out of his mouth as he spoke. He was at his most evil when he was being nice. She had learned that lesson soon after they married, and it had worsened with time.

"Just tell me what you want," Mercedes said.

"Be nice."

"You should take your own advice. Now tell me what you want. We're not allowed to stay on the ship-to-shore forever."

"Okay, listen. Someone on the ship will contact you during the first days of the cruise. He'll ask you to do a simple errand, like delivering a message, or showing him the way to a certain place on the ship. He won't require you to do anything illegal. But you have to do whatever he wants."

"And if I don't?"

"I'll take it out on Juan. It's as simple as that."

"Why would you hurt your own son?"

"How do I know he's mine, you whore? The little bastard doesn't look anything like me."

"You're right. He's a handsome boy."

"Shut up, bitch. Just do what you're told and you won't have to worry about anything."

Diego had already gambled away most of the advance payment and would soon be in need of the balance, but he couldn't tell Mercedes. He had to pretend in his swaggering way that he was in total control, or the little *puta* would sense his vulnerability and refuse to take orders from him.

"Do you give me your word that this little favor won't get me into trouble?" Mercedes said.

"Yes."

"All right, then I'll do it."

"Good. I knew you would. I look forward to your return to our home. I want us to have another baby together."

Mercedes was about to say something nasty that she might have regretted, but Diego had already hung up. She knew that his word was worthless, so she wasn't sure she could fulfill her promise until she met Diego's contact.

Niko had been conversing with one of his officers on the bridge just outside the communications center's open door when he heard the page for Mercedes León.

"So she's been assigned to my ship again," he thought.

He had tried to remain neutral about her ship assignment. He had left the decision entirely to chance. If she was on board, fine. If not, that was fine, too. When he heard her name being paged, he felt an unscheduled neuron tingle that undeniably gave his apathy the lie. Unfortunately when his thoughts had drifted off in that direction he had missed hearing what his officer was saying about the engineer who had been puttering around with the Sat/Nav for so long. He shrugged. The officer took the gesture to mean that the Captain didn't think it was unusual for the engineer to be there, and since the man in question was a bona fide representative of the electronics firm that built the navigation system, the officer let the matter slide. Two days to go, and Niko would take his new ship up to LeHavre where the passengers would come aboard. LeHavre was a traditional port of embarkation for large passenger vessels. The *Normandie* and the *Liberté* had sailed from the famous port, and now it was the turn of the *Controller of the Oceans*. The elegant old French liners had had to compete with the Cunard's *Queen Mary* and *Queen Elizabeth* during the time that people made trans-Atlantic crossings in ocean liners. Niko's ship had many more competitors for the cruising market, but for the time being it was the Queen of the seas, and the 600-pound gorilla in the cruising business. He was feeling in a celebratory mood. Perhaps he would have dinner in his cabin and see if he could arrange for Mercedes to deliver it.

By this time Rashid had arrived in Toulon and was ensconced in a hotel near the port. One of his wives had rented the room and had been waiting for him. She had brought him a fancy suitcase filled with Western-style cruising clothes. Traveling on a cruise ship was a form of Western decadence, and he could not wear traditional Arab clothing without calling attention to himself. He was booked aboard the *Controller of the Oceans* and traveling with a false identity. He would be passing himself off as an American Arab who had achieved wealth and status in the U.S. by deserting his duties to Islam and becoming a capitalist lackey. He would soon be joined by a young English-speaking Arab woman who was trusted by the SOA, and who would dress in Western clothes and pretend to be his wife.

He was in Toulon to make sure that the Algerian engineer had successfully programmed the navigation equipment as he had been instructed. He would meet him in the same café where he had met him the first time. Rashid, a.k.a. Ricardo, had a couple of hours to kill before he was scheduled to go to the café. He was a fundamentalist Muslim and took his duties very seriously. According to the Qur'an, he was to produce as many children as possible for Islam and Allah. His wife had given him four children, yet he had never seen her naked. It was considered sinful to gaze upon a woman's nakedness. As a result, women always wore long garments that completely covered them in bed, even during intercourse. Rashid did not permit wanton infidel sexual behavior on the part of any of his four wives. Islamic wives understood that any licentious behavior on their part would not be tolerated. Looking at an adult male without her veil in place called for beating with a stick, and the penalty for adultery was death by stoning.

Sex with one's wife was for procreation only. If, in the unlikely event that the woman enjoyed sex, she certainly was not to show it, discuss it, or make any sound during the act. Having children was her job, along with caring for them and keeping house for her husband. Rashid had been away on his trip to Chile for over a week. When he received word from his contact in the shipping company that a certain Chilean waitress now had special access to the Captain's cabin, he dispatched himself to Chile to make a deal with her to help him. While he was prowling around trying to find out as much about her and her family as he could, he discovered that she had a husband who was a gambler and a ne'er-do-well. He hit upon the idea of having her husband, Diego, make all the arrangements, thus keeping himself incognito in case anything should go wrong.

Rashid was quite pleased to have been able to arrange things for the piddling sum of $5,000. Money was the least of the problems of the *Scythe of Allah*. Contributions had been pouring into the coffers of the organization from all over Islam for many years. What was needed now was a big, successful, spirit-lifting attack on an icon of the infidels, and he was certain that he and Ali were on the verge of delivering the biggest one yet. He sent an e-mail to Ali's transportation company saying that the delivery to the ship would be made by Mercedes León.

Rashid was pleased with the way things were going. He had encountered no unanticipated problems with the plans that he had made. In his present optimistic frame of mind he thought maybe he should try to make another son for Allah. He told his wife to get into bed. She obeyed. She had foreseen that Rashid would want sex when he arrived so she had previously removed her undergarment. She slid between the sheets and raised her dress slightly above her knees, not enough so that he would see her naked, but enough so that he could get up under it. Most women used specially made female underclothes that did not have to be removed, but Rashid found them troublesome so she had devised this compromise for his benefit.

He sat on the bed and removed his clothes, then slipped under the sheets and got on top of his wife. She turned her head and averted her eyes. It was painful, but she was used to it. She told herself he was a good, fertile husband and had given her four children, more than any of his other wives, and that gave her status in the family. Rashid, like most Muslims, thought modesty in marriage was an Islamic custom, but the despised orthodox Jews had been doing marital relations in the same way for centuries before Muhammad. He finished so quickly that his wife thought he might want her again, so she remained in the bed. Rashid had other things on his mind, however, so he got up and went into the bathroom. In the morning he would put his wife on the train to Damascus, and he would take the train to LeHavre.

He emerged from the bathroom fully dressed. He quickly slipped out of the room, saying he would be back later. He gave his wife no explanation of where he was going. She presumed he would get something to eat and bring it back to share with her, but as usual she was not privy to his plans. Being a good Muslim, Rashid did not drink alcoholic beverages. He always felt wimpy when he was in a foreign bar and ordered coffee or tea while everyone else had a drink. As many times as he told himself to ignore the alcohol-addicted infidels, he still felt that his machismo suffered in this kind of environment. Still, he would walk into hell for Allah, so he entered the bar with confidence. He looked around for the engineer, and spotted him at a table in the rear. They shook hands, and Rashid sat down.

"Did you get it done?" he asked the Algerian.

"I did, but it was not easy," the engineer answered.

"Good. Allah rewards those who do difficult things on his behalf." Rashid reached into his jacket pocket and pulled out an envelope, which he gave to the engineer. "This is just a little token of appreciation from Islam. You see, Allah is great!"

The engineer didn't want to accept the money, but Rashid wouldn't take no for an answer. He wished the engineer well, left his tea on the table, and returned to the hotel. Along the way he passed a fish and chips place and picked up two orders to take out. With the bag of food in his hand he returned to the hotel and went up to the room. He found his wife in bed where he had left her. Apparently she had fallen asleep. She heard her husband moving around, smelled the pommes frites, and opened her eyes. They ate the fried fish and potatoes on the bed.

Ivan was reading the newspaper after breakfast while Marina was nursing the baby. It was a domestic scene that pleased both of them. Marina loved breast feeding.

"It makes me feel like total woman," she said, looking tenderly at the baby. "It is next best thing to how you make me feel when we are together. You know? Feeling is not as strong, but anyhow is very good, ya?"

"I guess it was meant to feel that way, or women wouldn't do it. As it is, many women seem to care more about how they look than about the nutrition of their children. I'm glad you're not like that. Just look at little Julia. She's puffing up like a body builder. Your milk is obviously agreeing with her."

"Yes, but are you going to leave me for younger woman while I am alone with my swollen breasts to raise child?"

"Ah, the twenty-first century mother's lament. Don't you know how much I love you? You personally and individually, I mean. Do you think I'd really prefer an anorexic, bleached narcissist for a wife?"

Ivan was about to make a speech about the questionable standards of female beauty that have been drummed into women's heads like so much brainwash, when he was distracted by an article in the newspaper he was reading. The headline read: *World's largest cruise ship prepares for maiden voyage.* The hairs on the back of his neck started to tingle. Here was a target for terrorists if ever there was one. The cruise ship, icon of Western-style dissipated living, was about to splash its message of vulgarity all over the world. Ivan remembered the attack on the U.S.S. Cole and the Arab penchant for piracy, stretching all the way back to the Barbary Pirates in the time of Jefferson. He sat bolt upright in his chair.

"What's wrong, Ivan?" Marina asked.

"I have an idea.," he said. "I've got to go right now."

He quickly kissed Marina and baby Julia, and took off running while he tried clumsily to put on his suit jacket. He started his car, jammed it into drive, and gunned the engine, screeching the tires as he blasted off toward the White House. He grabbed his cell phone as he was driving and pressed button one to get his office. Brooklyn picked up.

"Brooklyn, call all our staff at once. Get them in my office now. I'll be there in six minutes."

He hung up and tried to concentrate on not killing anyone or being killed on the streets of Washington. He could read that headline now. *Presidential aide killed in auto accident in front of White House.* He could also see the story behind the story that would come out later. *Tragedy at sea was avoidable.*

By the time he opened his office door he had mentally written the story of how the government had failed to prevent the greatest maritime disaster in history. The story would go on to describe how the aide to the President had vital information that could have saved the lives of thousands, but due to the red tape and inefficiencies rampant in government he had failed miserably to alert the proper parties. The article would call the President himself to account for this horrible failure of his administration, and of course there would be follow-up stories about the obvious conspiracy to cover up the whole affair.

Perspiration was dripping down Ivan's face as he stood before his staff. He wasted no time with trivialities.

"I believe I've identified the target of the next major Al Qaeda terrorist attack. It's the new super cruise liner *Controller of the Oceans*. This vessel is now in Toulon, and it'll be sailing to pick up its first passengers in LeHavre in two days. We must find out if this vessel is indeed a target, and we must capture the terrorists plotting to sink her. At the very least we must foil the attack. Thousands of lives are at stake, but take note that none is likely to be a Muslim aboard this pleasure ship. This would be a typical al Qaeda-motivated operation aimed at capturing the attention of the world, embarrassing the West, and proving how a few keen followers of the faith can defeat the perverted, immoral infidels in the midst of their debaucheries. And *of course* they don't care that thousands of innocent lives would be lost if such an attack were successful."

"How do you know this ship is their target?" asked one of the staffers.

"At this point I don't know for sure, but we can't ignore the possibility. We've spent untold millions in security measures over the years to protect large events from terrorist attacks, with or without having specific intelligence to indicate that attacks had even been planned. Look what happened with the Super Bowl games, for example. You can't get into the stadium with baggage, everyone is passed through metal detectors as they enter, guards and electronic surveillance devices are all over the place, and sharp shooters with telescopic sights on their rifles are posted on the roof. Lord knows what other steps have been taken, and it's all just in case of a *possible* attack."

"So what security measures are we going to take?" asked another staffer.

"What we'll be doing now is no different than what we regard as normal security for a bowl game, an Olympic venue, or a political convention."

"I still don't understand how you figure the terrorists have chosen this particular target from among all the choices that are open to them," the first staffer said.

"I could tell you, but then I'd have to kill you," Ivan shot back. "Seriously though, I've created my own little analysis tool that uses information provided by our colleague, Damian Rutledge. It takes historical terrorist attack data, psychological profiles, evaluations of the target's difficulties, and a whole slew of other criteria, and applies a form of Program Evaluation Review technique in reverse. Essentially it evaluates targets from the point of view of the Islamist fundamentalist jihadists. When I run the *Controller of the Oceans* through my computer analysis, it comes up as number one on the hit parade."

"That's fascinating," said the second staffer. "Does the PER technique put all the possibilities in order?"

"Bear with me," Ivan said. "There've been over 8,000 documented terrorist attacks worldwide. The vast majority of the successful ones – the ones that were successful from the terrorists' point of view – those attacks were carried out in Islamic countries or in waters bordering those nations. The list begins in 1979 with the Iran Embassy hostage affair. The attacks continued in the Beirut Embassy and the Marine barracks. Then there was an attack in Saudi Arabia on the military complex there, and that was followed by attacks on the embassies in Kenya and Tanzania. Then after that there was the attack on the U.S.S. Cole in Yemen. Do you see the pattern? The home team has the advantage. When we pass that huge, gleaming new ship through the waters of Morocco, Algeria, Tunisia, Libya, Egypt, and the Middle East, it's going to be a hate magnet. We now have a valid sample of events, and although they may not be perfect, our statistics could be of enormous value in predicting future targets. I'm not a prophet. I'm only working with probabilities here. But trust me, to a senior terrorist this ship is the juiciest morsel in his harem."

Then, pointing to the second staffer, he said, "So with that in mind, I'd like you to do the following: call the French Sureté. Don't panic them, but tell them we're interested in getting a passenger list and a list of the companies that were involved in any way with building this ship. Make it sound as though it's a normal security precaution, because so many of the passengers are American citizens. I'm sure the French are also doing some top level security policing on such a high-profile vessel. Now, as soon as you have this information, bring it to me."

The staffers began gathering up their papers.

"I need a volunteer to call the Secretary of the Navy," Ivan continued. "I need to get a list of all the U.S. ships that are scheduled to be within a hundred miles of the route to be sailed by the *Controller of the Oceans* on the days listed in their schedule. Get a copy of the schedule from the company that owns the ship. Let's keep everything outside this office in the routine mode, but inside we're in emergency mode."

"I'll be your volunteer," said the first staffer.

"I appreciate that," said Ivan. "Brooklyn, you continue working your lists. Use the algorithm we prepared to match our suspect lists to the passenger list, and the supplier lists that we get from the French. Bring me any anomalies that you discover at once. Please stay behind after the meeting disbands," he said, wondering if Brooklyn had noticed his use of the *please* word. He hoped that might indicate to her that he was trainable.

"People," he went on, "the welfare of this ship is priority number one for the next few days. Put everything else on hold until further notice. If you think anything is strange, or if you have ideas that might help, please bring them to my attention. Now let's get to work."

Brooklyn had remained behind. When the others had filed out of the office, Ivan closed the door.

"How did you find out that this ship is the target, if I may ask?" said Brooklyn.

Ivan looked at her and said, "I haven't found out anything yet. It's about 90% intuition and 10% paranoia at this point, but don't tell anyone else. Promise?"

"Promise. But I hope you realize that you've essentially shut down the whole department based on a guess."

"I do realize it, but if I'm wrong, then I'm like the shepherd boy who cried wolf the first time, except that there really was a wolf. If I don't cry wolf we may lose our flock. That's what a Security Advisor does – he protects the flock. If he inspects the perimeter of the pen and finds no holes in the fence, so much the better, but if he finds a weakness that might let the wolf get in and kill his sheep, then he's a good Security Advisor and he doesn't get fired. I don't want to get fired. I can't afford it. I have a new baby and a wife who's not working, so the wolf is already at my door."

"Why did you want me to stick around?" Brooklyn asked.

"I want you to arrange for standby passage on any military or civilian flights leaving for France during the next four days. See how many they can accommodate on short notice. Call Damian and ask him to prepare a report on all the instances of terror attacks involving ships in port or at sea. I need a complete rundown of perpetrators and suspects, caught or uncaught, and a comparison of explosives used in each case. Tell him this supersedes the other project I gave him, and tell him why."

"Got it. Anything else?"

"Call Abdul and tell him to keep his eyes and ears open. If he hears anything peculiar having to do with liners or cruise ships in the Middle East, he should let me know at once. You needn't tell him my suspicions just yet. I'd like to see what he comes up with on his own. Don't pull him off the project he's doing for me now."

"Okay." Brooklyn was making notes as fast as she could.

"Call David Feingold and tell him to keep a bag ready with three days' worth of clean clothes suitable for a cruise. We may have to make a trip on very short notice. Be sure to tell him it's not a vacation. And you get yourself ready, too."

"Who, me? I'm going on the cruise?"

"That's what I said. Please arrange for us to have real time communications capability when we leave the country. I want to be able to reach military top brass, as well as civilian police and any agency directors, even those only vaguely concerned with security. I may need total communication flexibility, and total inter-agency cooperation. I won't stand for any f-----g around with this one."

"Whoa! You must *really* mean business."

"Please call Marina and ask her to pack my things. Call a driver and instruct him to go by and pick up my suitcase. Tell her I won't be home tonight and possibly not for the next week, because something has come up. She'll understand, I hope, because you'll lie and explain to her that it doesn't involve any personal danger. Then call the Marine officer in charge of security weapons in the White House and have him issue and deliver three pistols with an ammo supply as soon as possible. One for you, one for David, and one for me. Got it?"

The orders had been flying out of Ivan's head as fast as he could talk, but Brooklyn had hung in there with him.

"Got it," she said, placidly.

CHAPTER EIGHT

A li and his son Amin arrived safely at the coastal town of Mostaganem, Algeria. They had delivered the ice cream in Algiers, and the balance in Oran. What was left aboard the truck was a little treat for the infidels. A brotherly connection of the *Scythe of Allah* in this city of 115,000 had made some precautionary arrangements on behalf of Ali's group to house his truck in an old vacant warehouse near the docks. Father and son had slept under the stars for several nights and were looking forward to having showers and eating some food prepared by someone other than themselves.

Ali had a long history with the FLN, the political entity that had arranged the rebellion from France that had resulted in the formation of an independent Islamic Algerian nation. The Detonator was deeply respected among Berbers for having transported badly needed weapons with which to fight the French colonists. Algeria was one of Ali's favorite countries because they had known how to win against the infidels who had invaded their homeland and held it captive for centuries.

People in the West seldom realize it, but Algeria is the second largest country in Africa, encompassing three and a half times the area of the State of Texas. Everything about Algeria was familiar to, and appreciated by Ali. Islam approved of the 99% Muslim purity of its 32 million citizens, and so did Ali. With its sand and mountains in the south and the Mediterranean coast in the north, Algeria had a recognizably comfortable ambience in which Ali felt relaxed.

Even the economy of Algeria was compatible with his experience. Oil generated 52% of the country's financial wealth. Algeria is the 2nd largest exporter of natural gas in the world, and it is the 14th in oil reserves. Ali fully expected that

Algeria would take an important role in the Islamification of the contemporary world. And with 30% unemployment it was a prime country for recruiting young jihadist fighters for the cause of Allah. Many of these young people emigrate to France to seek work, and whether they find it or not, they are treated as second-class citizens. Naturally they are disaffected with the treatment they receive from the French infidels.

Ali wasn't sure of the exact numbers, but he estimated that about 20% or more of the population of France was from North Africa. It gave him great satisfaction to think that Islam had placed so many of its own people in the midst of the French. The testing of French resolve and policing capabilities by the night riots in city streets all over France by these alienated Muslims was like honey to his lips. French authorities had been unable to put down the protests for weeks. The burning, looting and vandalism was just the beginning of what Allah had in mind for these infidel perverts.

Ali hated the French. He thought they were egocentric, effete, and sexually deviant, but clever in the ways of the world. He told his Algerian friends that in his opinion the French were masters of the military maneuver called retreat. The Gauls had retreated from the Romans, Napoleon had retreated from the Russians and the British, DeGaulle had retreated from the Germans and the Algerians, and next they would retreat before the strength of Islam.

Ali went to sleep happy to have his loyal son next to him, and with great expectations for the days ahead. He was looking forward to seeing his old friend and comrade in arms, Al Jaza'ir. His friend was called by the name Algiers in Arabic, just as many called Ali "Yemeni." They had both risen in the ranks of the Islamist struggle since their college days in the U.S. Ali laughed inwardly when he thought about the American conjecture that the terrorists were only a few rag-headed fanatic fundamentalist Arabs operating without a central organization. If they only knew how Allah controlled his forces and regulated his Islamist fighters, they would not sleep as peacefully as he would this night. As dreams began to fill his sleep-deprived head, Ali ran over his plans for the next few days.

The crew on the *Controller of the Oceans* was just about finished with the last minute preparations. Training classes had been concluded, and the administrators, managers, and officers in charge were crossing their fingers, hoping that the crew had learned their lessons well and that things would go smoothly for the maiden voyage. Most of the crew had been given the day off to go ashore as a reward for their work and as an incentive for them to be caring and accommodating when the passengers came on board in two days' time. The ship always retained a skeleton crew to cope with safety, security, and any unexpected details that might crop up. Included in this group was an officer in charge and a chef to provide meals for the few crew members who remained aboard. Niko had volunteered to be on duty so that his officers could have a last day ashore. He was a single man and nobody was waiting for him, so he was happy to let his subordinates enjoy their last day of freedom.

The chef answered when the phone rang in the galley. It was the Captain, asking about the choices for his supper. After some discussion, Niko made his selections and the chef agreed to have his meal sent up to his cabin.

Mercedes had volunteered to stay aboard and allow her shipmates to go ashore for many of the same reasons as Niko's. She had been sitting just outside the galley reading a newspaper. It was in French, so she was trying to puzzle out what it said, using her knowledge of Spanish. Although French was also a Romance language, she still found it difficult to understand. When the chef informed her he had a meal that needed to be delivered to the Captain's cabin, she asked if it could wait five minutes as she wanted to wash the newsprint off her hands. She hurried into the washroom, washed her hands, and looked at herself in the mirror. She tidied her hair and straightened her uniform. She knew she could pretend not to care whether or not he still wanted her, but her body was telling her that she did care. In a few minutes she would know what his feelings were, too.

She knocked on the door.

"Come in," came the Captain's voice.

"I've come to serve you again," she said, as nonchalantly as she could. She felt nervous and apprehensive about their first meeting after such a long separation, but her dark eyes had a coquettish twinkle as she delivered the double entendre. She approached the table and put her tray down.

Niko, too, had been wondering what would happen when they met again. When he had accidentally learned that she was on board his ship a couple of days before, he had realized that he was glad. But just as Mercedes had wondered how he felt, he had no idea what her reaction might be to a resumption of their relationship. Her comment, and the look in her eyes, told him that she was truly happy to see him again. He stood up and moved toward her. He took her in his arms and they kissed with feeling.

"No, Niko, you must eat your supper first while it is still warm."

Mercedes pushed him gently into a chair and removed the metal cover that overlaid his dinner plate. She poured him some wine from the flask that the cook had sent along with the meal. She put the napkin on his lap and sat across from him.

"Have you eaten?" Niko asked.

"Yes, all but dessert. I am watching my figure, but that piece of chocolate cake that the chef sent up is too much for one person, so I will share it with you."

"I'm watching your figure too," Captain Niko said.

Rashid put his wife on the train for Damascus. He had a couple of hours before his train came to take him to LeHavre. He put his suitcase in a locker in the train station, and went outside and called a cab. He had the driver take him to the port; not to the pier that the *Controller of the Oceans* was tied to, but close enough so he could walk to the great liner and look her over.

There was no denying it – she was an immensely impressive ship. The brand new white vessel stood in splendid contrast to the grey and dismal aspect of the port's surroundings. The sun ricocheting off the luminous glass windows was blinding. She was a horizontal floating skyscraper, thought Rashid. She must be as long as one of the twin towers of the World Trade Center, he observed with satisfaction. He noticed that she was riding high, and some of her bottom paint was showing. Rashid reasoned that she would be deeper in the water once she had taken her passengers and their luggage aboard, and topped off her immense water and fuel tanks. No doubt she would do that in LeHavre just before sailing. He concentrated now, trying to impress on his memory all the details of the ship, the number of decks, stacks, the position of the bridge, the number of radars and their locations, and every aspect of her outward appearance while she was still afloat.

After an hour of strolling around doing his assessment, Rashid hailed a taxi and returned to the train station. Once aboard the train he found a compartment, put his suitcase up on the overhead rack, and prepared to read the Toulon newspaper that he had picked up at the newsstand on his way through the station. A whole section of the paper was devoted to the massive ship that in one more day would be missing from the skyline of the port city. The *Controller of the Oceans* did, in fact, dominate the city that had built her. Many photos of the elegant interior furnishings were included in the articles about the ship's approaching departure. Descriptions abounded of the various design features, along with the amazing statistics of the technical details. The horsepower of the engines, the fuel and water-holding capacities, the length, width and height above the water were all described in extravagant terms accompanied by diagrams, charts, and graphs. Rashid thought all this data would make writing the obituary for the ship very easy for the reporter who got that assignment.

At the last minute, just before the train left the station, two young women and an older man joined him in his compartment. The two women were cheeky American hikers wearing shorts and boots as though they had just come down off a mountain. They lifted their backpacks up to the rack, and the stretching and reaching left little to Rashid's imagination. They spoke English loudly with a Midwestern accent, caring nothing about who overheard them. The man was wearing a nondescript gray business suit with a maroon tie patterned with a lackluster design. He noticed the newspaper that Rashid had put down on the seat next to him, and asked in French if he might look at it. Rashid passed the paper to him. The girls across from him were tanned, fit, and healthy looking. They sat like men; one with her legs crossed, and the other with her legs separated in an unladylike fashion.

The women presumed that the men in the compartment did not speak English, but Rashid was actually fluent in English, French, Arabic, and Spanish. He was in the window seat facing the unladylike young woman. He was looking out the window at the passing cityscape, and occasionally letting his eyes drift back into the compartment to look over at the women. They were chattering away about the upcoming voyage that they were going to make in the new ship. Apparently they had booked passage on the *Controller of the Oceans* and were going to Le Havre, just as Rashid was, to board the cruise ship for their Mediterranean voyage.

Rashid was glad he had been chosen for this mission. The gigantic Gomorrah of a ship filled with infidel perverts deserved to sink. The Christian morals of the West had slipped so far into degradation that women now cavorted shamelessly in public, granting themselves the same freedom that had been given to men. They flaunted their sexuality in front of a soldier of Allah in total disregard of the behavioral commands in the Qur'an. Rashid decided to ignore them. He hardened his heart against them, and his eyes went cold. He would wash himself thoroughly in LeHavre before he did his evening prayers.

CHAPTER NINE

Ali was up with the dawn. He made some strong coffee and set out some dates, figs, and unleavened Algerian bread, and then he woke his son Amin to share it with him. In a few minutes his old friend Al Jaza'ir would be arriving with the materials he needed for his mission. It was glorious to have comrades-in-arms all over Allah's Islamist world to share in the exciting work and the satisfaction of bringing the infidels to their knees in front of his throne.

Ali loved his work as the Detonator for the *Scythe of Allah* brotherhood. There was pride in it, to be sure. He had achieved great status from his fellow fighters because of his knowledge of explosives. In the Arab world he could go almost anywhere and be treated with respect and admiration. His anonymity had to be preserved, however, due to the dangerous business he was in, so his every move was cloaked in secrecy and mystery. Even his own sons were unaware of their father's immense reputation among those closest to the heart of Islam.

Al Jaza'ir arrived in an old, unmarked Renault truck that looked so ordinary that no one could be suspicious of it. The two old warriors embraced and kissed three times in the Arab fashion. They looked at each other and both remarked how well the other appeared. Ali introduced his son. He wanted to be certain that if something happened to him the organization in Algeria would recognize Amin and look after him. They began unloading the Renault onto the dirt floor of the building that housed Ali's truck, and in which he had slept the night before. There were three rolls of Dacron rope, each containing one thousand feet of half-inch diameter spooled line. Boxes of new nylon fishing net mesh were offloaded next, and then an assortment of various sizes of buoys, floats, chain, two anchors, and fishing gear were stacked off to one side. A large box of spooled, insulated copper wire was last to be off-loaded from the truck. Ali looked around him and smiled.

"Allah akbar," he said. "He has given us everything we need to put fear into the infidel dogs. I have with me the plastic explosives and the detonators. Let us get to work at once."

He began opening the boxes of fishing net material. Under his direction the men spread the netting out. They sewed each length of netting together so that they had one very long length of fishing net. It took thirty boxes of one hundred feet of net each to give Ali the 3,000 feet of length that he needed. When the thirty lengths were joined together and sewn, the men wove the Dacron line through the top loops parallel to the header rope of the nets. The three lengths of rope had to be joined end to end, and Ali had brought special clamps to hold them together. He would have liked to use steel cable to hold up the net, but the new satellite radar equipment could detect metal under the surface. It was dusty work, for they had to lay everything down on the dirt floor of the shed to do the assembling.

Yemeni and Jaza'ir worked well together. The Algerian had picked Mostaganem as the location to do the assembling because the shed they were in had two large entrances on either end of the building. The upper end faced the street that ran closest to the edge of the water, and this was the entrance through which the trucks had been driven. The entrance at the lower end led directly out to the beach, and was intended to be used by boats hauled in for repairs.

The Detonator's plan was based on the precision of the marine Sat/Nav equipment. The electronic firm that made the gear guaranteed accuracy to ten feet. It did not have to be that accurate in order for Ali's plan to work – fifty feet would be close enough. Many successful bombings using improvised explosive devices to ambush U.S. Forces had already proven their merit many times over. In these cases, the bombs were stationary, and the targets moved toward the bombs. Ali was simply adapting the principles of the IEDs already in use. He would suspend his explosives (in this case a series of plastic explosive bombs hooked together), at a place and at a depth in the ocean that he knew the *Controller of the Oceans* would intersect. All that had to be done now was for him to locate a place on the liner's course, and the navigation equipment would supply the address as surely as if it had been a letter bomb mailed to the President of the United States.

Every fifty feet they sewed a bag to the fish net. Each bag would contain a block of plastic explosive and a compression detonator. When they were at sea they would place the charges in the bags one by one as they let the cable out from the stern of the fishing boat. Each end of the cable was to be held in place by an anchor with a chain rode. The directional lay of the cable would be north to south to intersect the ship's course, which was east. If it was done correctly the huge ship would come steaming along and the bow bulb would hook under the cable, dragging the anchors, cables, fish nets, and explosive charges on both sides of the ship back against its hull. The tremendous forward motion of a vessel this size traveling at its cruising speed of 30 knots would slam the detonators against the steel hull of the ship down near the keel, setting off one shaped charge after the next on either side of the ship. The explosions would rip the whole hull off the vessel, and the forward motion would fill the ship with water, causing her to sink in minutes.

Al Jaza'ir had arranged for them to be picked up by a large fishing boat equipped with satellite navigating equipment. The net they were constructing was to be loaded aboard the boat that would back into the beach, which shoaled off steeply enough so that the boat was only a short distance from the back of the boathouse at high tide. Following the instructions that Ali had given him, Al Jaza'ir had located a large number of net floats, and had them painted a sea green-gray color. Ali's idea was to put just enough floats on the net to suspend it above the bottom, but keep it at a depth of twenty feet from the top of the water. Most ships drew less than twenty feet of water so they would pass over the net unharmed. He had done some calculations, but it would take some trial and error work to be certain they had it right. To anyone who saw them at work it would look like typical fisherman activities, mending nets, or setting nets.

Ali had thought to use several large rubber bladders in conjunction with the floats. These were fitted with rubber stoppers that could be pulled out in an emergency by light lines in the boat that were connected to the stoppers. When the cords were pulled, the stoppers would come loose and the air would leave the bladders, causing the net to lose enough buoyancy to sink it to the bottom, where it could be retrieved later. Nothing could be seen from the surface. The men on the fishing boat, if questioned, could just say they had lost their net and were trying to recover it.

While Ali and his associates were executing their plan of attack, Ivan Welland was in the unenviable position of having to organize a defense and a counterattack. The advantage was in the hands of Ali, because the defenders didn't know where or when the attack would take place, and usually they didn't even know what or who would be the target. In this case Ivan felt that he knew the target, and that could make all the difference if he could figure out how they were planning to strike the new super-liner.

At this time Ivan had absolutely nothing else on his mind. He sat in his chair, leaning far back and staring at the ceiling. He had taken it as a given that his principal enemy was a very experienced master terrorist. He would have a proven record of successful attacks and a talent for devising them, if indeed it's a talent to have an aptitude for committing wholesale murder. He'd have to be a highly skilled tactician, as well. The choice of the *Controller of the Oceans* as his target proved that his adversary had audacity and knew what would create outrage in the West, at the same time creating pride among the followers of Islam. Ivan figured that if his antagonist succeeded in sinking this iconic symbol of Western decadence without having a ship, bomber, or an army of his own, it would be perceived in the Middle East as an attack equal to 9/11 when the terrorists used

American airliners to collapse the World Trade Centers. After the Americans exterminated the caliphs from their lair under the Ka'bah in Mecca, the jihadist forces of terror needed a major victory to return them to the glory days they had enjoyed after 9/11. Ivan's intuition told him that the sinking of the *Controller of the Oceans* was intended to be that victory.

Ivan was astounded by the fact that the American attack on Mecca had been simply ignored by the entire Arab press. It was as if it had never happened. When it came to having a united front in protecting the extremist religious Muslim views of the world, the unanimity among Islamists was absolute. This blind allegiance in perpetuity to a faith badly in need of reform was to Ivan a sign of a fatal weakness that would eventually have to give way to modern ideas. He recalled something he had heard that was attributed to Will Rogers that went, "You can be on the right trail, but if you don't keep moving you'll be trampled from behind."

Everything in the universe is forever expanding. Nothing can stand still, not even the definition of the "Straight Path." Mapmakers and mathematicians long ago had their troubles with the concept of what "straight" is. It was time now for the ayatollahs to amend some of their opinions. The example of the U.S. Supreme Court, in recognizing that the U.S. Constitution is subject to occasional amendment, should be a model for people everywhere. No generation of thinkers can have all the answers for eternity, and it is equally true that interpretations of scripture will differ from age to age for the Torah, the Bible, and the Koran. The One we call Jehovah, or God, or Allah, did not dispense all his wisdom to man at one time, and we couldn't have handled it if he had.

Ivan thought this was irrelevant to his particular problems of the moment, but then he had an idea that changed his mind. If his adversary was willing to consider murdering thousands of people in the name of his religion, then his faith must be as hard as a diamond. His enemy's commitment was total. But a mind that seals off other ways of thinking is a mind that lacks flexibility. Such an enemy is susceptible to error, as we all are, but he is also unlikely to be able to adjust his concrete way of thinking to cope with creative methods of response. Ivan's job was to parry his opponent's thrust by the use of unanticipated action, and then to apply the coup de grace while his enemy dealt with the subtleties of the unknown territories outside the purview of closed minds.

Who was he dealing with here? A great mind would want to challenge the world openly with his ideas. Only an ordinary mind would wish to secretly subvert the truth so he could replace it with a violent, mediocre alternative that couldn't be justified in the open courts of the great minds of the world. He is clever enough, however, to try to overcome truth by replacing reason with fear, because what else has he to offer? Such men should not be allowed to condemn others to death, and the religions that sponsor them must be purged of the ideas that make heroes of such villains. Philosophically Ivan was so far from the deeds and ideals of the extremists that it was like taking a dip in the sewer to force himself to think like them.

How would a terrorist sink a civilian ship? There were many ways, of course, but *quickly, horribly,* and *dramatically* were adverbs that came immediately to Ivan's mind. If your motive is to kill people and get as much attention as you can, then explosions give you the best bang for your buck. You can't drop a ten-ton bomb on a ship if you have no air force. But how about mines? He thought about them for a while, but he decided that mines are too random unless they are placed in a channel where ships must pass in order to enter a port. But then it would be too easy for someone to see them being set.

Ivan was about to drop this line of thinking as non-productive when two things occurred to him that changed the equation. First, terrorists had a specific target in mind when they placed a bomb. Second, mining did not have to be done in a harbor, nor did the placement of the mine have to be random any longer. Nowadays with satellite navigation systems, even a small yacht can locate itself within a very close margin of error. If someone knew the course a great ship like the *Controller of the Oceans* would be taking, it might be possible to leave a mine in such a position that the bomber could be fairly sure that the ship would collide with it.

Leaving the *who* question aside, and assuming a mine at sea was the *how*, the *when* would be the time that the *Controller* was scheduled to be at the point of the course to intercept the mine. Ivan pulled out the sailing schedule of the ship. The first day at sea the ship would head out of the channel between England and France, and then go south to Lisbon, Portugal. A day of land tours in the Lisbon area would end in an evening sail around the Southwestern tip of the Iberian Peninsula to Gibraltar for some more land tours and shopping. The ship would then sail by night along the coast of Spain to Barcelona. During that night she would be off the coast of Algeria.

"That is where I would put my mine, if I were the terrorist leader," Ivan thought. "Darkness would hide the explosives, and also hide the escaping villains. Disappearing would be easy for a Muslim in nearby Algeria."

When he left his office his entire staff was on hand, waiting to give him the answers he had asked them to find. After an hour of hard thinking, Ivan was more convinced than ever that the target would be the *Controller of the Oceans.* He told his staff the that he believed the attack would take place in the Mediterranean Sea off the coast of Algeria, and the method of attack would be some sort of mine device.

"I know that some of you may be questioning the wisdom of going forward with these actions when we still have so little intelligence. I can only say that terrorists don't advertise. They kill squealers, so there are not many of them. Our government is always being accused of not having enough intelligence after some terrorist event. We should have known that 9/11 was coming and stopped it, we're told. Well, that's easy to say. My opinion is that we'll never have enough intelligence about the plans of this type of enemy. Our problem is that we must have enough *intuition* to make up for the lack of intelligence. What we do know about this enemy is that he's blood-thirsty and merciless. Before 9/11 we probably wouldn't have believed a source that informed us that a group of terrorists was going to fly our own airliners into the World Trade Center buildings. Now we can have confidence that if we expect unspeakable acts from this enemy we will not be surprised, and just maybe we can be proactive in our defensive measures."

Ivan's staff said they had received the list of passengers scheduled to be on board when the cruise left LeHavre, and it had lots of good ID information. The U.S. Navy had provided its list of ships in the area. Unfortunately only three ships assigned to NATO would be on patrol anywhere near the coast of North Africa during the coming week. An aircraft carrier would be in Marseilles, France on a friendship visit. The carrier's personnel would be on leave during the time in port. A nuclear submarine was stationed in the Eastern Mediterranean, but that was not of much help for Ivan's purposes. Damian had supplied a list of past terrorist actions against ships. Brooklyn told Ivan that his clothes and his weapon had arrived, and that all his other orders had been discharged.

"Good work, all of you," Ivan said. "Take a quick break, then Brooklyn will pass out some new assignments. Brooklyn, if you wouldn't mind accompanying me back into the TC's office please, I would very much appreciate it."

Once inside his office Ivan said, "I'm trying to be as polite as I can, Brooklyn, but I'm under a lot of pressure now so I'll just say one *please* and hope it will do for all the duties I'm going to assign to you. Okay?"

"No problem. Fire away."

"Please call the State Department and have them alert the Brits on Gibraltar that something big may be coming along and that we may need some support from their Naval detachment. Please call the Chief of Naval Intelligence and ask him to use the Operations Room to monitor the voyage of the *Controller of the Oceans* from Lisbon to Barcelona. Call Admiral Sadler and have him locate the Navy Seal team that worked with me on the Caliph operation. Tell him I need them immediately. They should be fully equipped with scuba gear, rubber boat, and the full complement of weapons. One of the Seals should be a woman. Tell her to pack a few things suitable for a cruise, and the same for Lieutenant Mercer. Have the Admiral call his NATO contact in Lisbon to clear the team for landing and immediate transfer to the *Controller of the Seas*. Call the owners of the liner and have them arrange to have the Seal team board in Lisbon as unobtrusively as possible. I'm sure the maiden voyage is completely booked, so we're going to have to bump someone in order to use their cabin for Mercer and his Sealette to play house in. Call whomever you have to call to arrange the bumping. Try to get a cabin for the happy couple as close as possible to the bridge. The other members of the Seal team can be bunked in with the crew of the ship. Send Mercer a copy of the layout of the *Controller of the Oceans*. He should study it and be familiar with the ship before he gets aboard."

"Hang on, hang on," said Brooklyn, writing as fast as she could. "A cabin near the bridge… Seals bunk with the crew… send Mercer the layout… Okay. I'm with you."

"Have the commanding officer of the carrier in Marseilles schedule some high altitude surveillance flights to monitor the progress of the liner and keep track of any suspicious vessels, particularly in the area off Algeria. Convey my apologies to the boys who'll miss their shore leave. Call the president of the company who manufactured the satellite navigation system used on board the ship and connect me ASAP. I'll need some time to go over all the information I got today, so keep me out of the day-to-day business of the office. I think that's it for now, unless you have any questions."

"I'd just like to say that everyone on your staff is 100% behind you, and we'll do everything we can to help."

"Thanks, Brooklyn. Please thank the others for me, too."

Niko and Mercedes were sharing the Captain's dessert. First one and then the other would take a forkful of the chocolate cake. Niko studied Mercedes' lips as she savored the dessert.

"Please tell Chef René that the cake was superb," he said.

"I will tell him," Mercedes promised.

"I must say you are looking very beautiful," Niko told her, taking her hand. Mercedes thought it was unusual for him to be complimentary. She had tried to do everything he asked of her in a matter-of-fact way. She hadn't expected anything from him in return except a certain sexual maturity. His usual women were probably tangled up in the "great man syndrome," which made them expect that as Captain of the ship his sexual prowess would be pretty close to extraordinary.

She was not far from the truth. The women who sought him were almost always narcissistic and were more interested in making a conquest to satisfy their vanity than they were in making even the slightest effort to offer him anything in return. So Niko did indeed welcome Mercedes' quiet, undemanding attentions, and his performance was even better in her relaxed company. As for Mercedes, the attentions of a kindly older man brought her peace and reminded her of her father, who loved her. Perhaps for this very reason there was no romance in this relationship as far as she was concerned, and she was not ready for Niko's wooing.

For his part Niko had been acting as Captain night and day for many weeks as he prepared his ship for its final shakedown cruise from Toulon to LeHavre. During this time there had been no infatuated women on board to indulge his urges in return for a bit of fanciful charm. He was more than a little surprised to notice that he didn't miss this aspect of his life. He had not abstained for such a long period of time since he was a teenager. The few times during the sea trials when his mind had briefly turned to women, it was the image of Mercedes that had prevailed. Now that she was with him in his cabin, he noticed a strangely calming feeling of contentment within himself. He was comfortable with her. That was it. His wife, and all the succeeding women, had not given him the peace he felt as he just quietly sat with this woman, eating and talking. There was no reason to hurry, no expectations, no obligations – yet a bond had grown between them. He wondered if she felt it, too.

Mercedes had always felt close to this man, but she had regarded him as an incorrigible Don Juan. She didn't really blame him for it. She just believed that was the way he was before they met. She had no grand illusions about his wanting to change, or being able to change even if he had wanted to. She had felt about him the way a favorite daughter feels about a father whom she knows to be a rake. In her mind she was ambivalent about him – on the one hand she disliked his faithlessness, yet on the other hand she was fascinated by him as well. It was strangely flattering to be with a man that many women wanted, but it was impossible to consider a permanent relationship with such a person. She was a serious woman, she told herself, with a son to support and a rotten husband that she couldn't get rid of. Niko was twice her age and still a playboy. He was kind and gentle, but he was single and had no incentive to reform, or none that she could see. She had resolved to share the moments of tenderness, but not to expect them to continue for very long. On the surface she would be cool so that when the moment came for them to go their separate ways, the break-up would not be too traumatic for either one of them. She had convinced herself that she had chosen the wise course.

Niko was suffering the pangs of being an aging roué. He was not a complicated man, but he was not stupid. He noticed his declining libido, and knew that he had passed his prime. He understood that his license was not bringing him contentment. These days he was valuing contentment more highly than he had when he was younger. Ten years before he might have said contentment is for cows, but lately he was wishing he could get more of it. He began looking at Mercedes in a new light. She was there and he felt content. He might not be able to explain it fully, but he was serenely happy when he was with her. His problem was not with his understanding of the situation; it was with being able to convince Mercedes that his affection for her was growing and solidifying. His history with women was well known to her, and she had been very good about it – never showing any jealousy, and never speaking about his dalliances. The trouble with converted Don Juans was that they had too much experience making lies sound like the truth, so they could no longer make the truth sound as though it were not a lie. If

Niko tried to make love to her instead of just having sex with her, he didn't think she would believe him. She might even regard it as phony and dislike it thoroughly. They had had a certain amount of honesty in their relationship up to that point, and the last thing he wanted, now that he was starting to really care for her, was for her to distrust him.

She was stacking the dirty dishes on her tray in preparation for returning them to the galley, when Niko stood and came up behind her. He placed one hand on her stomach, and with the other hand he moved her shiny black hair away from her neck so he could kiss it. It was one of her sensitive spots and she shivered as his lips ran from behind her ear to the nape of her neck. She put her hand over his to make him feel welcome to touch her. His other hand slid from her hair to her small, firm breasts. He cupped first one then the other, and unbuttoned her blouse so he could put his hand inside her shirt. She reached in and unhooked her bra so that his hands and fingers could freely move over and around her nipples.

Just at that moment the speaker in Niko's cabin cut in and a voice said, "Captain Constantine, please report to the bridge at once. Repeat, Captain Constantine, your presence is required on the bridge at once."

Niko could not imagine why he was needed on the bridge so urgently. The ship was in port, after all. He kissed Mercedes on the forehead.

"I'm sorry, my dear, I was so looking forward to being with you," he said, with genuine feeling.

"I will return this tray to the galley and perhaps I can come back later. You can call me if you want me," Mercedes said.

She left with her tray, and Niko donned his captain's hat and followed her out into the empty corridor. They went off in opposite directions. He watched her go, admiring her tight little body, and not relishing the idea that duty came first.

Niko entered the ship's bridge and asked with some degree of annoyance, "What is it? Why was I summoned?"

"It's a call on the hot line, sir," his second officer said. "They asked for you personally."

The hot line was a special phone that Captain Olaf, Niko's immediate superior, used when he needed to talk to him about some special situation. Niko was very surprised to hear a woman's voice ask, "Is this Captain Nikolas Constantine?"

"Yes," Niko answered.

"Please hold on for Dr. Welland, sir."

Ivan's voice came on the line. "Captain Constantine?"

"Yes," Niko replied.

"This is Ivan Welland. I'm the National Security Advisor to the President of the United States. My reason for contacting you is not a happy one. I have reason to believe that your new ship is under threat of attack from Islamist terrorists. I'd like to discuss this matter with you in detail. I've been in touch with your company's headquarters, and it was from them that I got this number. I've received permission from your CEO to take a few precautionary measures."

"How may I be of service?" Niko asked.

"We have over 2,000 American citizens scheduled to board your ship in LeHavre, and we need to insure their safety and the safety of the other passengers and crew, so do not discuss this matter with anyone but me. Your vessel is in no danger until you enter the Mediterranean Sea. I'll join your ship in Lisbon, along with a small contingent of U.S. Navy Seals. We'd like to come aboard as secretly as possible while the passengers are ashore. We'll stay on board until the danger is past."

"I shall instruct may staff to work out accommodations…" Niko began.

"Accommodations for my team have already been arranged by your management, so don't worry about that. All you have to do is take us aboard in Lisbon. As for the rest, you're the Captain. You'll be in complete charge of the operation of the vessel at sea, as always. We'll only be there to advise and protect, should it be necessary. There may be a few preventive measures that we can take to avoid an attack, but we can discuss them when I see you in Lisbon. Captain, do you understand me completely?"

"I understand everything you have said," he replied, in his accented English.

"At this point there's no need to get everyone riled up. I could be wrong about the impending attack, and starting a panic won't help, in any case. You have an excellent reputation for passenger safety, and I'll be glad to cooperate with you to keep everybody safe. So I'll see you in Lisbon, where we can go over things in detail. If you have to get in touch with me you can use this number. It's my personal number, and I can be reached on it at any time."

Niko took down the number and said, "I'll look forward to meeting you in Lisbon, Dr. Welland."

Niko was torn between his roles as lover and Captain. He was annoyed with himself because of how strongly he felt the urge to call Mercedes and finish what they had started, but his duty as Captain obliged him to review his security program for the ship. He couldn't ignore the fact that his duty to the safety of the passengers and crew in his care had to come first. His call to Mercedes would have to wait for another time.

He said nothing to the skeleton crew on duty on the bridge, but he went straight to the cabinet that contained the emergency procedures to be followed in the case of any of the possible disasters that could occur to a ship at sea. He found the folder marked S*ecurity* and flipped through the pages until he came to the section labeled *In Case of Attack*. There were several pages of instructions that were sensible, but they were suggestions more than they were instructions. Niko had not been told by Dr. Welland what kind of attack to expect. He read on. *How to deal with acts of piracy. How to deal with terrorist attacks on board, from the sea or from the land.* There was a lot to know, and know it he must before the Americans arrived. They would surely ask him what contingency plans there were to deal with attacks of various kinds. He must know them in detail, and commit them to memory.

CHAPTER TEN

Ivan thought that Captain Constantine sounded like a good man – cautious perhaps, but that was understandable under the circumstances. He would no doubt check with his bosses to make sure that all he had been told was true.

The phone buzzed on Ivan's desk and Brooklyn announced that she had Mr. Dick Gregoire, the President of Concentco Navigation Equipment, on the line. Ivan cleared his throat and picked up the receiver.

"Good morning, Mr. Gregoire. I'm Dr. Ivan Welland, the President's National Security Advisor. I would like to ask you or your chief engineer some questions about the Sat/Nav system on board the new cruise ship, the *Controller of the Oceans.*"

"I'm an engineer," Gregoire informed him. "I should be able to help you. What would you like to know?"

Gregoire shook his head and smiled to himself. He was used to people thinking he didn't know anything of a technical nature because he was now an executive of the company.

"Can you tell me how secure your largest Sat/Nav sets are? For instance, could an outside programmer get into your code and change a function, or write a subroutine that would not be discovered by an end user?"

"Well, that would depend on a number of things. First of all it would be highly unlikely because all our equipment is pre-programmed in our factory and requires a password in order to get into the code. There's a special level of specific knowledge that requires training and experience unique to the programming of Sat/Navs. Ordinary hackers or commercial programmers wouldn't have this background."

"Do you have technicians stationed around the world to repair this kind of equipment? If so, do they have the ability to program the devices?"

"All commercial vessels have redundancy equipment these days, so if they lost one Sat/Nav they could easily use another unit. Some of our technicians might be able to program the equipment, but we've found it is easier to slap a new disk into a unit rather than try to reprogram it. Each of our models has slight differences in the software it requires, so it's more cost effective to replace them than to train people to be programmers or engineers. Modular design allows us to replace a faulty system either in part, or in its entirety. I must tell you, though, that our equipment is extremely reliable and repairs are seldom necessary. Repairs and maintenance represent a very small portion of our business."

"I'm sure you're right. But I need to know whether it's possible for a knowledgeable person to put some sort of default routine into one of your standard Sat/Navs. For instance, could the equipment be made to steer a ship to a specific latitude and longitude regardless of the information put into the equipment by the navigator of a ship? Could a programmer put a 30 second error into the course of a vessel at sea? If I were going from Marseilles to Rome and I wanted to steer due east, could the Sat/Nav intentionally take me off course and make certain I went on a course of 90.00.30 E. to make my ship intersect a specific point just south of my planned course?"

"Well, I suppose it could be done, but it would require a good bit of navigational knowledge and programming ability. But who would want to do something like that when the whole point of the Sat/Nav is accuracy within a few feet?"

"I can't tell you that. But I need to find out if it's possible to force a ship to meet a certain point on the earth's surface whether it wants to or not. I'd also like to have a list of all of your employees in France, and especially any who may have worked on installing equipment on the new cruise ship called the *Controller of the Oceans.*"

"It'll take me some time to contact my Managing Director of French Operations and get that information, but of course I will do it."

"Please do it at once, and call me with the information, Mr. Gregoire. I'd be very grateful if you could get back to me within half an hour."

He left his number and returned to work on his plan. It was probably only twenty minutes before Gregoire called back.

"I have the information you requested," he informed Ivan. "Fortunately I was able to locate my manager in France on the first call. He gave me the names of those who worked on the installation of our equipment on board the new cruise liner just completed in LeHavre. Would you like me to dictate the names to you or fax them?"

"Thank you for the fast action, Mr. Gregoire," Ivan said. "How many names are we talking about?"

"Three," replied the CEO. "These units are practically turnkey when we deliver them. Just a few test runs and we're out of there," he said proudly.

"Have you got their addresses and job titles right there in front of you?"

"Yes, Dr. Welland, two technicians and one engineer. The engineer would have been in charge of the work. They all work out of our office in Toulon, where the ship was constructed."

"Please give me the engineer's name, address and phone number, Mr. Gregoire."

Gregoire dictated the information and Ivan wrote it down. *Murad Al Bejalo, 46 Rue des Petits Bateaux, Toulon.*

"Do you know if there anything unusual or different about this particular installation?" Ivan asked him.

"My manager in France told me it took longer than usual to make things work properly. He didn't think it was significant, just some little glitch. He told me Murad is a good man. He's been with us for twelve years. He is one of the millions of Algerians who have migrated to France to find work. Is there anything else I can do for you, Dr. Welland?"

"No, Mr. Gregoire, that's all. Please don't tell anyone about our conversation. It's a matter of national security."

Ivan was about to get in touch with the security forces in France when he thought better of it. The damage was already done. He could always arrange to have the engineer picked up later. It was clear to Ivan that this man had probably tampered with the Sat/Nav on board the *Controller of the Oceans*, but he may have been acting under duress. Terrorists have their ways. Right now what was important was that he instruct Captain Constantine not to rely on his Sat/Nav, and to change course from what would be the normal path through the shipping lane. He would arrange that when he went aboard in Lisbon.

Rashid got off the train in LeHavre in the afternoon. He called a cab and asked the driver to take him to the Alhambra Hotel. The hotel was frequented by Arab travelers, mainly because they liked the architectural details of the place.

The Algerian desk clerk spoke to him in Arabic. While he was checking in, the clerk advised him that his wife had arrived that morning. Rashid received the room key, and took the ancient elevator up to the third floor. He looked up and down the corridor to find room 328. When he found the proper door he inserted his card and opened it. Once inside, and before he could put down his suitcase, he felt a gun in his back. An armed assailant had stepped out from behind the door and had him covered. He raised one hand over his head, but he was still holding the suitcase with the other.

"Put down the suitcase slowly," a woman said in Arabic. "Now lower your pants." Rashid followed her instructions. "Now your underwear." Rashid complied. "Now turn around." The woman looked at his genitals dispassionately, then said, "Okay, you can pull your pants up now."

While Rashid was adjusting his clothing, he stared at this woman who had been so bold and cold. She had olive skin, and was dressed in traditional Arab women's clothes, with her hair and the lower half of her face covered. Her eyes were dark, and they had a feral aspect to them, darting quickly from one thing to another. She was small of stature, but full of self-confidence. Rashid knew why she had insisted on seeing his privates before letting him speak. It was because of the second circumcision. She wanted to see the scar.

Men chosen by their religious leaders to be captains in the fight for the new Islam were marked in a special ceremony. Those given authority in the inner sanctum of the brotherhood bore this seal. It was a symbol of bravery and total commitment to the cause to submit to this ritualized scarring. Once so identified, these men carried great status among the warriors of Allah. The young woman would not have followed orders from Rashid had she not seen evidence of his rank in the movement. It was no longer sufficient for Arab men to be circumcised, because the Jews and others also did it.

Many attempts by Jews to infiltrate terrorist cells had been attempted, and some had succeeded, but no moles had gone undiscovered since the installation of the rite of the second circumcision. For the recipients of the rite (done at age twenty) it was unpleasant in the extreme, but it did accomplish what it was designed to do, which was to prove the loyalty and dedication of the bearer of the scarring, and to identify those whose orders were to be followed.

Rashid's assailant put away her gun and introduced herself as Fatima. She was known in the organization by this single name only. Rashid spoke to her in Spanish, as he wanted to be sure she could pass herself off as a Latin American woman.

"How did you learn Spanish?" he asked.

"I was born in Andalusia," Fatima told him. "My parents were Moroccans who lived in Spain for years, and I went to school there. Later we moved to Palestine to help our Islamist brothers to regain their territory and put an end to the Zionists. Both my parents were killed by Israelis while they were there working for Hamas. Naturally I would like to do anything I can to avenge their deaths and remove the illegal occupiers of the Arab lands and their supporters, the Americans."

"On the ship you will refer to me as Ricardo, and as your husband. We will occupy a cabin together, and we must pass as a Chilean couple on a vacation cruise. Have you brought appropriate clothing to wear on the ship?"

"Yes," she said. "I have observed the tourists in Spain and I have acquired the right things to wear for such a voyage. Would you like to see them?"

"Yes, put some on. I would like to make sure that we look the part. I will change into the clothes I have brought as well. Then we will go out to a restaurant, and practice acting like husband and wife."

Fatima picked some clothes out of her suitcase and went into the bathroom to change. Rashid put on a Hawaiian shirt that he thought was suitable for a Western tourist going on a cruise. Fatima had to forego wearing the veil and head covering, but the cause they were fighting for took precedence over rules of modesty. She told Rashid he was to regard her as a fighting comrade and not as a woman.

They went out to look for a place to eat, and discovered a Spanish tapas restaurant. They decided to dine there, presuming they could speak Spanish with the staff, but it turned out that the people who operated the restaurant were from Barcelona and spoke Catalan as a first language. Like most Catalonians, they preferred to speak their own language. They knew Spanish, of course, but they preferred French as a matter of pride. Many people in Catalonia hated the Spaniards, and wanted to have their independence in the same way as the Basques. Although Rashid and Fatima could understand their feelings, they were disappointed not to get the opportunity to practice their Spanish.

When they arrived back in their room, Rashid took two passports out of his suitcase. He handed one to Fatima. They were Chilean documents – his was issued to Ricardo Manuel Ruiz, and hers to Consuelo Luz Lopez de Ruiz. Rashid had studied them carefully and thought the forger had done a very good job. She looked at her photo in the passport and realized it was the same one used by the forger in her present passport, which was Spanish. If they had used their legal passports they would have been hassled everywhere they went. Hers would have been Palestinian, and his from the U.A.E.

Since the European Union had come into effect, travel restrictions between European nations had been lifted. One could move between countries without passports or customs declarations, which was an even bigger boon for terrorists and criminals than it was for ordinary citizens. Rashid reached into his suitcase again, and this time he pulled out a wad of U.S. bills. He counted out ten one hundred dollar bills and gave them to Fatima.

"You should have some American cash in case you need it," he said. "You never know, we may be separated, or we may need to be in the casino for tactical reasons, and these Western floating pleasure palaces require money for everything."

"You're right," she replied, slipping the money into her bra.

"Now let's go over our stories so we don't trip ourselves up. We live in Santiago. We have a condominium in the down town area of the city. I am a fruit broker. I buy various fruits from the growers and arrange to ship them all over the world to processors and retailers. Most of our fruit gets shipped to the U.S. in the winter season when Florida and California growers are unable to supply their customers. That is why we can take our vacation at this time of year. We have one child, a son called Juan, and your mother is caring for him so we can get away for a few days. You were trained as a nurse, but you have been staying at home with our child for a while. We will pretend to be a typical Westernized South American couple. I may have to touch you occasionally in the way of the depraved infidel devils. As a Muslim woman you must forgive me, as I would never act this way except that it is part of our taqiyyah. As you know, the Qur'an sanctions whatever lies we need to tell to trick unbelievers."

"I have had to prove myself worthy of being sent on a mission such as this many times before. I do not have the scar of the second circumcision as you do, but I assure you I will carry out my assignment. I am capable of suspending normal decent behavior if it is clearly an assignment from the *Scythe of*

Allah. In my mind I am still a virgin even if I use my body to advance the purposes of Allah. I am sure a true Arab believer such as yourself will understand that."

"I do understand that. I am married, and I have four wives and eleven children. I would never knowingly dishonor an Arab woman, so you can depend on me to make any distasteful behavior as minimal as possible."

"I have been on assignments before. On some of them, the men seemed to think that my part of the mission was to take care of their sexual desires. I found that behavior unacceptable, and at its root hypocritical, because loyalty to our cause should equate with obedience to our moral code. When our actions do not agree with our beliefs, we are like the perverted Western infidels. I have seen your scar and I respect what it signifies, so I expect you to treat me according to true Islamic principles."

"And so I shall," Rashid promised. "Muslim men should not have treated you that way, and I will certainly not do the same. It is clear that you have earned the right to perform this mission, or our leaders would not have sent you on it. We are both soldiers of Allah, and our gender difference does not enter into the mission."

"That is it exactly. I just wished to make it clear. Putting on their clothing and showing more of my skin than I would like to does not change my wish to dress in our cultural way. The Qur'an does not give specific instructions about how women should dress except to say that we should be modest and not entice men, who I must say are portrayed as lacking self-control. Muslim women have accepted this picture of how things are and have taken the route of extreme modesty, covering themselves from head to foot. This act of submission on the part of Muslim women is done in the expectation that men will curb their desires and function within the moral parameters of our faith. It is the Straight Path that leads to paradise with Allah."

In her tiny cabin in the bowels of the great ship, Mercedes was busying herself with the task of making things comfortable. She noted that the elegance level of the new vessel was raised for the passengers, but the crew's quarters were essentially the same – stark, dark, and tiny. As she puttered around she hoped that Niko would call her back to his cabin. As it got later and later her expectations petered out, and she got into her bunk to go to sleep. She was thinking about the fact that he had seemed to be more affectionate with her than usual. Then, when he didn't call her back, she felt that she had misjudged his signals. In dealing with a man with a history of womanizing, it is confusing when attraction turns to affection. She sensed this time that Niko really liked her and had missed seeing her. She had in the past, by her own actions, discouraged him from getting too attached to her because she felt their relationship had no real future.

Niko, for his part, had not tried to define his feelings for her. He realized that he missed her, of course, but he attributed the fondness of his heart to her lengthy absence. Yet he was surprised by the degree of joy he felt at seeing her again. He was trying to blame it on his abstinence of the last few months. She had been the last woman he had been with before he moved to his new command, and now she was to have been the first after their separation. Still, this explanation did not perfectly describe those aspects of his feelings that were not sexual. Being torn away from her in the present emergency, however, did nothing to clarify his feelings for her. Those sentiments would have to wait.

Now Niko had to focus on how to keep 3,000 souls alive and how to keep their water-borne home afloat. Had Mercedes known what Niko was doing she would have felt differently about his failure to resume their tryst. Throughout history men have been required to do great things while their wives and lovers were kept in the dark. This case was no different. Mercedes assumed that Niko was apathetic about their relationship, and that it didn't matter much to him if she visited him or not. She knew he was not callous, but he might have the common tendency of the ladies' man to vacillate and be indecisive in his dealings with the opposite sex. While she pondered the subtleties of their rapport in her tiny corner of the ship, Niko was facing the worst nightmare that a man in his position could be called upon to deal with.

Ivan's problems were of two types – strategic and tactical. He must design a response to the immediate tactical problem of preventing the terrorists from sinking the greatest nautical icon of the decade. At the same time he must devise a long-term strategy to prevent all types of terror attacks from occurring in the first place. He felt his ideas about how to disarm those who would use weapons and explosives to cow the world into silent compliance had taken a temporary back seat to the immediacy of the safety of the ship and its passengers.

He called Damian and Abdul to ask about the progress they were making on the weapons project. He encouraged them to continue their work, advising them that he and David would be away for a few days, but that they would all get together when he returned. Then he called Marina and tried to sound calm and normal as he explained that he would be gone for a while. He asked after Julia, their new baby, and promised to be careful and come back as soon as possible.

Brooklyn came into his office with an armload of papers. "These are just some routine matters, correspondence to sign, staff assignments to make, and a list of calls you should take care of before you leave," she said.

"Before *we* leave," Ivan corrected her.

"Speaking of leaving, we're going on a military transport that will be delivering equipment and supplies to NATO in Portugal. The Navy Seal team will be boarding with us at Andrews Air Force Base. All the arrangements for boarding us in Lisbon have been made according to a confirmation received from Captain Constantine on the ship. I have spoken to the Chairman of the Joint Chiefs and he assures me that we'll have the support we need in all areas of our mission. I'll be the contact point for all communications between our mission and the military services that may be required to support us."

"What news do you have about the four men from the academic lists?" Ivan asked.

"I don't think we're going to get anything useful from this list. I mean, it's interesting in the sense that we know that we've educated a few guys to be experts in explosives and that they live in hot spot areas of the Middle East. We know they've been using false IDs for a long time, but until we catch them red-handed, a terrorist by any other name is still a terrorist. I'm sure it's a source of great amusement to the terrorists that they get their know-how and their choice of targets directly from our educators and our media. They must think we're very stupid, and perhaps they're right."

"Did you get the list of nautical attacks from Damian yet?" Ivan asked.

"Yes. Here it is. I don't know about you, but I'm surprised by how many terrorist incidents have taken place on ships."

Ivan took the list and scanned it. "I agree, but it's probably not so surprising. After all, they've been operating afloat since the Phoenicians, and the Barbary Pirates, and right up to today. My biggest worry is that they'll come up with some new way to attack a ship, perhaps using some method we haven't thought of yet. We don't want to find out about it after the fact.

"Do you have any ideas about what kind of attack it might be?" Brooklyn asked.

"I have some ideas, but I don't have time to talk about them. What I need you to do right now is to call someone in the Navy and get them to send me a nautical chart of the Western Mediterranean. Make sure it shows soundings off the Algerian coast. And one more thing, get the guy at the CIA who reads the satellite photos of the Mediterranean on the phone as soon as possible, please and thank you."

His phone buzzed. It was Brooklyn. "I've got the CIA guy on the phone for you. His name is Daniels."

"Thank you Brooklyn," Ivan said, and switched to the other line. "Daniels, for the next five days I'd like you to be especially watchful of the waters off Algeria. Please report to me any anomalies that you observe, no matter how small. We're keeping an eye on the new cruise ship, the *Controller of the Oceans*. She's scheduled to pass through those waters on her maiden voyage, and we don't want anything to happen to her."

"Aye, aye sir."

CHAPTER ELEVEN

A li and his son had a great deal of respect for water. They were desert Arabs, Bedouin nomads who trekked all over the parched areas of the earth in search of oases. When they reached a great body of water such as the Arabian Gulf, The Red Sea, or in this case the Mediterranean Sea, it was soul-stirring to them. They loved to walk along the shores, smelling the moist air and letting their humidity-starved lungs breathe in the moisture. On a visceral level they were enjoying their mission. It would be nice to be sailors of the sea instead of sailors of the sand for a little while.

Father and son had slept on the beach under the stars and had been awakened by the throbbing sound of diesel engines approaching. A commercial fishing vessel 60 feet in length was slowly backing toward the beach in front of the large shed in which they had been assembling their contraption of death. A man on the bow of the boat was setting an anchor to hold the boat off the beach. The captain was backing the engines against the anchor to make sure it was holding.

In a minute a smiling Al Jaza'ir jumped off the stern of the boat into the shallow water and walked up the beach.

"Good morning," he called out to Ali.

"Good morning, old friend!"

"I have brought the boat so we can load it today," said Al Jaza'ir. "Tonight we will leave with the fishing fleet, and being one among many, we will be unseen. My lifelong friend, Captain Muhammad, whom you see now tying a stern line to that tree, will take us where you want to go."

When the Captain had finished securing the line he used to counter the swinging effect of the wind and the lapping waves, he approached the threesome on the beach.

"May I present Captain Muhammad? These gentlemen are Ali, and his son Amin."

The Captain had heard of the reputation of the Detonator, and was very respectful toward Ali.

"I have been navigating my way through life following the star of the Prophet Muhammad, peace be unto him," Ali said. "It will be my pleasure to navigate under Captain Muhammad."

The four men went into the rough shed in which the gear was warehoused. Ali explained to Muhammad what everything was, and how he planned to use it. The Captain nodded as the plan was revealed to him.

"Allow me to ask a question," he said, when Ali finished.

"Please," Ali said.

"Have you taken into account the drift of the currents?"

"The anchoring system will be sufficient to hold the long net against any current."

"If I may beg your indulgence, I have a second question, then," the Captain said.

"Please," Ali said again.

"How can you be sure that some other vessel will not pass that way and be accidentally destroyed before the *Controller of the Oceans* comes along?"

"The anchors will keep the nets at a depth that will allow all other vessels to pass over the trap, except perhaps an aircraft carrier. If an aircraft carrier *did* hit the line of explosives, however, that would be even better for Arab public relations purposes than sinking a civilian ship."

"One last question, then," said the Captain, in an almost obsequious tone.

"Of course," Ali said.

"Are the explosives deep enough for our oil supertankers to pass over?"

"They are. But to be on the safe side, all our supertankers have been routed around the area. Their captains have been privately informed to avoid the shipping lane in question. They have also been sworn to secrecy about this information."

When the Captain was satisfied by Ali's explanations, they began to load the gear into the fishing boat. Ali had planned the loading in as meticulous a manner as the operation itself. They would load the nets and their deadly contents aboard the boat on the wooden pallets that had held the ice cream off the floor of the truck so the refrigerated air could circulate under them and keep the product frozen. First they would move the pallets to the sides, up against the gunnels of the boat. The pallets were wrapped in tarpaulins that covered the plastic explosives disguised in individual strawberry ice cream containers. Since the shed had been used for years in the boat repair business, it still had the ways over which they launched and hauled fishing vessels.

Captain Muhammad found three long connected tree trunks that the fishermen used in cases just like these to provide an incline. He placed one end of the primitive ramp on the stern of the boat, and the other end on the beach so that it touched the last greased log of the way. Using gravity, greased logs, and manpower they pushed the first pallet down to the water's edge. Captain Muhammad affixed cables to the pallet when it reached the lowest point of the way. Then, by means of the power winch that the Captain used for hauling nets into his boat, they gingerly hauled the heavy load of plastic explosives onto the stern deck of the fishing boat, first one pallet and then the other.

Ali had secured three neatly coiled nets to the pallets with light pieces of line, which allowed them to move down the ways much more easily than the first two heavier pallets. Gradually, through the clever use of blocks and cables, the pallets were slid securely into place. The last thing they wanted was for the cargo to shift or fall overboard while they were motoring to their destination, so they made sure every pallet was belayed. Lastly, all the floats, wire, bladders, and tools were put aboard using a crib that Ali had built out of pallets to hold this gear. The men had taken the sunny, calm weather during the loading as an omen of good luck for their mission. Ali walked to his ice cream truck and removed the box of detonators from behind his seat in the cab. He reverently carried the box aboard the boat as though it contained a sacred relic.

It was Friday, the Muslim equivalent of the Sabbath. The men all went to a nearby mosque to pray for the success of their mission and to hear the words of the imam's sermon. After their ablutions, they doffed their shoes, entered the sanctuary, placed their rugs on the floor and settled themselves on them to pray and hear the traditional midday Friday message which dealt with the way Muslim believers should comport themselves in order to keep favor with Allah. The imam's preaching of fire and brimstone for all those who ignore the words of Allah was a fear-provoking experience for the sinful, but for those obedient ones a paradise of unimagined beauty and pleasure awaited.

The sermon also pled for believers to resist the debauched ways of the infidels. The imam reminded his audience that everything that favored Islam was good, and everything that impeded the infidels was also good. Ali and his henchmen all took note of how much the success of their mission would impede the despicable merchants of Western aberrant sexual mores. In the future they would be afraid to trot their lascivious lifestyles all over Allah's world to tempt believers into impure and lustful thoughts and behaviors.

The self-styled warriors retreated to the shed to have a nap. They would likely be up all night, resting during the heat of the day. In a few hours they would be joined by two young divers whose regular jobs were underwater ship repairs, and whose sideline occupation involved underwater demolition. One of these men was a son of Al Jaza'ir's. Now both these leaders had their sons with them. Providing sons to be soldiers for Allah was the duty of all Muslim fathers in the view of these sincere fundamentalist men, and it was considered an honor to serve with them in the fight to defeat the infidels.

The swimmers would load their scuba tanks and gear aboard the boat. Then at dusk, the traditional time of departure for Mostaganem's fishing fleet, they would all set sail for the appointed spot in the shipping lanes off the coast of Algeria.

* * * *

In his short, regular meeting with the President of the United States the next morning, Ivan had discussed the various matters that the President needed to know. Included in these was the suspected attack on the *Controller of the Oceans*. He informed the Commander-in-Chief of his plans and told him that he would be going to Lisbon to take charge of the measures to protect the great ship. When he had finished his explanation, the President fully understood the magnitude of the problems that would occur should a terrorist attack on this vessel be successful, and he agreed that Ivan should follow through with his plans to thwart any such attack.

Having the complete support of POTUS was a great boon to Ivan. Now he could push any government button and receive immediate support to prevent what could be the largest disaster at sea in the modern age. He walked down the hall to his office.

"Get hold of David Feingold," he said to Brooklyn, "and tell him to come to my office. If I'm correct, we're leaving in two hours. Please check with our flight to make sure of the time we should be at Andrews, and order a limo to get us there."

"I did that already."

"Good. Also please verify that our Seal team will be on the plane with us. I don't want to go to the O.K. Corral by myself. Do we have any feedback from the security checks I ordered to be done on the passenger and crew lists?"

"They're on your desk."

"Thanks, Brooklyn. There's no certainty, you know, that the attack will come from outside the ship. There could be terrorists on board the ship, either among the passengers or the crew, for that matter. Furthermore, there's nothing that says the attack couldn't be coordinated with some elements on board, and others coming from the sea. That's the advantage the attacker has – he knows what he's going to do. But we have to guess what he's up to, until he actually does it. Just this once, though, I'd like to be there waiting for him."

"I hope your instincts are right. If they are, we'll be able to stop the unthinkable from happening. Feingold was here earlier and left his suitcase. He's around somewhere, probably hiding and hoping you'll change your mind about taking him. I'll go look for him and make sure he makes it on time. I'll also let you know about the plane and the Seals."

Ivan felt bad about having to drag David Feingold along. David had had a hard enough time relocating from New York to Washington, and Ivan knew that taking him to Europe was going to be upsetting for him. But Ivan needed his brain and his programming skills to deal with the Sat/Nav issue. He needed David to get into the guts of the equipment and find out if it had been tampered with.

Ivan pored over the passenger manifest and it occurred to him that simply reading names and nationalities was not going to be very helpful. If he could be present when the passengers were issued their plastic identification cards with their pictures and signatures on them, perhaps he might be able to recognize an anomaly such as someone claiming to be from one country but having an accent from a different country.

Arabs, unfortunately, were among the best in the world for mastering accents in foreign languages. But Ivan was a trained linguist, and he knew the typical idiosyncrasies of language that are nearly impossible for a foreigner to overcome. An Arab, for example, will always pronounce the letter *p* as a *b*. So *Grand Rapids* becomes *Grand Rabbits,* and a *lap top* becomes a *lab top.* But Ivan could not speak to every boarding passenger, and those employees of the cruise line who issued the cards would not be concerned about foreign accents. Besides, the passengers would be boarding in France, and Ivan had no jurisdiction there.

There was something about the use of these cards that could be helpful, Ivan thought, but he wasn't sure what it was. The cards took the place of a credit card on board the ship. Any purchases could be charged to the passenger's account. At the end of the cruise the purser's office tabulated all the charges and issued a bill that included every item purchased on board the ship, as well as the suggested tips for service staff. The bills could then be paid to the purser by credit card or cash. It was all done rapidly by the computer, and usually without errors. Ivan decided to put David to work on this to see if the system could be used by his team to sniff out people who were not who they said they were. One thing that occurred to Ivan was that Arabs don't drink alcohol, so theoretically anyone who ordered drinks containing alcohol, which would be most people on a cruise, could be removed from suspicion. Of course they could order drinks but not drink them. Ivan didn't think this was very likely, unless they were totally paranoid or had been forewarned. Anyway, anything David could do to reduce the number of suspects would be helpful. Ivan thought his team should be highly motivated, because if they failed to discover the terrorists, who might be suicide bombers, they could go down with the ship along with the Captain, crew, and passengers.

In due time Ivan and his little band of smart but relatively inexperienced terrorist hunters got into the limo and headed for Andrews Air Force Base. When they arrived they were driven directly to the huge transport plane. There Ivan encountered his old friend, Lieutenant Mercer, standing over a pile of gear that included scuba, weapons, and a rubber boat. He was directing the loading of the equipment aboard the plane. The two men greeted each other with warm affection. Ivan observed from his uniform that the Lieutenant had been promoted, and was now a Commander.

"Well done, Mercer," Ivan said, "I'm glad to see the Navy is rewarding its best and brightest."

"Well done yourself," Mercer smiled. He was referring to Ivan's promotion to National Security Advisor to the President.

Ivan maneuvered him away from the others. "As soon as we take off," he said, "you and I have a lot of planning to do. I've arranged for us to have a table to work at during our flight over the Atlantic."

"That's fine, sir. I look forward to working with you again. I'll just finish supervising the loading of our gear, and then I'm all yours."

Ivan found an Air Force Colonel standing nearby whom he assumed was to be the pilot of their plane.

"May we board the plane now, Colonel?" he asked him.

"Yes, sir. Go right ahead."

Ivan gathered his little group of stalwarts and chaperoned them onto the plane. They found seats in a small section of the cavernous interior of the cargo plane. He took his usual outside seat so that he could extend his long legs into the aisle. He asked David Feingold to sit next to him. Damian and Brooklyn sat immediately behind Ivan and David. Ivan had intentionally left the seats in front of him for the Navy Seal team, as he wanted to observe them and get familiar with their faces. A second reason for this seating arrangement was that Ivan presumed the Seals would be cool in their demeanor, and therefore have a reassuring effect on David.

"Did you bring your laptop?" Ivan asked David.

"Yeah, I never go anywhere without it," David replied.

"Good, get it out. I've got a project for you to work on during the trip. It's important, and it needs to be done before we get to Lisbon."

Ivan dug around in his briefcase and got out the list of passengers and crew for the maiden voyage of the cruise liner. He handed them to David. "See if you can figure out which ones of these are terrorists. Each of these passengers will be issued a plastic card like this one."

He handed David the sample card that the cruise company had sent him. "The purser on board the ship has a computerized system that tracks every card and every purchase charged to each card. Everyone leaving the ship must have his card scanned, and when he returns, his card is scanned again. You've been granted admittance to their system on a read only basis. You aren't to make any entries or changes. Your password is written on the card I just gave you. These cards are being issued right now in LeHavre to the boarding passengers. So let me know right away if anyone attracts your attention."

"Brooklyn," Ivan said over his shoulder, "call that British Admiral on Gibraltar and ask him to have a meteorologist, the one most familiar with conditions in the Alboran Sea, call me ASAP. And please call the Spanish officer in charge of security for Isla Alboran and warn him to be on the lookout for pirates from North Africa for the next ninety-six hours. You may have to clear this through the Spanish military hierarchy."

"Damian," Ivan continued, "I need you to think about the historical big picture. Let your mind wander freely over all the previous seaborne terrorist attacks you know of. Think about who masterminded them, and what they might be up to now. Try to think like a terrorist. Write me a scenario of what you think they'll do in this case. We're out of valid intelligence reports so we're going to have to rely on our intuition. I need your best guess of the worst-case scenario. If you think I've overlooked something, or I haven't thought of something, I need to hear from you *tout de suite*."

During the time that Ivan was issuing his orders to his team, the out-of-uniform Navy Seals had boarded the plane and were now casually seated just in front of Ivan. The jet engines had started up and the plane was racing up the runway while David clung to the arm of his seat. He was silent, but his white knuckles gave him away. In a minute the huge plane was wheels up and steeply climbing into the skies over Maryland. As soon as Ivan felt the plane leveling off into its cruising altitude he leaned forward and asked Commander Mercer if he was ready to go to work. The young officer indicated that they should move to the other side of the plane where there were two seats side by side behind a table.

Ivan led off by telling Commander Mercer everything he had done, thought, and said about the possible attack.

"You realize that there's not a lot of hard evidence in those details, right?" said Mercer, after Ivan had finished.

"I know," Ivan said, "but I'm interested in preventing terrorism, not reacting to it. It's always too late if you can't be proactive in these cases."

"Gotcha," said the Commander. "So, how do you see this attack coming about?"

Ivan spent the next two hours conferring with Mercer, except for a few minutes when Brooklyn advised him that she had a Lieutenant Briggs on the phone, calling from the British Naval Base in Gibraltar. After the requisite introductions Ivan asked the lieutenant to tell him the general geological and meteorological conditions in and surrounding the Alboran Sea.

"Well, sir," the officer began, "the Alboran Sea comprises the western part of the Mediterranean Sea. The principal characteristic of this body of water is its proximity to the Strait of Gibraltar where the connection to the Atlantic Ocean is narrowed. Cold, and therefore, heavier tidal ocean water flows into the Mediterranean and passes under the warmer water of the Mediterranean Sea, which flows out into the Atlantic when the tide changes. This exchange of waters has a lot to do with the weather patterns and the water temperature of the area."

"Tell me Briggs, what are the currents like?"

"The currents are strong and circular. The movement of the tides and the exchange of warm and cool water keep things stirred up, and it's often foggy. Reportedly this is a good fishing area, and it's also the playground of the largest known grouping of bottle-nosed dolphins."

"What can you tell me about Isla Alboran?"

"The small island is really the top of a mostly underwater mountain. There is an automatic lighthouse on the highest point. It contains no harbor worthy of a name, but there are a couple of piers that fishing boats tie up to occasionally. The Island is claimed by both Spain and Morocco. It's closer to North Africa, but a Spanish army garrison occupies it to guarantee possession. Alboran has a history as a hideout for pirates. There's a second island nearby, but it's really not much more than a rock. It's well charted and appears on the nautical charts. That's about all I can tell you about the island, sir."

"Thank you, Lieutenant Briggs. Your information has been very helpful," Ivan remarked as he disconnected the call and returned to his mission planning with Commander Mercer.

* * * *

Niko had spent the morning doing a last minute walk-about during which he had spoken to each of his division heads and received their assurances that they were ready to receive passengers that afternoon and sail as scheduled for Lisbon that night. He was confident that his ship was in readiness to do what it was designed for, but was it ready to repel an attack? Neither its Captain nor its crew had military training, nor was the ship built for war. Like all men in positions of public trust, Niko had developed a persona that radiated confidence. But like anyone else, he was susceptible to inner doubts when confronted by matters of life or death. He hoped the Americans he would take on board in Lisbon would be experienced in combating threats and attacks of the kind they had warned him might be coming, and he prayed to his much neglected God that no harm would come to his ship and its human cargo.

Captain Niko's new bridge officers were a capable group of ambitious seamen who had been chosen for promotion to the new flagship. They had been deemed capable of promotion and were working their way up to commands of their own. They had all been around long enough to know that their futures depended on their getting good recommendations from their captain. From the most junior to the most senior of his officers, there was a lot of respect for Captain Nikolas Constantine. After all, he had been chosen over all the other experienced captains to receive the command of the most expensive civilian piece of sea-going machinery in history.

The work of commissioning the vessel and training the crew was finished. In a few hours the passengers would be boarding the ship and the regular schedule of work for the crew would begin. Niko had decided to host a coffee break meeting for his bridge officers, and all were present and accounted for. Many of the junior officers were hardly more than boys, just as he had been when he had started his sailing career. There were no women bridge officers – not because women were incapable of doing the job but, Niko supposed, because as senior officers they would too rarely be home to manage child and family matters, so the work did not appeal to them as a career. Women who sought the responsibility of command positions would be better off doing faster trips as airline pilots, often returning home the same day. There certainly were women on board in various capacities, including executives, but the vast majority was young and single. Most were doing work on board that they might have done on land, but for their desire to see the world. In this category were the waitresses, bartenders, casino dealers, clerical workers, sales clerks, baby sitters, child-care workers, nurses, and stewardesses. Some were married, but because they came from less developed countries, they couldn't find work that paid as well as the cruise ships, so they signed on to help support their families. Mercedes de León was one of many in that position.

Due to her seniority and her willingness to tackle anything, Mercedes was often assigned extra or unusual tasks. Niko's bridge party was such an event. The ship was in port in LeHavre so there was no work that couldn't wait to be done later. She was well known to the bridge personnel, having brought them coffee and snacks at sea innumerable times. So when she arrived with her assistant José (a Filipino with a long service record) pushing a cart laden with Danish pastries, fruit, donuts, and coffee, no one was surprised except possibly Niko himself. He thought perhaps she would decline serving at this affair so she wouldn't have to see him, but she nonchalantly went about her business pouring coffee, offering pastries, and bantering with the flirty officers.

Niko was proud of her poised way of handling them. She was never snippy, though at times what the men said called for a little show of attitude. When she got to the Captain she looked at his handsome, cheerful face, smiled, and passed him his coffee. He winked at her, hoping that none of his men would catch him in this act of familiarity. If he had been seen, however, most of the men would have just accepted it as a gesture of a typical male acknowledgement of female charms.

But to Mercedes and Niko, the wink was more. It was a sign to them both that things were all right between them. Mercedes continued distributing the coffee and goodies until everyone had been served. Then she sent José back to the galley and positioned herself in the rear of the bridge area so that she could serve anyone who wanted seconds.

Niko stood and addressed the men. "I'm very satisfied with your performances up to now. However, our customers will be boarding soon, and we want them to be impressed and pleased with our cruise ship. It is our responsibility to introduce this vessel to the world, and good public relations means lots of explanations. People always want to know how the ship works, and what is unusual about her. I'll try to handle as much of this responsibility as I can by making announcements over the Public Address System, giving on-board speeches, and visits to the bridge.

"You have all noticed the special viewing gallery that has been added to this ship's bridge area to accommodate more visitors and move them along comfortably. A visit to the bridge is a big attraction, particularly for male passengers. It may seem like a nuisance to have to deal with the passengers' questions, but I remind you that we are in a very competitive business. It is not a necessity for our passengers to take a cruise. We are not delivering food, or medicine, or essential supplies – we are delivering a good time. We must never forget that. If I were to write the book on how to succeed in the cruise captain business, it would contain far more pages about passenger relations than seamanship."

Niko looked at the attentive seamen gathered before him, then continued his address. "On a successful cruise, a good time is had by all. But the most important, mostly unseen chore that we have to do is to keep the passengers *safe*, while they are being made happy. And it is to this element of the passengers' welfare that I would especially like to call your attention. Alas, in this day and age, happiness and safety are usually tied up with security. Our beautiful ship is for some people a beautiful target. It may be hard to believe, as we seldom see acts of terrorism because we are prepared to deal with violent attacks. But if we let down our guard we will see them more frequently.

"So in the next few hours before we set out to sea with thousands of lives in our hands, I am going to ask each of you to get out your procedure manuals and go over the security section. Don't do so casually and expect me to ignore it. This matter is critical, not casual, and your job performance reviews will be tied to your knowledge of the security portion of the procedures manual. Gentlemen, I am very serious about this. Your alertness and your knowledge of security will be directly related to the speed with which your career progresses. Do not forget this."

The audience was a bit startled by the severity and passion of Captain Niko's words. His team had never seen him so stern. Usually he led with grace and humor, but this time he was almost threatening in his demeanor and attitude. Mercedes, being more familiar with Niko on the personal side, was more taken aback than anyone at his change in attitude. She knew him to be curt sometimes when giving orders, but she had never heard him threaten that if his orders were not obeyed there would be career consequences. She was happy to have received his wink, but she was puzzled about his steely attitude on the issue of security. Had there been some sort of threat against the ship? It occurred to her that this might explain why he had left his cabin in such a hurry the night before.

CHAPTER TWELVE

The throb of the diesel engine called out to Ali, Amin, Al Jaza'ir, and the two divers. It was Muhammad's way of saying *all aboard*. The men who had been resting inside the shed came out of the building, holding their arms to their faces to shield their eyes from the setting sun. The ramp had been removed when the cargo was on board the boat, so the men had to wade into the sea and walk waist deep to approach the vessel. Muhammad had placed a makeshift ladder over the side, which the men climbed to get aboard the fishing vessel.

Once on board, the dripping men heard the call to evening prayer coming from the mosque's minaret. Automatically they faced the southeast, fell to their knees with the sun at their backs, and prayed. Their prayers were short but fervent, as they were anxious to get on with their mission, the success of which they felt would be worth a thousand prayers to Allah. These were men of action, given to earning their rewards. When they rose from their knees, dripping wet from the waist down, they were ready to die for their Allah and his promised paradise.

Muhammad lifted the hatch-cover in the cabin and proudly showed Ali and the others its contents. Inside were automatic rifles sufficient to arm them all. In addition there were three RPGs, a missile launcher, a .45 caliber machine gun, and a large metal box containing ammunition for the weapons. With the plastic explosives stacked on the stern deck, the fishing boat was far better armed than most coast guard vessels patrolling in the area. Ali's plan called for the use of none of these weapons. If he could set his string of plastic explosives in the correct spot and leave the area before the *Controller of the Oceans* came along, their mission would be a success, and they would easily escape without firing a shot.

Ali walked around the vessel, familiarizing himself with every detail of her construction, while Muhammad moved the boat ahead very slowly so his son could pull in the anchor rode and retrieve the anchor. They were disconnected from the land now and were on their way. The diesel engine increased its RPMs and they headed north, picking up speed.

In a few minutes Ali looked over the port side and noticed a similar vessel heading on the same approximate course as the one Muhammad was steering. Then one by one a flotilla of such boats appeared. It was the fishing fleet leaving the harbor and heading for the fishing ground, as they did nearly every evening in this season.

"These are our unwitting accomplices," Muhammad said to Ali. "We will hide among them until it is time to set your net, then we will slip away. After you have done your part to provide food for the fish, we will return to the anonymity of the fleet and go home. You don't suppose the fish will refuse to eat infidel dog meat, do you?"

Ali gave his shoulder a playful shove and said, "I have arranged to grind it into very small pieces, and I'm sure the fish will enjoy it."

Rashid and Fatima had slept fully dressed on top of their beds in their hotel room. Rashid could hear Fatima urinating in the bathroom through the closed door. It was strange to hear that noise emanating from a woman sharing his room – a woman he had not enjoyed in the Qur'anic fashion.

When her turn came to listen to Rashid, Fatima was put off by the noise and the memory of his noisemaker. In Muslim society a woman married young and produced children. An unmarried woman of Fatima's age was looked upon with suspicion. Was she a deviant? Was she so ugly that no man wanted her? Was her family so poor they could not provide a suitable dowry?

Fatima considered herself special. Indeed, most Muslims would also have made allowances for her if they had known that she was an esteemed member of the *Scythe of Allah*. Most Muslims who didn't know her, however, and to whom she could not explain herself, felt she was probably either a Lesbian or a whore. She envied nuns who wore a uniform that spoke for them. She wasn't attracted to women sexually, and if she were a whore, she would be Allah's whore only. Why did she have to endure the disdain of the ignorant, and the condemnation of the self-righteous among her own people, when she had done more for Allah than nearly all the Muslim women in the world? What had these self-proclaimed virtuous ones ever done besides lie on their backs for their men?

Fatima had dressed herself in Western clothes while she was in the bathroom, and Rashid had done likewise in their room. He was startled by her appearance when she stepped out into the bedroom area. She looked like a totally different person. She had on a bright blue blouse cut to reveal a modest décolleté, and a white pleated knee length skirt that for some unknown reason Western women thought was particularly appropriate for cruises at sea. Italian pumps with high heels accentuated the muscles in the calves of her bare legs. Her black hair was pulled back and tied with a small white silk scarf.

For his part Rashid looked quite natty in a navy blazer, grey trousers, and an open necked pale blue shirt. To most observers their olive Semitic skin would enable them to pass for Chilean mestizos. They assumed their Latino personas and went down to the lobby for breakfast.

In a French hotel frequented by Algerians it was possible to order breakfast a la Algérienne, but the couple declined in favor of the more typically French menu – croissants, butter, jam, and café au lait. They spoke Spanish together and tried to see if the waiter and the other diners would detect their Arab background. They thought they had passed the test, but it was impossible to know for sure.

In France there was a strong sub-culture of North Africans whom the French ignored as much as possible. The French might easily be capable of looking down upon Latin Americans too, so Rashid and Fatima weren't sure just which type of condescension they might have been experiencing. From the point of view of a terrorist trying to make his way in the world, the haughty superiority of the French was convenient. The French thought themselves too good to talk to foreigners, and the terrorists preferred not to talk to them either, for reasons of their own.

The real test for the pseudo Chileans would come at dinner time, when they would be expected to make conversation with other guests. They hoped the other guests would be Americans or Canadians, as they usually had less linguistic sophistication than most other nationalities. Since both Rashid and Fatima had accents in English and Spanish, they had to create a cover story to explain them.

Rashid evolved a story that the couple had escaped from Chechnya as refugees and had moved to Chile. In this way it would appear that their accents were Chechen, which very few people could distinguish from the Arabic underlying their Spanish and English, and it would enable them to be Muslims without being seen as Arabs. In this way they would not need to know anything about the nearly universal Catholicism of South America. Ideally they would never have to use this story, but they both needed to have the same explanation in case they were ever questioned.

Rashid wanted them to board the ship as soon as possible, but at the same time he didn't want them to attract attention by being among the first passengers. It was bad enough that they would be photographed twice before they went aboard – once for creating their credit/ID card, and the second time by the ship's photographers. Hoping to sell the photographs to the passengers, the photographers magically materialize at the gangplank every time passengers leave or board the ship. If the vessel sank, as Rashid hoped, then these photos would go down with the ship. If for some reason the ship did not sink, the photos would be in the name of Ruiz anyway. If they never picked up the pictures, as some passengers don't, they would simply disappear along with all the unwanted photographs.

Boarding was to begin at 2 PM and finish at 5 PM. Sailing was at 6 PM, corresponding with the first seating at dinner. The huge glass windows would afford the diners a panoramic vista of the harbor as the great ship pulled away for her maiden cruise. Rashid figured that he and Fatima would arrive at 2:20 PM for processing. In that way they could go aboard early, but not be at the head of the line. He wanted there to be as few passengers as possible on the ship when he and Fatima arrived so he could retrieve the guns that had been left on board for him by the Algerian who had worked on the ship in Toulon.

At 2 PM he and Fatima took their luggage down the rickety old elevator to the desk and paid the bill in French currency. The concierge called them a cab and they were whisked off to the dock where the *Controller of the Oceans* waited, dominating the harbor like some enormous white swan swimming in a dingy little pond.

There were ten people ahead of the Ruiz couple standing in the line leading up to the reception clerk who was charged with registering passengers whose names began with the letter R. The excitement of the huge number of people in the cruise ship boarding area adjacent to the pier was palpable. Every passenger was anticipating a good time and wanted it to start immediately. Unfortunately, checking in over 2,500 people and their baggage takes time. Passport procedures, luggage tagging, and processing of credit information, even with a computer terminal for nearly every letter of the alphabet, proceeded at a pace that was more stately than swift.

When Rashid and Fatima reached the desk, the registration clerk was pleasant and efficient. She requested an imprint of Rashid's credit card, processed their passports, put tags on their two pieces of luggage, told them the luggage would be delivered to their cabin in due time, and passed them through to have their pictures taken for their plastic shipboard ID's. Cards in hand, they proceeded to the gangplank and walked aboard the great ship, holding hands as if anticipating a wonderful cruise. Boarding the ship could not have been easier.

They took one of the elevators in the central column in the part of the ship called the atrium. The elevator had glass walls, and as it slowly rose to deck D it provided the passengers with a view of the various central areas of each deck. The decorations were elegantly dispersed, and each deck had a different country theme. D deck was named for Denmark, and the decorations featured the Little Mermaid from the story by Hans Christian Anderson. When the elevator doors opened at level D, there was a statue of the young mermaid that was a perfect likeness of the one in Copenhagen.

Fatima observed that the uppermost deck would no doubt be named after America instead of Arabia. She was right. Rashid read the signs and proceeded to cabin 414D. The door was open, but nobody was in sight. He told Fatima to have a seat and he would be right back. He hurried off to find cabin number 610. The Algerian who had hidden the guns had chosen cabin 610D because no Muslim could forget the number of the year when the Prophet began to receive the revelations from God that eventually became the Qur'an.

As he hoped, Rashid found the room located on the port quarter, and as yet unoccupied. It was a much larger room than his, with its large glass observation windows and a door that led to a small outside balcony from which the occupants could see astern and also along the port side of the ship. He proceeded to the closet that was located just off the entrance. In it he found a stand that held an ice bucket for cooling wine. In the bucket, wrapped in a white towel, he found a bottle of champagne, or so it appeared. Rashid felt the towel and decided it contained what he was looking for. He cradled it in his arms and turned to leave the cabin, almost colliding with the cabin steward. The Indonesian steward cast a suspicious eye on him, perhaps thinking that Rashid was swiping the bottle of wine.

"There's a complimentary bottle of champagne in every cabin," said the steward, meaning that there was no need to steal one. "Would you like me to bring ice and chill that for you?"

Thinking on his feet, Rashid said, "No thanks. We're having a bon voyage party in my cabin and I was sent to get my friend's bottle as a back-up in case we need more."

The steward was a wily, experienced little man who had seen many petty thefts performed by rich passengers on cruise ships, and he didn't believe Rashid's story for a minute. He didn't dare get nasty and confront Rashid, however, as there might be truth in his story and he didn't want to start the inaugural voyage off with an unpleasant incident that could result in disciplinary action being taken against him. So he nodded and smiled. His mind was working on finding another bottle to replace the one this guy was stealing. He couldn't allow the passenger who belonged in this cabin to be cheated out of his complimentary bottle, as it might be reflected in his tip. He was glad that this man was not his passenger.

Rashid returned quickly to his cabin and explained what had happened to Fatima. He looked in the closet and found the bottle of champagne there and handed it to Fatima, instructing her to quickly return it to cabin 610. If possible she was to replace it without saying anything to the steward, but if she did encounter him she could explain that they hadn't needed the extra bottle after all. In this way Rashid hoped no one would be the wiser, and the steward would forget the incident.

While Fatima was off on this errand he unwrapped the bottle and found nothing but the neck, with the barrel of a pistol and a silencer stuck into it. The Berretta handgun and another like it were wrapped together to simulate the shape and weight of a wine bottle. Rashid examined the guns closely. They were fully loaded, and seemed to be in excellent working order. It was too bad, he thought, that the guns could not have been in their cabin instead of 610, but he realized that the weapons were placed in Toulon long before cabin assignments had been made to the passengers booked on the voyage. He was lucky, he supposed, that they had at least been on the same deck.

Fatima returned looking a little annoyed. "I had just put the bottle in the bucket and turned to leave the cabin," she told Rashid, "when along came the steward with *another* bottle of champagne. I told him that my husband did not need the extra wine after all. He seemed to buy my story as far as I could tell. Obviously he didn't buy yours, though, as he had evidently gone away to find another bottle to replace the one he believed you had stolen."

"Don't worry," said Rashid. "The result is good, I believe. Since there is no missing wine, there can be no repercussions. I think we have overcome our first problem. Let's hope that everything else is resolved this easily."

"You are probably right," Fatima agreed. "Now, let me see our bottle of champagne."

Rashid passed the guns to Fatima. She handled them almost reverently. She disassembled them, examined each part, and reassembled them. He was impressed at her complete familiarity with the weapons. Allah had chosen wisely when he sent her to him to be his partner in this most important mission.

Niko had finished his meeting on the bridge. Mercedes had cleaned up afterwards and collected all the dirty cups, stacked them on the cart, and was preparing to leave for the galley. The officers had departed, and for a minute they were alone.

"You look very beautiful this morning," Niko said. "Do you have any time off today?"

"No, I am sorry, Captain. We are preparing for our first dinner at sea. There are menu meetings, a service review, and the setting of tables to be done. Chef Claude and the dining room manager are very busy organizing a gala first meal for our passengers."

"Of course," Niko replied. "You have much to do, I know. It was just that until we leave the dock this evening, I am free. I miss you very much, Mercedes," he added, gazing at her with a serious expression.

Mercedes felt herself blush.

"After a few days, when things settle down, I will come to you," she said, looking down at the floor. "Meantime you must keep all of us safe," she added, trying to get a grip on herself.

"I couldn't help overhearing what you told your men, and it made me uneasy. Have you received a threat against the ship?" She raised her eyes again, searching his face. "Nothing specific, but we are a big target and I can't take any chances. Keep your eyes open, and if you see anything unusual about the passengers, report it to me right away." "I will," Mercedes said as she walked away, pushing her cart in front of her.

"I'm glad you're on the ship with me," Captain Niko called after her. He was taking a chance, speaking that way in a public place where he could be overheard.

Mercedes felt her heart beat faster, but she was too shy to look back at him or reply to his comment. After so many years of knowing her Captain, she was amazed at the feeling of uncharacteristic bashfulness that he had aroused in her.

A few hours later there was quite a lot of fanfare in the port as the huge ship made ready to depart. Niko was on the narrow balcony that winged out from the bridge, permitting an officer to see the docking hawsers.

"Let go the spring lines," he said, speaking into a walkie-talkie. On the dock two men lifted the heavy rope off the bollard and let it fall into the water. An unseen winch on board the ship wound the line in. The second spring line followed the first into the water and was taken aboard ship.

"Fore and aft thruster engines on, but keep in neutral," Niko ordered. "Point thrusters to direction 90 degrees to heading, and let go stern line," he continued. "Let go bowline," he said into his hand-held radio. The winches rolled the heavy docking lines in, first one then the other. "Engage thrusters bow and stern, and set to half power."

Inside the bridge his officers were attentively following his instructions. There was only one thing more exciting than undocking a large ship, and that was docking one. Captain Constantine was in his element doing both. He had developed an impressive reputation among his junior officers for the skill he demonstrated at these times.

He had begun to develop this talent when he was a small boy sailing a dinghy in the harbors of his island home in Greece. He was fond of telling his officers that docking a big boat was no different than docking a small one. The wind is the same, the current the same, the objective of putting the boat gently up to the dock is the same – the only difference might be that you can't fend off an ocean liner if you approach too fast or too hard.

The thrusters would hold the ship off the dock, but in order to reach the channel he had to move the ship sideways. He would do this by running his port and starboard engines in opposition to each other, port ahead, starboard in reverse, so that the angle that the propellers bit into the water moved the huge vessel imperceptibly away from the dock and out toward the channel, without moving the ship forwards or backwards.

A stream of commands issued forth from the Captain to his crew. He was controlling five separate engines and moving one of the heaviest vessels afloat so subtly that one could barely detect any motion at all. All around the *Controller of the Oceans* was a sea of small vessels nearby. Fireboats aimed their water hoses into the air, creating an arc of cascading water. The cacophony of horns and whistles blowing was deafening, as seemingly the entire population of LeHavre bade goodbye to the floating sister city that had been docked there for two days.

In the midst of all the noise and excitement, Captain Constantine coolly guided his ship to the right center of the channel, from where he would keep the green lights on his starboard side all the way out to sea. When he judged that he had reached the position he sought, he ordered all the auxiliary engines to stop, and commanded the main engine to go to work, ahead one eighth. It took a tremendous amount of force to move the ship, and it took an equal amount to bring it to a halt. In fact, from a cruising speed of thirty knots to a dead stop would take two miles of distance to accomplish, so braking to avoid small boats in her path was not an option.

Soon the big ship passed out of the harbor and headed into the wider part of the English Channel in a Westerly direction.

The passengers were summoned to their various assembling areas for the mandatory lifeboat drill by the urgent sound of the ship's horn. Following directions on the door of their cabin each passenger found and donned his orange-colored life jacket, and reported to their designated staging area where in an emergency they would be directed by a crewmember to the appropriate life boat. The passengers received an explanatory lecture on the use of the features of their life jackets, and after a few minutes of milling around they were dismissed to return to their cabins to store their lifejackets away. Not one of the 3,000 persons on board ever thought they would see the jackets again.

The passengers scheduled to eat at the first serving at 6:00 dressed casually for dinner and found their way to the dining room. The table seating had been pre-assigned and the scrum to find the proper tables began. Directions from the headwaiters guided everyone to their appointed tables with a minimum of confusion. Seating at each table was random, but those people at the table would be there for the duration of the voyage. Larger parties or family groups might occupy a whole table, but in most cases dinner partners were pre-selected by the luck of the draw. The people that passengers met at dinner would become those whom they knew best for the length of the cruise, so finding a convivial table grouping was important, if not essential, to having a good time on the cruise.

Rashid and Fatima found their table for six. The other four diners were already seated when they got there. The headwaiter pulled Fatima's chair out for her, and she seated herself. The gentlemen at the table stood and introduced themselves.

"I'm Sidney, and this is my wife, Miriam."

"I'm John, and this is Louise."

"Hello. I'm Ricardo, and this is my wife, Consuelo."

Rashid was happy with the seating arrangements. He immediately saw that the other guests were Americans, older, and seemingly benign. Fatima was on his left, and Miriam on his right. He was, of course, not a bit interested in any of these people. All he wanted from them was to be left alone to do what he had come for, but if he had to be with any strangers, these would do nicely. He felt confident that he and Consuelo could hide their Arab ethnicity from these ordinary-looking people.

A waitress appeared with a large pitcher of iced water. She filled their glasses and distributed the menus.

"Hello, my name is Sandy, and I'm from Scotland. I'm your assistant server for the duration of your cruise."

After the people at the table had taken some time to look over the menus, another server made her appearance.

"Hello, my name is Mercedes, and I'm from Chile. I'm your server, and I'll be taking your orders."

The hairs on the back of Rashid's neck tingled with apprehension. Of all the servers on this huge vessel, why had they been assigned one from Chile? He would have wagered, and won, that there were not a half dozen crew on board from this remote South American country.

After the introductions, Rashid had told the table that he and his wife lived in Santiago, Chile. He decided that he would rather attack than play defense, so when he heard that Mercedes was from Chile, Rashid immediately feigned pleasure and spoke to her in Spanish.

"Where in Chile do you come from?" he asked her.

He was taken aback when she replied, "I'm from near San Bernardo, south of the capital city."

This was too much of a coincidence. Mercedes must be the wife of that worthless cur Diego, and the very one who was to assist them in their mission. He had hoped to meet her once, and only just before he needed her. He did not want her to have a chance to know him, and possibly identify him in case the plan went awry. Rashid had spent a few days in Santiago, but he didn't know the city well enough to pass himself off as a resident. He decided to keep the conversation directed to San Bernardo, a smaller city which he actually knew a little better, having been there longer in order to track down Diego, and through him, this very woman who was now asking him for his dinner order.

Mercedes was busy taking the orders for drinks, starters, and the main courses for this table and the others in her station, so she didn't have time to think about the couple who spoke Spanish well, but with a peculiar accent. She sent Sandy to the bar to bring back the bottle of wine that the American couple had agreed to share. The Chileans did not order wine, a rare event for someone from Chile. In his mind Rashid was dusting off his story about being a Chechen refugee who lived in Chile, which accounted for what must be a strange-sounding Chilean accent to Mercedes.

There were many European immigrants in Chile; Mercedes would know that, so his story should convince her that he was a Chilean citizen now. It was unlikely that she had ever come in contact with a Chechen or an Arab who spoke Spanish, so Rashid did not expect her to be able to tell the difference in accents. Fortunately everyone else at the table was an English speaker, so that became the lingua franca of the table and enabled him to speak as little Spanish as possible to Mercedes. She would know he was an Arab soon enough, he thought.

The meal was very good, as Western cooking went. Rashid had fish, and Fatima ordered lamb. The conversation was general, mostly concerning upcoming activities on the ship. Ricardo and Consuelo said as little as possible without being anti-social. The servers were busy shuttling food out of the galley, and bussing dirty dishes in. All conversations with the servers were in English until after the dessert and coffee were served. Then, with a few minutes to spare before the first seating was over, the two servers became more talkative.

Sandy was a chatterer and kept her tables entertained with her Glasgow burr. Mercedes was more demure, but very pleasant about answering the questions of the Americans, most of which concerned her family and conditions at home in Chile. The two American couples were retired people, and were planning to go to the nightly theater performance. When the faux Chileans were asked what they were going to do, they said they thought they would take a walk and retire early. The tables around them began to empty, and Rashid followed their example, taking Fatima's arm and making a polite exit.

Night had fallen, and they did indeed take a long walk on the upper deck. The couple sauntered along, discussing their companions at the dinner table and especially the server from Chile. They agreed that they had probably not given her any hints as to their real origins. Rashid told Fatima that Mercedes was the very one who had been coerced into helping them. She agreed that the odds were great against sitting at her table.

"Allah must have wanted it to happen this way," she murmured. "There can be no other logical explanation."

Rashid grunted his assent and they walked on, speaking Arabic softly together. They looked up at the bridge and thought about how surprised the officers of this proud ship were going to be in just about thirty-six hours.

It was cool. Rashid took off his jacket and put it around Fatima's shoulders. This was a very nice thing for an Arab man to do. Rashid had seen it done in some Western film. He couldn't remember the name of the picture, but he remembered thinking that he would use that tactic whenever he wanted to impress a woman. He had used the technique on his third wife once when he wanted sex from her. It had worked. That night she had unbuttoned her nightdress so he could see her naked even though it was against their religion. The next morning he had prayed, and had made his wife pray, for forgiveness for their sin.

Rashid questioned his motives for putting his jacket on Fatima. Did this signify that he desired her in spite of the conversations and agreement they had had? He convinced himself that he had done it because there was a good chance they would die on this mission, and by keeping her warm he was demonstrating that he was proud of her and appreciated her willingness to sacrifice herself to help with this great deed on behalf of Islam.

If the dark waters rushing along the hull and the almost starless sky overhead could have spoken, they would have acknowledged that this was the great Atlantic Ocean and it was not about to be bested by any ship, not even the magnificent *Controller of the Oceans.*

Nearly all the passengers had either gone to dinner or to the show or to the casino, so Rashid and Fatima had a feeling of being alone together under a black and endless sky. Their shared mission gave them a certain unity of spirit. When they heard the burbling of conversations and saw groups of people joining them on deck, they knew that the second sitting in the dining room was over. Whenever one of the automated doors slid open, the faint sound of Western music competed with the whooshing sound of the sea rushing along the hull to join the wake astern. It was time for them to go below.

Rashid opened the door of their cabin with his plastic card. The steward had made up the beds and placed a chocolate on each pillow. Fatima took a blanket from the closet and went into the tiny head, where there was just room for her to have a shower and dry herself. She decided to sleep wrapped in the blanket, as she would have done in a tent in the desert.

When she came out of the head, Rashid went in. She lay down on the single bed on the right side of the cabin and went to sleep right away, even before Rashid crawled into his bunk and turned off the lights.

The ship skirted the headlands of France and passed on into the North Atlantic. It would sail outside the mouth of the Bay of Biscay while the passengers slept, proceeding in a southerly direction down the Iberian Peninsula and passing the Spanish city of La Coruña at the northernmost tip of Spain. Then, sailing south into Portuguese waters, the ship would pass the charming city of Porto.

At dawn the *Controller of the Oceans* appeared at the entrance to the port of the capital city of Lisbon and picked up the harbor pilot.

Niko, who had slept through the night so that he would be fresh for the docking procedure, was on the bridge and would guide the great ship to her berth. Fingertip controls, thrusters, electronic communications and hand radios had made tug boats almost redundant, but they stood by anyway, just in case they were needed. When the majority of the passengers awoke, the ship would already be alongside the dock.

CHAPTER THIRTEEN

Ivan and his little group were happy that the flight was almost over. The seats they had been using weren't the equivalent of first class airline seats by a long shot. They didn't recline, they weren't sufficiently padded, and they weren't intended for comfort during a trans-Atlantic flight. Whatever was merely uncomfortable for others, however, was torture for a man of Ivan's size. Several members of the group had managed a few hours of sleep, but the majority had not slept at all. Ivan wasn't very pleased about that because he wanted everyone to be fully alert for the next two days.

As their plane approached the Lisbon fly space the Captain, who in this case was a Colonel, pointed out the *Controller of the Oceans* on their port side, occupying a large space along the dock. Everyone on board had a good look at her before they strapped their seat belts on for landing. The sight of that huge, white, shiny new ship had a unifying effect on all of them. There was no way that they could allow that beautiful vessel to be sunk by rag-tag militants of any stripe. No one, no religion or group that used religion for its own purposes could be allowed to kill innocent people and sink this huge ambassador of peaceful American capitalism.

Commander Mercer and his Seal team oversaw the unloading of their equipment. It had been carefully packed into wooden crates labeled *Air Conditioner Parts* to disguise the true contents.

"Why air conditioner parts?" Brooklyn asked Mercer.

"Well ma'am, it's because everywhere we go we bring a breath of fresh air."

She liked and respected the Commander. He had a sense of humor. He was confident, but not overbearingly so, like many of the Marines she had met before. He was essentially the All American Boy – tall, dark, handsome, and polite. That was all right with Brooklyn as far as it went, but the real test for her was that Ivan respected him, and she knew he didn't suffer fools gladly. Brooklyn was an independent woman, a thinker, and a bit of a cynic when it came to trusting people, but Commander Mercer was one man she felt she could trust with her life, if it ever came to that.

The other man was Dr. Ivan Welland, her boss. Ivan had saved the entire U.S. Government, the Civil Service, and the American system of government, as far as she was concerned. He was the first and only, elected or unelected, government official she personally knew to be entirely worthy of the trust that had been placed in him. That was saying a lot, but it was her opinion, and she was sticking to it.

The "air conditioner parts" were put on an unmarked Portuguese truck and taken to the dock to be loaded aboard the cruise ship. The people, also bound for the ship, were taken in a van along with their personal luggage.

Brooklyn boarded the van first. She, whose real last name was Brocklin, had suffered a name change at the hands of her civil service colleagues who had combined her similar-sounding last name with her New York accent and had arrived at the nickname of *Brooklyn*. Actually she was from the Bronx, but sorting out a Bronx accent from a Brooklyn accent required the skill of a veritable Henry Higgins, so she was consigned to be called by the name of the better-known borough. Her accent persevered, and the nickname stuck.

David Feingold, the pride of the Department of Statistics at the City University of New York, followed Brooklyn into the van. David was Ivan's linguistic and mathematical muse, and a significant talent as a computer programmer. Ivan was counting on him to probe into the Sat/Nav on the ship to see if it had been tampered with. He had been Ivan's right-hand man on the Council of Caliphs caper, and his proficiency was needed again on the present mission.

Next to board the van were the Seals, dressed in civilian holiday clothes and feeling less comfortable in them than Ivan and his subordinates. Lieutenant O'Neal, the only female on the Seal team, stepped in and took a seat. Commander Mercer, who knew her slightly because she was a year behind him at the Academy, had chosen her for this mission.

Katherine O'Neal preferred to be called Kate or Lieutenant. After the brutal physical training that is part of the qualifying regimen to become a Seal, Kate had attended language classes. She had chosen to study Arabic because she thought it might come in handy in light of the instability of the Middle East. Kate had chosen not to become an academic, however, partly as a teenage act of rebellion, and partly because she was very fond of physical activities. Early on in high school she had become a long distance runner. She participated in sports of all kinds, but she excelled in those requiring endurance. She ran marathon races and competed in iron man events, but it was her untiring ability to push on, not any overpowering strength, that had seen her through the Navy Seal physical training school.

The other members of the Seals were Lieutenant Peter Pugni, second in command, who was an up-through-the-ranks Naval officer. His forté was the handling and navigating of small boats. He navigated himself into the van, followed closely by the Chief. The Chief Petty Officer was an expert in defusing explosive devices, as well as being the team medic, strange as that might seem.

One after another the three enlisted men boarded the van, bringing with them an assortment of skills, including weaponry, underwater photography, and computer instrumentation. When they were all aboard, the English-speaking Portuguese Naval representative to NATO drove them to the dock where the *Controller of the Oceans* awaited.

It was the middle of the morning, and the majority of passengers had gone on land tours of Lisbon. Those in the crew who had time off were similarly doing the tourist circuit. While the six who would be intermingling with the passengers went up the ramp, the five who would stay with the crew of the ship entered the vessel along with the gear crates. The crates were put into a separate compartment. The space had been designed to hold a small fleet of jet-ski boats that would be put aboard on future cruises to tropical climes for the use of passengers. The room was ideal for assembling and inflating the Seal boat. In a pinch the boat could be launched from the stern of the liner, even while she was underway. One of the Seals would be on guard to secure the weapons and the equipment at all times.

The ship's security officers had been expecting Ivan and his team, so Ivan and Mercer were shown to the Captain's cabin, while the other four were shown to their quarters. In the late afternoon, when the shore-side revelers were back on board, they would mingle with the passengers. Ivan hoped, but didn't expect, that his people would be able to sniff out any terrorists who might be on board.

Meanwhile, inside the elegant cabin, the men shook hands warmly. Ivan made the introductions, and thanked the Captain for all the cooperation that had already been extended to him and his men. As Ivan looked around the cabin he thought it must not be such a bad thing to be the captain of a huge cruise ship. The accommodations were conservatively elegant, and decorated in a maritime theme. The accoutrements were of high quality, and the space was the equivalent of a suite in an expensive hotel. Ivan imagined the food and service were excellent as well.

The thing that most appealed to him about the Captain's job was that the level of authority was completely unimpeded. He was sure there were some areas in which he was subject to supervision, but the Captain's command was enviable compared to his own situation in the White House where public scrutiny, the influence of self-seeking senators and congressmen, and political advantage were pressures bearing heavily on him, to say nothing of having to report to the most visible man in the world.

"My I have a brunch sent up for us?" Niko asked.

Ivan and Mercer had eaten very little since they had left Andrews, so they were pleased to accept the Captain's offer.

Niko lifted the phone and called the chef. He ordered them as
fine a selection of breakfast and light lunch items as could be
found in any of the best restaurants in the world.

"Dr. Welland," said the Captain, looking directly at Ivan,
"what makes you think my ship is going to be attacked?"

The burden of convincing the Captain was Ivan's alone, so
he began explaining how he had come to the conclusion that
terrorists were targeting the *Controller of the Oceans*. He did
not have to go into much detail to point out that the vessel was a
superb target. The publicity, the photos, and the symbolism of
Western decadence that a cruising pleasure vessel of this scale
represented to Islam was an irritant of great magnitude and a
temptation too great to pass up. Ivan ranked the sinking of
Niko's ship, if they could pull it off, with the destruction of the
twin towers of the World Trade Center. He recounted to Niko
how al Qaeda tried unsuccessfully once before to bring down
the towers. Osama's boys had no compunctions about trying a
second time. Ivan suggested that the same sorts of "boys" had,
over the years, made several attacks on cruise ships and other
large vessels, and had even tried to sink an American warship
docked in Yemen. Ivan believed that the terrorists lusted after a
victory at sea, and the affront represented by this new pleasure
palace sailing into their waters was too much to resist.

Niko, being a Greek, raised an eyebrow at the mention of
the Mediterranean being an Arab sea. Ivan caught the almost
imperceptible expression on Niko's face and quickly mentioned
the historical incidents of piracy committed by the North
African Barbary Pirates.

When he finished with the historical perspective of why a
naval attack could be expected, Ivan began to discuss the
change in recent terrorist tactics that had been noticed
worldwide. He called Niko's attention to the IEDs that had
proliferated in Iraq and quickly spread from there. He pointed
out how much more efficient it had become for the terror
merchants to leave their bombs in one place and let the enemy
come to them, instead of chasing around trying to find the
enemy in a vulnerable position. Ivan mentioned how similar

this kind of thinking was to the technique of mining the waters. Then he came to his most important point, namely that with satellite navigation it was now possible to place a mine exactly in the course of a great ship like Niko's. A terrorist need not even be present when the explosion occurred.

"Furthermore, we're on the trail of a known terrorist demolition expert who is working in the Middle East," Ivan said. "So when you add it all up, it seems that this ship is a very high-profile possible target. Our job is to prevent any attacks at all, and that means anticipating anything that the enemy might throw at us. There's no way we can wait until we're absolutely sure there'll be an attack. We have to take steps now."

"What exactly are you advising us to do?" Niko asked Ivan.

"We have to defend against an attack by persons on board the ship, as well as protect it against an attack from the sea, and possibly both simultaneously," Ivan said. "In the first case we have gone over the passenger and crew lists and matched them against our statistical data base of suspected terrorists, and those whose profiles demand further scrutiny. We may need the cooperation of your stewards to allow cabin searches and that sort of thing. I've brought my computer expert with me, and I'd like you to allow him to examine your Sat/Nav to see if it has been tampered with. You can see how convenient it would be for the terrorists if they could find an opportunity to take the ship off course just enough to run it into a well-placed mine."

Ivan continued to outline his plan to the Captain.

"Commander Mercer is a graduate of our Naval Academy, and a trained Navy Seal. He and his men have brought along weapons and equipment, but they will be acting under cover out of uniform, and passing as civilian passengers until there is an attack or an overt threat of an attack, at which time they'll repel it. We've slotted some of them into spaces at the dinner tables of those we identified from our databases as possible risks. This was arranged by agreement with your management. I personally will stay close to you as an advisor, but you are to be in complete control of your ship, as usual. However, I'd like to go over your security staff's normal functioning. Do you want us to meet with your security people so that we can all be on the same page in the event that something does occur?

"Certainly," Niko said. "I'll call a meeting of my security personnel so that you and your men may meet with them. This is a good time for that, as most of the passengers are ashore."

He went to the phone and called his chief security officer to order the meeting at once. Just then a knock signaled the arrival of the brunch. Niko opened the cabin door. Mercedes had arrived with a cart loaded with food and a pot of coffee.

"Please come in, Mercedes," he said.

The waitress spread the food and water out on the table along with the silverware and napkins. The three men stood up and moved to the table. Mercedes nimbly got out of the way of the huge American man who was finding his place at the table. She served the men and poured the coffee.

"Will there be anything else, Captain?"

"No Mercedes," Niko said. "Thank you."

As she was closing the door she heard the Captain say, "Mercedes is from Chile, and is a model of our company policy, which states that we live in one world and we can all work together in peace. I am not sure about this trip yet, but we usually have about 45 nationalities working on board."

Mercer said, "No doubt you're working together better than the United Nations itself."

"That is my line. I usually say that," Niko smiled.

"Oops! Sorry about that, sir," said Mercer cheerfully.

"Captain," Ivan said, "I'd like to outline for you what we'll be doing in the event of an attack from outside the ship. Our world satellite surveillance system has been alerted. We'll be contacted at once if there are any vessels approaching the ship. The U.S. Navy has also been alerted and will be flying periodic air cover flyovers. The British Navy at Gibraltar has been keyed in so that nothing untoward happens in or near Gibraltar when you're there. The Spanish Navy has also been advised to keep an eye out for anything suspicious. The Spanish Army contingent on Isla Alboran has been asked to report any strange boats operating in the nearby waters.

"Fishing boats and pirates occasionally have tied up on that tiny inhospitable island, so we thought it best to keep them in the picture, too. As you know, the Moroccans claim the island belongs to them because it's closer to North Africa than to Spain. They might have a case, I don't know. I don't think it's likely that there'll be a war over such a small, inconsequential island. The Muslims probably think they'll get it back when they take over Spain again, which they also claim is theirs.

"I'm sure you've been kept apprised of the pirate attacks off Somalia in the Indian Ocean. You probably heard about the boat that got close enough to fire rocket-propelled grenades at a U.S. warship. That was an insane attack, and they were subdued in minutes. Commander Mercer has brought along his fast little Seal boat in the event an attack of this sort materializes. Should there be anything strange in the water ahead of your ship, Mercer and his boys have brought their diving gear with them. In the meantime, please use your forward-looking radar at all times after we leave Gibraltar."

"I planned to use the forward radar anyway, but thank you for the reminder," Niko said. "It is very good to know that we will have so much cooperative support from the various navies. I want you to know that my number one concern is safety. I have never had the experience of being attacked by pirates or terrorists, but it can probably happen to any ship that is in the wrong place at an inopportune moment. Anyway, gentlemen, I look forward to working with you. Personally I don't see how Islam expects to convert people to their point of view by frightening them, or killing them. The compulsion and severity offered by Islam are a hard sell compared to the pleasant alternatives of the innocent fun of a cruise. Now, Mr. Welland, perhaps you will attend the meeting with my security staff?"

"Of course, Captain, I'll be happy to accompany you. But please call me Ivan."

CHAPTER FOURTEEN

Rashid awakened early the next morning. The first thing he saw was the semi-naked body of Fatima in the other bed. She had apparently unrolled herself from her blanket while she was sleeping. Rashid silently studied her body and found it very attractive. One breast, with its dark nipple, was completely visible to him. He was surprised to find it so full. He would have expected her body to be boyishly small-breasted. Her legs were long, firm, and shapely, leading up to a dark, tangled, partly concealed place of mystery.

Rashid had all he could do to keep himself from moving over to her bed. Surely Allah would not have put this woman with him in this place had he not wanted him to have her. Why would the deity make a woman like this, if not to produce children? He would have married her if he hadn't already fulfilled his quota of wives. He finally decided it was a test to see if he was strong enough to resist temptation. He sat up and continued to stare wistfully at her nubile body.

Awakened by the sound of Rashid's movements, Fatima opened her eyes and saw him looking at her. She realized she was exposed, and quickly covered herself. She wished he had not seen her, but it was too late. She remembered, though, that within one minute of setting eyes on him she had forced him to show himself to her. Perhaps it was fair that now he had seen her, too. She suspected that the sight of her in the bed across from his had aroused him, but she was glad he hadn't tried to have sex with her. That would have put their mission at risk. She would have rejected him, but he would have resented her or been terribly embarrassed by the incident. It was better this way. They needed clarity of mind to bring Allah's revenge down upon this modern-day mechanical leviathan.

Fatima came to the conclusion that Allah was testing them. In the Islamic tradition of earned rewards from Allah, piety in this world leads to paradise later. She smiled inwardly at the thought that men will try to have sex at any time, in any place, with any woman willing to accommodate them. The use of this one piece of knowledge has allowed women to manipulate their men throughout the eons. It has also caused the male gender to be in universal denial, blaming women for their own weakness ever since Adam told God that it was Eve's fault that he ate the forbidden fruit.

Rashid was feeling pleased with himself for not having taken her. Fatima, for her part, was feeling good that he had not tried. Together they went to the dining room for breakfast. They decided to take a walk through the streets of Lisbon by themselves. The less they had to do with the others on the ship, the less chance they had of being discovered to be Arabs. They walked around in the city, which resembled an Arab settlement in many ways. The neighborhoods, with their narrow streets, and the architecture of the buildings had a distinctive flavor of Moorish influences.

Portugal's admittance to the European Union had brought up the level of prosperity. It was comical to see the number of expensive cars that had to fold up their mirrors in order to crawl through the narrow streets. The policy of equalization payments to poorer countries entering the union had resulted in many modern transportation benefits of improved roads and vehicles, but nothing could be done about the hilly neighborhoods that crowded the city.

In the modernized harborside area the apotheosis of Prince Henry the Navigator and his clan could be seen in the statues and the nomenclature of streets, businesses and restaurants. The couple, silently miffed that there were so many churches in a place that rightly belonged to Islam, found their way into the Maritime Museum.

The Museum housed an enormous collection of superbly crafted ship models. Vessels built to scale from the most ancient to the most modern were on display in myriad glass cases.

Ships of many nations were represented, and there was even a display of Arab dhows. The captains of these dhows were no doubt the teachers of the Portuguese sailors who came after them. Rashid and Fatima suspected that Magellan, Da Gama, and the lesser-known nautical navigators, so acclaimed in this museum, owed much to the unsung Arab sailors of the past. How unfair that the Arabs, who had named the navigational stars as well as used them, should receive no credit for it at all!

In spite of the misgivings they had about the loss of the Iberian Peninsula to the infidels in the past, Allah assured the future of Islam in Lisbon. They decided to relax and have lunch before doing more sightseeing and returning to the ship before 5:00 PM.

They had wrapped their pistols in articles of dirty laundry and left them in the cabin. They had to leave their weapons behind so that they could pass through the metal detectors at the head of the ship's gangway. There was no reason that the cabin steward should discover them there, but Rashid was a little nervous even so. He would check on them first thing when he got back to the cabin. In the meantime they would enjoy the city, which was much to their liking. All it needed were a few large mosques on the skyline to rival the great port cities of Islam.

Ali's boat stayed on the periphery of the fishing fleet throughout the day. The men rested. The younger ones fished with hand lines and managed to catch their dinner. Al Jaza'ir and Ali pored over charts and consulted their shipboard Sat/Nav. They reckoned they were about one and a half hours from the point of interception with the course of the *Controller of the Oceans*. Ali had to estimate how long it would take them to set out the long line of explosives. He wanted to operate at night in the dark so they would not be discovered. His plan was to separate his boat from the fishing fleet immediately after sunset and proceed to the exact latitude and longitude where the cruise ship's Sat/Nav was programmed to take it.

He encouraged the younger members of his crew to rest, as they had a lot of work ahead of them. It would probably take them until dawn to finish setting the trap. Laying the better part of a mile of netting exactly perpendicular to the ship's course would be difficult under any conditions, but at night, with no lights, and with plastic explosive charges set every one hundred feet (each one powerful enough to blow their fishing boat out of the water), they would need all the strength they could muster.

The currents in this part of the Mediterranean were an added worry for the group of jihadists. They had seen to it that the liner's Sat/Nav was set to allow for the widening of the Alboran Sea at the point where the trap was to be placed. The currents closer to Gibraltar were said to be stronger and to move in a circular motion due to the confluence of the exchanging of waters back and forth as the tides moved through the straits. Floating the net at just the right height was a matter for the divers, and working underwater with flashlights was going to be difficult, but they had depth meters and plenty of buoys from which to suspend the nets. Ali was sure that with the help of Allah it could easily be done, so he stopped worrying and just concentrated on the work.

Al Jaza'ir had computed the exact position for anchoring the net at the northerly end. He would simply go to that point, drop the net's anchor, make sure it was holding, and then go south, very slowly letting the net off the stern so that Ali and Amin could put the detonators into the plastic explosives and the deadly packages into the bags that they had sewn onto the net back in the shed in Mostaganem. As the net ran out behind the boat it would sink to the depth that Ali calculated would be enough to hook the net over the bulbous nose of the ship. It would be the loudest nose-blowing in the history of the world, he thought, chuckling with glee.

The ship would be proceeding due east. His net was to be laid pretty well in a north to south direction. The cruise ship had to cross his line if it was anything close to being on course. If it crossed close to the center it would drag the charges back along both sides of her hull under the water line, and one after the other the explosions would come as the detonators struck the metal hull of the ship. The great speed of the boat's forward motion and the enormous thrust of her passing through the sea would fill the ship with water through the penetrations made by the blasts, and each succeeding explosion would blow another hole in her hull aft of the one before.

Ali could imagine many holes in the hull of the ship, but he could see no holes in his plan, as long as they were not detected while laying their net. Even so, he reviewed all the precautions he had taken to avoid failure. The boat he was using was made of wood, and therefore was less detectable by radar than a metal boat. Darkness would also help to cover their movements. Traveling with a group of similar boats would shield and confuse any pursuers. The trap was set deep enough under the water for all vessels except the targeted one to pass over without detonating the charges. The ship's navigation equipment was perfectly programmed to lead the vessel to its death. Once back in Algeria, he and his son would simply drive away in his ice cream truck.

The passengers in the first seating were being served in the dining room, and Mercedes was cheerfully taking orders at her tables. Wanting to be friendly, she addressed Rashid and Fatima in Spanish. They replied unenthusiastically in Spanish, giving their orders in halting fashion and with an accent that Mercedes just couldn't make out.

"What was your original language?" she asked them, with a warm smile. "Your Spanish is very good, but I don't recognize your accent."

Rashid felt angry that she would be so bold as to ask such a personal question, but it would have looked suspicious, he felt, if he had shown his annoyance. Westerners were happy to explain their business to nosy females, it seemed. All the other people on the cruise were talking to one another in just this sort of way.

"My wife and I escaped from Chechnya during the fighting there," he said, trying to sound cordial. "We settled in Chile a few years ago. That is why my accent sounds strange to you."

Mercedes gracefully acknowledged his explanation. She watched him carefully as he spoke, and she could tell he was trying to decide if she believed him or not. She broke off contact with him as she moved to the next person to take her dinner order. She was speaking English to the others at the table, none of whom understood what she and Rashid had been saying.

She could feel his eyes burning into her as she moved around the table, but she didn't make eye contact or act as though she were paying attention to him in any way. Sandy came along, pouring water and joking with the Americans at the table about her accent being the only true English accent. This kind of talk continued for a few minutes, while Rashid smiled affably.

Mercedes had no way of knowing what a Chechen accent in Spanish would sound like, but she had the distinct impression that this passenger did not want to discuss it. She noticed the serpentine coldness in his eyes as he watched her. It was as if he had something to hide, and he was trying to find out if she was onto him.

She decided she would mention her observations to Niko. While she was in the kitchen placing her orders she picked up the phone and dialed the number for the bridge. Mercedes knew the Captain would be there, as the ship was just leaving the port of Lisbon, bound for Gibraltar. He was always on duty whenever the ship left or entered any port.

"Hello, bridge," said the communications officer.

"May I speak to Captain Constantine, please?" Mercedes said. She could hear the officer telling Niko that the call was for him.

"Captain speaking," said Niko, in his familiar accent.

"Niko, it's Mercedes," she said, keeping her voice lowered so that nobody would overhear her. "I just want to report that

I'm serving a couple of people at my table who seem suspicious to me."

"What are they doing?"

"It is not what they are doing, it is how they speak. The man claims to be from Chile, but I am from Chile myself, as you know, and their accents in Spanish are very peculiar. I asked the gentleman what his native language was, and he told me that he and his wife escaped from Chechnya and settled in Chile a few years ago."

"What struck you as being strange about that?"

"It was not so much what he said, but the cold way he looked at me. It was as if I had hit a nerve by asking him that simple, ordinary question. But worse than that was the way he continued to observe me as if he were searching my expression to see if I believed his story. Well, I don't believe him, so I am reporting this incident to you, because you specifically asked us to be very watchful and to report anything unusual."

"Thank you Mercedes. What is the passenger's name?"

"His name is Ruiz. That is a reasonably common Spanish name, but I doubt that it is also a Chechen name."

"I'll check into this at once, Mercedes. Just act normally, and try not to provoke him in any way."

"All right. Thank you for taking me seriously, Niko. A lesser man might have verbally patted me on the head as though I were a child. But I must go now. My food is ready to be served."

As soon as Niko hung up the phone he explained what she had said to Ivan, who was standing nearby watching David Feingold working on the Sat/Nav program. Together they went to a computer terminal and flashed up the passenger manifest. They ran their eyes down the list until they came to Ruiz. Ricardo and Consuelo Ruiz were in cabin 414, D deck. They had come aboard in LeHavre, as had most of the passengers. They had Chilean passports. The photos that had been taken prior to issuing their plastic ID cards were staring back at them from the computer screen.

"If you don't mind, Captain," Ivan said, "I believe this would be a good time for us to search their cabin, while the two of them are eating dinner."

"Of course. I'll call my chief of security and send him to their cabin at once."

"I'd like Commander Mercer and Lieutenant O'Neal to go too, if it's all right."

"Certainly," Niko replied.

The Captain got on the phone and called his man, telling him to meet Ivan's officers immediately at cabin 414 D, with a passkey. Ivan paged Commander Mercer with the silent pager instrument that they both carried. As soon as Mercer felt the vibration of the pager he feigned a bit of sea sickness and excused himself from the dinner table. His pretend wife, Lieutenant Kate O'Neal, followed him out of the dining room, ostensibly to look after her husband.

As soon as they were in a quiet place, Mercer called Ivan and was told he was to search the cabin of a couple that was thought to be acting in a suspicious way. He was instructed to check for anything that could implicate the people in a plot against the ship.

In a matter of minutes Mercer and O'Neal met the chief of security in the companionway in front of the Ruiz cabin. They went inside and in practically no time at all Lieutenant O'Neal found the two pistols in a plastic laundry bag containing dirty clothes stowed inside a suitcase on the floor of the closet.

"Bingo," she exclaimed. "Call Welland and tell him I found two 9 millimeter hand guns with silencers and ammo."

Mercer contacted Ivan immediately and reported the news.

"Good work, Commander. Can you locate their passports? They boarded the ship with Chilean documents according to the manifest, but I'll bet they're forged."

"We'll have a look, sir."

"Mercer, hold on a minute. I want to discuss this situation with Captain Constantine. It's his ship, we're in international waters, and the *Controller of the Oceans* is not a U.S. flag vessel. I want everybody on the same page on this one, so we can make any charges against these two passengers stick."

"Very good, sir. I'll wait for further instructions, but I'll impound the weapons," Mercer replied.

Ivan turned to face Niko. "Captain, the Commander has discovered hidden weapons in cabin 414D. We have several decisions to make about how to handle the situation. I'm not versed in the laws of the sea with regard to an incident such as this, but it seems to me that we have to arrest this couple."

"Smuggling unauthorized weapons aboard is a crime. We must take them into custody at once," Captain Constantine agreed. "I can hold them pending verification of their papers, and any background investigation that you may wish to conduct. Cabin 414D is an inside cabin. That means there are no windows, portholes, or other means of escape. We can hold them right in their cabin if we secure the door and keep a guard outside. I don't want to alarm the other passengers if we can arrange not to.'

"How long do we have before making our decision?"

"We have until noon tomorrow to decide what to do with them. We'll be in Gibraltar at dawn, and we can have them held there for questioning if we want to get them off the ship. My security staff can handle this matter, and it will leave your men free to continue with their work. We need not indicate that this is a case of suspected terrorism until we are sure who these people are and what they are up to."

"Very well, Captain. Your men can make the arrest and confine them to their cabin. If these people are terrorists, as I suspect, there may be more of them on board, and it doesn't preclude there being an attack from the sea, either. Do any of your security men speak Arabic?"

"Yes, one of them does. He is an assistant to the security chief. A Lebanese, I believe."

"Then I'd like to request that Lieutenant O'Neal be present at any and all the interrogations of these suspects. She speaks Arabic, but she won't say anything. She'll just be present to monitor the conversations in Arabic so that nothing transpires that we don't know about. Can you lend Lieutenant O'Neal one of your security officer uniforms?"

"You are a very clever man, Dr. Welland. And you are thorough, too. I like that very much. Yes, we can supply the Lieutenant with a uniform, and we will station her close enough so she can hear the questioning of these suspects. Now I must call my security chief and put all this into action."

"One more thing, Captain, before you go. I'd just like to be sure that these two are not Chechens. I was in Chechnya once for a time, and I'm also fluent in Russian. I'd like to see if this couple understands these languages from the country of their claimed origins. I'll go down to the dining room and stand behind them, but well within earshot, and speak with one of your dining room captains. All he needs to do is nod as though he understands what I'm saying. Can you also arrange for this little performance as well?"

"What will you say to make them give themselves away?"

"I'll think of something, don't worry," Ivan said.

Ivan called Mercer again. "The ship's security personnel will handle this from here on. Did you locate their passports?"

"We did."

"Bring them to the bridge and we'll check with Chile to see if they're authentic. Tell O'Neal she needs to put on a ship's security uniform and be present during the questioning of these faux Chileans. The chief there will be getting orders from the Captain about now, and he'll get her a uniform. She mustn't say anything. All she has to do is listen while an Arabic-speaking security guard questions the suspects. I don't want any communications between Arabs, even supposedly friendly ones, which we aren't tuned in to. Got that?"

"Got it. See you on the bridge in a few minutes, sir."

While he was walking towards the bridge, Mercer suddenly had an idea, and called his second in command. He ordered Pugni to organize the team members who were in the crew's quarters to provide a little unannounced backup for the ship's security officers outside cabin 414D.

Captain Constantine returned. "Our security officers will wait for these suspects in their cabin and sequester them there. I have spoken to the dining room captain, and he will listen to you speaking Russian and nod as though he understands you. My security chief will find a uniform for your lieutenant. Dinner will be over soon and the suspects may go directly to their room, or they may not. In any case, we will wait for them in the cabin in order to make as little fuss as possible among the passengers when we arrest them.

"Very well, Captain," Ivan said. "I'm going to the dining room to run my scam. I'll return to the bridge immediately to meet with you and Commander Mercer so we can decide what to do next."

Ivan strode off the bridge and quickly walked to the stairs, descending them two by two in his effort to save time. He met the servers' captain at the entrance to the dining salon, and they nonchalantly walked to a position that was immediately behind Rashid and his companion. Ivan chattered away in Russian, a language that the dining room captain didn't understood, but he pretended to agree with every word Ivan was saying. The couple in front of them was eating dessert and drinking coffee. Neither the man nor the woman showed the slightest interest or sign of comprehension.

After a minute or two, Ivan took his leave of the dining room captain.

"Sank you wery much, Kaptink," he said over his shoulder to his mute partner in conversation.

Ivan went to the bridge to rendezvous with Mercer and the Captain Constantine.

"Those two don't speak a word of Russian or Chechen, I promise you that," Ivan told them.

"How did you find out?" Niko asked.

"I stood right behind them so they couldn't help hearing me, and I announced that two guns had been found in cabin

414D, and the couple was going to be arrested at once. I said all this in Russian."

"Maybe they only spoke Chechen," Niko observed.

"I tested them on that, too," said Ivan. "I said in Chechen that we should all be very careful that this bomb doesn't go off. They didn't even flinch or turn around, so I know they didn't understand a word I said in either language."

CHAPTER FIFTEEN

Mercer and the Captain looked at each other and smiled when Ivan told them how he had called the Chilean couple's bluff.

"So they're about as Chilean as I am," said Captain Niko.

"Let's see those passports please, Commander," Ivan said.

Mercer handed them over, and Ivan looked at them intently for a minute.

"I'll bet you a hundred bucks these are phony," he smiled.

"How can you tell so quickly? They looked official to me," said Mercer.

"Well, look at the passport numbers."

Mercer looked at them, and Captain Constantine as well, but both men remained puzzled.

"If this couple is married," Ivan said, "and if they are naturalized citizens of Chile as they claim, then wouldn't they have applied for passports at the same time? And if so, wouldn't the passport numbers be consecutive? This may not be conclusive evidence, but taken with the lies, the guns, and the inability to comprehend their own native tongues, I think we have good reason to doubt everything about these two."

"I guess you're right," replied Mercer.

"Traveling with false documents is also reason to hold them. I'll ask my assistant, Brooklyn, to check with the Chilean government to verify the passports. Meanwhile, we have to assume this ship is in danger of being attacked. I can't believe that only these two were meant to take over a ship of this size. There must be others. Are the others on board now? Are others planning to come aboard at the next port, or from a vessel at sea? If two people got aboard with guns, couldn't others have done so, too? Gentlemen, I need a few minutes to consult with my team. Please let me know as soon as the culprits have been sequestered. In the meantime, put your thinking caps on and let me know how you believe we should proceed."

Ivan headed over to the Sat/Nav to see how David Feingold was making out.

"Any indications of tampering yet?" Ivan inquired.

"These things are preprogrammed," David said, "and it's impossible to get into them without a password. We have a redundant Sat/Nav and we've been running it in conjunction with the main one, but there don't seem to be any divergences. Maybe there's some sort of default routine that might have been inserted to override the standard software on this device, but I've got to have the password in order to do it."

"Okay, here's what you do," Ivan said. "Call Mr. Gregoire, he's the CEO of the company that builds these Sat/Navs. Brooklyn can get you his number. Tell him you work for me. Say you have to examine the code. I think he'll be cooperative. Let me know if you encounter any problems. I have to have an answer before we leave Gibraltar tomorrow afternoon."

Damian and Brooklyn had just finished their dessert when they felt the vibrations of their pagers. "Please come to the bridge, IVW," the text message read. They left the dining room and went up to the bridge deck, where they found Ivan waiting.

"Brooklyn," Ivan said, "Please take these passports and check them with Chilean Passport Control to see if they're legit. You can use the fax. Also, please give David a hand. He needs to get the password for the Sat/Nav from that executive I spoke to recently. His name was Gregoire. He'll explain."

"Damian," he continued, "you come with me. I'd like to see what you've been able to come up with from your analysis of the passenger and crew manifests. A crew member noticed something unusual about a couple of passengers, and the Captain authorized a search of their cabin, which turned up guns. We're in the process of arresting them now, but we need to know if they have accomplices on board."

Damian began by showing Ivan the steps he had taken, and the logic he had used, to reduce the 3,000 passengers to just 47 suspects whose backgrounds required further investigation. The crew, some 800 in number, had been processed too, leaving 21 with insufficient background information. Damian had run the manifests against the list of known or suspected terrorists that he maintained in his database, and had gotten no hits. That was not surprising to him, as no self-respecting militant ever used the same name twice, but he had to check just to be sure.

He was about to refine the process of elimination further by conducting what he referred to as his "survivor's politically incorrect examination." This included citizenship, religion, birthplace, ethnicity, native language, race, age, gender, and the other personal bits of information that could help him uncover murderers. These killers were counting on their victims not to dare ask any questions that could be deemed embarrassing. Damian, who was known as Doctor Disaster by his colleagues because he kept all the mortality statistics caused by terrorist atrocities, was not ashamed to ask any question that might help him uncover a plotter and save innocent lives.

Ivan took the list of 21 crewmembers that Damian had questions about and went over them himself. Meanwhile Damian continued his work with the passenger list. Aside from some peculiar-sounding names of Indonesians, Africans, and Turks, Ivan had insufficient information about these people. He would need to see their personnel files.

He returned to Captain Constantine's side and asked him if he could access to the crew's personnel records. The personnel records included a skills inventory that allowed the files to be searched for specific talents or knowledge. Ivan keyed in Arabic under native language spoken, and was immediately provided with a list of seven names. Four were among the 21 that Damian had wanted to explore further. What about the other three? Ivan would check with Damian to see why they weren't among the 21 suspects. Each of the four Arabic speakers was from a different country – Lebanon, Syria, Algeria, and Morocco.

Was nationality a valid criterion for suspicion? Not a sufficient one, Ivan decided. But if the attack on the ship was to occur near the countries of the terrorists' origins, it would be an escape advantage to be from the nearest country. Perhaps mutinous crew members were planning to leave the ship after they did whatever they were planning to do. In which case, the two from Morocco and Algeria would be likely candidates for closer examination. Ivan didn't want to exclude any citizens from Islamic nations, since he now knew, after discovering a council of caliphs at a communications center in Mecca, that a centrally-controlled militant international Muslim brotherhood was at the root of all the terror attacks. Nationality was not sufficiently incriminating in and of itself to build the profile of a terrorist, but together with other factors, it might point the investigator in the right direction.

How about gender? Ivan knew that two pistols were discovered in cabin 414D, which suggested that the couple was both involved and armed. In this case, therefore, women were active participants in the plan. That made it a bit unusual, as normally terror is a man's business and, except for the odd suicide bomber, women were not expected to be warriors. The macho character of an Islamist terrorist fortunately reduces the number of possible soldiers of Allah by half. Was this true enough in general to eliminate as suspects the two women from among the male Arabic-speaking crew members? Ivan believed that in a case like this, no chances could be taken.

Thinking of another criterion to use to narrow the search, Ivan began to consider occupation. Now here was something interesting, he thought: one Moroccan woman and the Lebanese man were security officers. The other two were servers, a Syrian man in the dining room, and an Algerian woman was a waitress in the lounge. He knew he had to investigate the security staff. He would start with the two Arabic speakers who worked in the security department of the ship. Did they have access to firearms? How, and under what circumstances, would they be carrying guns? He flashed up the files of the two security employees on the monitor screen. He memorized their names and other information, then summoned the Captain.

"Can you tell me what firearms are kept on the ship?"

"We have an arms cabinet. I'll show it to you."

Ivan followed the Captain to a cabinet that was pretty well hidden from view. He took a key ring out of his pocket and opened the cabinet. Inside were three rifles, a shotgun, four pistols, and ammunition.

"I have the only key," Niko said, "and my first, second and third officers have been trained to use these weapons."

"What about the security staff?" Ivan asked.

"The chief and his two assistants are licensed to use hand guns, but I must personally issue the guns from this cabinet and give my permission for them to be used. You met the security department in its entirety earlier today. You see, Dr. Welland, on board his ship the captain is the chief executive."

"A sort of Controller of the Oceans, you mean."

Niko understood his word play. He realized that Welland understood that without wise leadership and assistance from others, the great cruise ship could be a great catastrophe, and the absolute ruler an absolute fool.

"Have you heard from the arresting officers yet? Are the occupiers of cabin 414D under our control?"

"Not yet. My people are still inside the cabin awaiting their return from dinner," the Captain replied.

"Have you thought about what you'd like to do with these people once they're in custody?"

"No, I haven't come that far," Niko admitted.

"May I suggest that we drop them off in Gibraltar? The British shore police can hold them until they're brought to trial. In the meantime we won't have to use our limited resources to guard them. I suspect we're going to need all the security staff we've got for more important tasks."

Rashid and Fatima decided to walk around the deck after dinner as they had done after their first night at sea. They were in no hurry to return to the cramped, windowless cabin. They casually discussed the dinner they had just eaten and the older American people who shared their table. Rashid asked Fatima if she had understood what the tall guy standing behind him was saying to the headwaiter. She hadn't understood a word, but she thought they were speaking Russian. Rashid agreed, and admitted that he hadn't understood it, either. It was comfortable for the two of them to be able to speak Arabic together. They were developing a certain rapport with each other that was born of familiarity. They felt that they had been drawn together by the will of Allah.

After a while the Arab couple decided to retire to their quarters, as there was nothing for them to do on this floating pleasure palace of the depraved. Their religion forbade them to gamble, and drinking alcohol was also forbidden to practitioners of Islam. Watching the obscene Hollywood films was hateful to them. The half-dressed dancers in the live performances were lewd, and in the opinion of Rashid should have been stoned for what they were doing. Board games did not interest them. Swimming in a pool full of nearly naked Western harlots and their overstuffed men was a disgusting prospect for them as well. In reality they hated life as it was being presented to them on this ship. They could not understand why anyone would enjoy it, but they had to admit that many of the passengers did seem pleased. Let them eat, drink, and be merry, for tomorrow they die.

Rashid put his plastic identification card into the door, and received the blinking green light from the lock to indicate that the door could be opened. He pushed it open and stepped in first, which according to Arab culture is correct etiquette, for women are to follow behind the men.

As soon as the cabin door closed, two security officers stepped out of the water closet and said in Arabic, "You are under arrest. Resistance is useless. We have armed officers outside the door."

At the sight of them Fatima fell to her knees, ducked behind Rashid, and dug into the suitcase to find the guns. The security officers let her look, knowing that they had already removed the weapons from the cabin. Hearing a scuffling sound from inside, Lieutenant O'Neal, along with one of the

Seals dressed in ship's security force uniforms, quickly entered the room. Faced with the fact that they would be overpowered, if not shot, Rashid and Fatima surrendered without a fight. The first two officers, a man and a woman, removed handcuffs from their belts and had the prisoners put their hands behind their backs to receive the cuffs. The ship's police searched the two offenders and removed the ID cards that also served as room keys. Rashid and Fatima were asked to sit on the beds.

The officer in charge spoke. "You have been arrested for bringing guns aboard this ship. You will be kept isolated in this cabin. The door will be locked and armed guards will be posted outside. There is no use trying to escape. Someone will be along later to ask you a few questions."

Not realizing that Lieutenant O'Neal understood Arabic, the officer said, "Allah akbar, he knows all his people." Then he and his female assistant left the room, leaving the Lieutenant and the Seal to follow them out.

O'Neal wondered exactly what the ship's security man meant by that last sentence. It could be nothing, but it could mean that Allah would send someone to release them. She would report it to Mercer, and they should all be on their guard for more terrorists or criminals to appear on board. She called Commander Mercer to report in.

"Sir, O'Neal here. The passengers in 414D have been secured in the cabin. They are definitely Arabs. I don't think they will tell us anything, but I will stand by to listen in if someone decides to interrogate them. Something the third officer in charge of the security unit on board said makes me think that there may be others on board. Just as he was leaving he looked at them, handcuffed as they were and said, 'Allah akbar, he knows all his people.' That doesn't seem appropriate to me. Maybe we should look into this guy's background."

"Dr. Welland is on that now."

"Good. I'll stay put here, then, until the interrogator arrives. Unless you have something better for me to do."

"Roger that. What the hell did we ever do before we had these little mission communications devices?"

"I don't know, sir, but I agree they're great until the perps learn to scramble them. O'Neal out."

Under cover of darkness Ali and his co-conspirators had begun to locate the one point on the face of the planet Earth that would fatally intersect their line of nautical IEDs with the course of the largest cruise ship in the world. Al Jaza'ir was hunched over the Sat/Nav readout. On the bow, his son was kneeling over the anchor, prepared to shove it overboard at his father's command. Fortunately the sea was calm, which was a significant aid in accurately placing their trap.

They began by letting go of the first anchor and its chain at the northernmost point. As soon as the anchor found the bottom, the young man in the bow signaled his father to back off. He snubbed the Dacron rode around the cleat on the deck until he was sure the anchor was holding, and then he released it and let the coiled line disappear under the water until he came to the first glass buoy. He refastened the anchor rode to the deck cleat and led the spool of anchor rope outboard back to the stern where he fastened the rope to the stern cleat. Then he went back to the bow and let go the anchor line from its cleat. Slowly the boat turned end for end, and was ready to proceed away from its anchored point. Now the father could give the order to let the long line of net with its bags of plastic play out over the stern into the water.

As the long net passed slowly overboard into the dark water, Amin inserted the plastic explosives into their bags. Ali affixed the detonators. Muhammad, the captain, steered the due south course, and Al Jaza'ir and his son slowly let the net with its floats play out off the stern. It was slow work handling the explosives in a sloughing sea in the darkness, and the long net was requiring some attention to prevent snarls. Eventually they reached the end of the line and had to set the anchor on the far end. When this was done they checked to see how far under the surface the net had been suspended. If it was too deep it would pass under the hull of the Controller of the Oceans and she would never know the fate she had escaped. If it was too high it might be seen from the surface, or it might be set off by another vessel by mistake.

The fishing boat stood by, keeping clear of the net while the young divers donned their wetsuits. They strapped their depth gauges to their wrists, put the breathing tanks over their shoulders, adjusted their masks and regulators, and hung their flipper-clad feet over the stern. They took the waterproof flashlights from the hands of their comrades, and pushed off into the sea. It would be some time before they returned, as they had to swim the entire length of the net, checking the depth of the net that was hanging twenty feet below the surface of the sea.

The fishing boat, now acting as a mother ship to supply the needs of the divers, had to make short trips in answer to pre-arranged light signals from the swimmers in the water. The divers let some air out of each of the main bladders in order to sink the net a bit, as it was riding too high. Al Jaza'ir had carefully computed the rise and fall of the tide so that the net would always be within reasonable tolerance levels to assure that the nose of the liner would pick up the line as it passed. He had favored the high side in his calculations, for if the net lay too low the ship would pass over it.

Even with their wetsuits on, the divers got cold after long periods in the water. Fortunately they never had to go deeper than twenty feet or so. When Ali and his son pulled the divers out of the water they were chilled through and through, but they had completed the work. With the first light of dawn the fishing boat motored back to the safety of anonymity among the fleet of Algerian fishing boats. There they would wait until the next evening to view the fireworks they hoped would light the sky.

The exhausted Arabs on board the fishing boat were happy that they had been able to lay their trap without being detected. They enjoyed being in the relative safety of the other fishing boats. The sound of Arabic words wafting over the water from the nearest boats was reassuring. They stretched out on the thin hard mattresses of the bunks and slept deeply. It was pleasantly cool now in the early morning sunshine. Inside the cabin the temperature was bearable. By midday it would be hot below, and blazing up on the deck, and then sleeping would become difficult. Al Jaza'ir maintained the watch while the others rested. He kept the boat from becoming tangled up in the drift nets of the other boats. As he thought about the mission, he wondered just how good the American electronic detection equipment was. Their boat was made of wood, and he had taken care to have as little metal on board as possible to avoid showing up on the radar screens of the infidel ships. He had maintained radio silence during the time that they were setting the trap. They had worked by the light of the moon. The overhead satellite photos would only show one fishing boat at a distance from the fleet, and he hoped that was not enough of an anomaly to arouse suspicion. The little battery-operated Sat/Nav didn't draw enough power to be detectable from anywhere except at the closest distance, and no boats had approached during the night. As far as aircraft were concerned, he had seen none that aroused his suspicions. A few planes had gone overhead at high altitudes, but these seemed to be commercial flights, as far as he could tell. The canny old fisherman believed he had reason to be cautiously optimistic about their chances of having a successful mission.

CHAPTER SIXTEEN

A board the *Controller of the Oceans* things were outwardly calm as she proceeded south off the coast of Portugal. The passengers were happily unaware of the arrest of two of their number for possessing illegal weapons. Had they been cognizant of the worried state of mind of their Captain, they might not have been partying so enthusiastically.

Niko now had sufficient reason to believe that some sort of attack against his ship was being planned. Up to that point he had had no real evidence; only the suspicions of an American government official who might have been paranoid on the subject of Islamist terrorists. Constantine had no idea what to expect next, and that was not the frame of mind that he wanted to be in for the maiden voyage of his wonderful new command.

Welland had been terrific at sharing plans and advising him of things he needed to know, and he had not threatened to take any actions without the Captain's consent. On balance, he was glad to have the Security Advisor to the President of the United States on board his ship. It was a comfort to have trained Seals on board too, and to have access to the military might of the American forces. Normalcy was what was missing in Niko's life at that moment. The backgrounds of his own security staff were now being brought into question. Had his own little police force been compromised? Were two of his staff members actually traitors working with other operatives among the passengers to capture or sink his ship?

Brooklyn received word from the Chilean government that the passports taken from Rashid and Fatima were forgeries. No one was surprised to hear that. It was another charge that could be brought against the couple, however, for it is a crime to knowingly traveling with false documents.

At her little desk in the communications room, Brooklyn had more outgoing and incoming messages than all the rest of the employees of the ship combined. She had managed to track down Mr. Gregoire on the golf course and had transferred the call to David, who had persuaded the executive to give him the password he needed in order to get into the guts of the computer program that controlled the Sat/Nav. She had put the CIA into high gear, checking out the backgrounds of the two Arabic-speaking security officers. She had also been in touch with the manufacturer of the pistols that they had confiscated from cabin 414D, and requested that the serial numbers be checked against their sales records to see if they could be tracked. The Chief of British Military Operations on Gibraltar had been contacted regarding whether he would be able to take charge of the two passengers that were being held in their cabin. Brooklyn was awaiting a call back from him, as he needed permission from his superiors in Whitehall to take possession of prisoners from a foreign-registered vessel.

In addition to all this, she had called the Secretary of the Navy and informed him of the situation on board the ship. She had obtained his permission to contact the Chief of Naval Operations in the Mediterranean and receive progress reports on the results of air reconnaissance flights being conducted in the western part of that Sea. The Spanish Navy was cooperating, but they had only been asked to report anything unusual in the Alboran Sea, and so far they had no sightings or radar contacts.

Ivan was at Captain Constantine's elbow most of the time, either receiving or giving information. They knew they needed each other if they were going to get through the situation. It was clear that they were both leaders and uncomfortable with sharing command functions, but in this case they would have to divide the responsibilities or be accountable for the potential consequences. Fortunately, although both of them were near the top of the alpha bull list of male authority figures, both of them had two character traits that made working together possible. The first was the ability to see a situation clearly and to place things in perspective. The situation that they were in called for them to be selfless, and both men were capable of doing it for the right reason. The second was that they both were inherently good men. The safety of people in their care was of the utmost importance to them both. Although each of them demanded obedience from their subordinates, both had earned it by being fair-minded, not by bullying people. In the case of the story of the *Controller of the Oceans*, neither of them wanted to be the author of a tragedy. Their mutual desire to save the ship and all on board was primary in both their foci, and no amount of ego gratification would stand in the way.

There was a natural division of responsibilities between the two leaders. They each had staffs. They each had specific duties, and there was no real need for a single supreme authority over all areas of responsibility, since Ivan knew little about managing a large ship and Niko knew nothing about deterring worldwide terrorism. Cooperation was the obvious answer, and the men both accepted that fact whole-heartedly.

"I think there is plenty for both of us to do," Ivan said to Niko. "Your chief concern must be what happens on board your ship, and I must think also of what's going on outside the ship. If I had to guess, I'd say that we're facing a coordinated attack from within and without. What we've accomplished so far is to interfere with a portion of the onboard attack. We don't yet know how many assaulters may be on board in addition to the two we've caught. We don't know what they're planning, but I expect the worst from these people, and I hope you agree."

"My desire is to protect my passengers and my crew first," Niko replied. "The second thing that concerns me is the incredible investment that my employers have made in this ship. I see little reason for unbridled optimism. The two we have captured reveal that something is going on. If we find that some of my crew is involved in a plot against this ship that has provided them with secure jobs and a future, I will be shocked at their disloyalty. But I will not be lulled into a false sense of security, even if the traitors come from my own security force."

"Good, Captain. We must try our best to think like these people, and that means putting nothing past them. I assume we're dealing with the most extreme circumstances. Sinking, or hijacking, a ship full of innocent people is about as bad as evil gets. I also assume that we're dealing with the most extremist elements of the Islamic Brotherhood here. These jihadists believe it's an order from Allah that they kill as many infidels as possible. They believe we have no value whatsoever, so they don't hesitate to kill us if they can. We must put our heads together and think of the worst things that could be done to a vessel like this one, and then we must get the Commander to help us work out plans to defend against those kinds of people, and those kinds of treacherous attacks."

"I agree fully."

Ivan called Commander Mercer over, and the three men put their heads together to plan for the defense of the great ship.

In cabin 414D, Rashid and Fatima were both feeling deflated. Somehow the infidels had managed to find out about them, and in so doing had taken away their weapons. They could have stood the ignominy of failure if they had been able to shoot it out with these infidel devils and gone out in a blaze of glory, but this way, held prisoner and kept in handcuffs, they could not earn Allah's approval. They sat facing each other with their hands behind their backs, looking and feeling miserable. Their only hope was in the statement made by the security officer as he was leaving the cabin.

"Allah akbar, he knows all his people," said Rashid.

"What do you think he meant by that?" Fatima asked.

"I think he meant we will be rescued, if it is Allah's will."

"Do you think the mission can succeed without our help?"

"I do. There are more of us on board than you know."

After a time the cabin door opened and Commander Mercer came in. He had been designated to conduct the interrogation of the couple, even though it was generally recognized that he would get no information from them. Originally they had planned to have the Arabic-speaking security officer ask the questions, but Niko and Ivan no longer trusted him to do it.

Mercer interrogated Rashid and Fatima for almost three hours, but after receiving nothing but silence, lies, or protests about violations to their civil rights in answer to his questions, he finally went to the cabin door and rapped sharply. It was opened immediately by the Navy Seal posted outside.

"Since you refuse to cooperate," Mercer said to them on his way out, "you will be taken off the ship in Gibraltar and held there until you can be moved to Guantanamo Bay, where you'll remain until you're brought to trial."

Rashid just glared at him and said nothing.

"I'm giving you one last chance," Mercer said evenly. "If you confess now, you'll only be charged with illegal possession of firearms and you'll get an abbreviated sentence."

Mercer said nothing about the false passports, so even if they took it easy on them for the gun charge, they could still sock it to them for forgery.

Rashid continued to glare at him sullenly.

"All right, have it your way," Mercer said, in a controlled voice. "You'll be charged with attempted terrorism, then. You realize that if you're found guilty you could get a life sentence."

Receiving no answer from the prisoners, he returned to the bridge to report the expected news of his failure to Captain Niko and Dr. Welland. Mercer got a call from a Colonel in Gibraltar, saying that they would send their paddy wagon down to the dock to pick up the detainees at 0700. The Brits on the Rock had gotten permission from HQ to keep the prisoners in their brig until a more permanent disposition could be made. It was agreed that the handguns and the forged passports would remain as evidence in the hands of the security forces on board the *Controller of the Oceans,* to be turned over to the prosecutors of whichever court ended up with jurisdiction over the case.

"Well, Commander, we haven't had much sleep since we left Andrews Air Force Base," Ivan said. "I suggest we all turn in and report back here at 0600. We'll be docking in Gibraltar at that time, and we can go on with our investigation then."

At 4:00 AM Mercedes heard a knock at the door of her tiny cabin on the lower deck in the crew's quarters. It was far too early for her shift to begin. The knocking was not loud, but it was persistent, as though the knocker didn't want to arouse anyone but Mercedes. Finally the pajama-clad waitress got out of her bunk and went to the door. She opened it a crack to see who it was. There stood the third officer of the security staff. "What is it?" Mercedes asked.

"Let me come in and I'll tell you. It's important, and I don't want to wake the crew by talking out here in the corridor." She stood aside to let him enter.

"Well, what is it?" she asked him, closing the cabin door.

"Are you Mercedes León, the wife of Diego León?"

"Yes."

"You have agreed to do an errand for someone on board this ship. I am that someone, and tonight, right after you serve dinner, I will find you in the dining room and tell you what it is I want you to do. I am instructed by Diego to report to you that your family is fine for the time being."

The swarthy little man was reading Mercedes' face. He could tell that she was very concerned about her family back in Chile. This man Diego, her husband, must have a strong hold over her, he thought. He decided to push her a little bit to see just how much she would do to protect her family.

"Take off your pajamas," he said.

"No! I promised to do an errand, and no more."

"Yes, Mercedes León, but I work in security, and part of my job is to be alert and notice everything that happens on board this ship. And I have noticed you entering the Captain's cabin and staying for long periods of time." He licked his lips in a disgusting, lewd way. "If you don't do what I say I will tell the company of your trysts with the Captain, and you will both be fired. And, of course, Diego will not be happy if he doesn't receive the other half of his payment, and who knows what he will do to your family when he is angry."

He spoke as though he knew Diego well, but in fact he had never met him. Ten years ago he had played the refugee card and left strife-torn Lebanon to join some distant members of his family in Canada. In due time he had achieved a modicum of respectability, and had been hired by the shipping company that owned many cruise liners. He was familiar with weapons, and claimed to have been a police officer in Beirut. The naïve Canadians had bought his unverifiable explanation, and had promoted his candidacy for the job on the cruise ships. He kept his nose clean, and advanced in the security department until his present position as third in charge. At last, after all the waiting, the real reason he was on board this ship would become evident. The infidels never failed to underestimate the ability of Allah's warriors to plan long in advance. As the memory of 9/11 faded in Western minds, Islam's patience would soon give Allah another enormous victory. He could feel the surge of power that would be his for his part in the attack on the present prime icon of Western depravity. Why should he wait to exercise his power? In less than twenty-four hours this little infidel whore would most likely be dead, anyway.

"Weren't you listening? Take off your pajamas. *Now!*"

Mercedes began unbuttoning her top, all the while thinking about the safety of her young son, Juan, and the well-being of her long-suffering parents. She decided to turn off her feelings and force herself to go numb.

The man smiled lasciviously when he saw her breasts. He was full of himself for realizing her vulnerability, and now he was going to exploit his advantage to the limit. Mercedes had made the mistake of showing weakness to a weakling, and no one knows better how to capitalize on the defenseless than a coward. The security guard pointed impatiently at her pajama bottoms, indicating that he wanted them down at once.

At last it was his turn to dine at the Captain's table.

Mercedes took one look at his disgusting, thick, parrot-like tongue moving over his wet, salivating lips, and suddenly she was galvanized into action. Her darting eyes settled on the metal lamp sitting on her bedside table, and she snatched it up at the same time as she uttered a piercing, desperate shriek, the like of which the security guard had never heard in his life. He stood frozen by the sound of her loud, primordial scream, and a split second later he saw sparks and flashes as the lamp came crashing down on his repulsive bald pate. The security guard reeled for a moment, struggling to regain his balance, giving Mercedes just enough time to open her cabin door, stick her foot into his soft, protruding paunch, and shove him out into the corridor. As his body smashed up against the wall, he heard the door slam and the lock click into place.

One by one the doors opened up and down the corridor as sleepy heads emerged from inside the cabins.

"Go back to bed," the security officer yelled. "I've taken care of it. Go on, close your doors. It's all over."

He walked quickly away, doing his best to maintain the appearance of a dignified security guard who had just conducted himself according to the requirements of his job, and in the best interest of everyone on board the great ocean liner. But the little whore of a waitress would pay for this. He would see to it that she never messed with him again.

Ivan slept fitfully. His mind was humming with life and death issues. He felt that if any action was necessary it was because things had not been thought out well enough. After tossing and turning most of the night, he finally climbed out of his bunk at the first hint of dawn. He washed, shaved, dressed, and worried. By the time his whiskers had surrendered for another day, he had worked out a mental "to do" list. He decided to find out if David Feingold was awake and working. He knew David hated traveling, so perhaps he couldn't sleep either.

Sure enough, when Ivan arrived at the bridge, there was David working on the Sat/Nav.

"How's it going?" Ivan inquired.

"Actually it's going quite well. I can say with certainty that the software has been tampered with, but I can't tell yet exactly how much. In other words, I can't tell you if the navigation system is off by a little or a lot, or if it's inaccurate under all conditions, or just some, but I'm working on it."

"Keep going, Dave. I've got to know where they intend us to be, so we can avoid being there."

"I'm on it, boss," David said.

Ivan checked with Damian to see how he was making out with identifying the bad guys from among the other passengers. "The suspects on my list are occupying nine cabins," said Damian. Do you think we could have those cabins searched?" "I'm sure we can. I'll run it past the Captain." "If Cabin 414D is any indication, we'll probably come up with some more weapons, if nothing else."

"I have a hard time believing that those guns were walked aboard through the metal detector. They must have been put here during the construction of the ship."

"I'll bet you're right," Damian replied. "They may have been on board for a year or more just waiting for the right guy to come along. In fact, there may be a hidden arsenal on this ship, for all we know. Since we found weapons caches all over Iraq, even in mosques, there's no reason to think this ship is any exception."

"If we can find the gunslingers in time, the guns won't matter. Keep working on that, and let me know at once what the cabin searches turn up."

Ivan could see that Captain Constantine was very busy with docking maneuvers, so he decided to see what Brooklyn was up to. She was on the phone when he arrived. Ivan took a seat near the desk where she was working. As she was listening to her caller, she passed Ivan a note that she had written just before he came along. It said that the pistols taken from cabin 414D were part of a shipment sent to Syrian police headquarters in Damascus ten years earlier.

"The manufacturer was very defensive in answering my questions," Brooklyn continued, after she had hung up. "The transaction was perfectly legal, he said. I hadn't even hinted that I suspected his company of illegally selling weapons. I was just trying to ascertain the source of the handguns, and the date of the sale. I explained this to the gun maker's rep, but he was still fairly nervous, I thought."

The well-respected company had been making guns for over a hundred years. The thrust of their business had moved away from hunting rifles, and was now mainly law enforcement and military in nature. They were not intentionally breaking the law. Dealing with gunrunners, smugglers and terrorists was definitely not the way they chose to do business, but it was hard to tell the good guys from the bad. After all, they were just making a product, not operating Interpol.

Ivan had heard many protestations of innocence from this company, as well as a good many others in the same business. That was just the party line from an industry that dealt in death. It was a lot worse than the tobacco companies, who claimed the choice was up to the customers and they were only supplying a demand for the product. In the case of the armament companies, their customers wanted the guns to kill others, not themselves. Ivan was sorry to have had to pull his people off the arms limitation project that he had just begun, but the threat to the *Controller of the Oceans* was an emergency that had forced him to put everything else on hold.

When the enormous ship was safely nestled against the pier, Niko went to the bridge while his officers made her fast. There was always a peaceful moment in the life of a captain just after his ship was at rest. Ivan took that opportunity to get permission to search the nine cabins that had aroused Damian's suspicions. Niko agreed that the searches should be conducted while the occupants were on shore. With the famous stone outcropping that was synonymous with the rock of Gibraltar, this port was one of the most popular destinations for the cruising public.

The town's military airport was between the ship and the shopping mecca that served the passengers, so they could be viewed from the decks of the *Controller of the Oceans* as they walked across the airport runway to be met by the taxi drivers offering guided tours of the "Rock." Few would remain on the ship when offered a chance to walk the streets of Gibraltar or visit the interesting fort, so the searches could easily be done by three teams of security personnel accompanied by one Navy Seal each. The stewards would knock on the door, and if no one answered they would enter to make up the room while the search was conducted.

Soon after breakfast the passengers would leave the ship. Having the town so handy to the dock was a temptation too great for real tourists to resist, but Ivan wondered how terrorists would behave in this situation. He finally decided that they would try to appear as much as possible like the rest of the tourists, and go along with the crowd. If they did that, it would indicate that the attack was not scheduled to take place during the ship's stay in Gibraltar. Since there had been no fuss during the arrest of those in cabin 414D, Ivan believed that if there were others in the gang, they would not yet realize that their cohorts had been captured unless the security guards whom he suspected had found a way to alert their henchmen.

Ivan was no fan of the concept of luck. He believed in meticulous planning, not fate or chance. But the best-laid plans are open to the vagaries of luck, good or bad. Those smiled upon are considered heroes or geniuses. Those frowned upon become failures, or in this case, dead.

Ivan's chief suspect, the third officer in security, had been on his way to tell his co-conspirators of the capture of Rashid and Fatima, and to devise a plan to rescue them. He had no reason to hurry because as far as he knew everything, except for the foul-up in 414D, was proceeding according to plan. So why wake his friends so early? They would need their rest for the long night's work ahead. And so it was that he had decided to stop and visit Mercedes in her cabin. That was very bad luck for Mercedes, and as it turned out, for him as well, but for Ivan and the *Controller of the Oceans* it was quite the opposite. How many times in the lifetime of one person does a seemingly insignificant action turn out to be critical in the life of so many? And how often are the many unaware of the selfless acts of others who have spared their lives, or changed them radically?

The passengers had flooded off the cruise ship soon after it docked. The schedule only allowed them a maximum of seven hours to visit Gibraltar, and most wanted to take advantage of the opportunity to see it while they had the chance. Damian had flagged the nine cabins that he wanted to have searched, so when the occupants used the plastic ID card it registered on the manifest to indicate that the passenger was off the ship.

In an hour the nine cabins had been carefully searched. Seven were found to have nothing suspicious in them. Two, however, revealed hand guns hidden in the luggage. The two couples in possession of illegal weapons would be arrested, as had been the couple in cabin 414D. As soon as Ivan and Captain Constantine were advised of the discovery of additional weapons on board, they requested that the paddy wagon from the brig in Gibraltar stand by to receive four more prisoners.

The Chief of Security had exempted his third officer and his female accomplice from the cadre of officers sent to arrest the passengers who had hidden guns in their cabins. The Chief found it hard to believe that any of his people could be involved in a plot against the ship, but he followed the Captain's orders.

The first weapon discovery had reassured Niko that Ivan's judgment was sound, and he resolved to cooperate with him completely. Ivan was planning to capture the four suspected terrorists as soon as they were back on board. He wanted them off the ship before it sailed from Gibraltar. He had visions of a gun battle on board that could result in casualties, and possibly even a loss of control of the ship. *The Controller of the Oceans* was not going to be controlled by terrorists – not on his watch.

The four conspirators had occupied themselves in Gibraltar by surveying the fortress. They believed that Allah would some day send them back to the "Rock" to recapture it and return it to Islamic control, along with the entire Iberian Peninsula. The four Arabs had pretended to be Spaniards, and in fact had lived in Spain for years as a sleeper cell just waiting for the call to action that they had recently received. They carried Spanish passports. They had worked at menial jobs, and had been looked down upon by the average Spanish citizen. Hatred for the Spaniards, whom they regarded as depraved lackeys of a Western civilization destined to fall to Islam, oozed from every festering sore spot of anti-Arab prejudice that they had endured. Now they were about to get even with the Iberian infidels. They were bursting with pride and anger, which in a few more hours, or so they thought, would be vented on the nautical icon to which they were returning. As soon as their ID cards were inserted into the scanning machine that awaited all returning passengers, they were asked to step out of the line of people waiting to pass through the metal detector archway. The four were taken to a room next to the incoming passenger reception area that was used to inspect any purchases or baggage thought to need open inspection. They were met by a mixed team of ship's security police and U.S. Navy Seals, who quickly took them into custody. In a short time they were handcuffed and led away through the crew's corridor to the gangway used by the crew.

As luck would have it, Mercedes' would-be rapist appeared on deck just as these prisoners were being shunted out the back door to be loaded into the riot van provided by the British. He already knew that Rashid and Fatima had been caught. That left only himself and his female accomplice in the security staff to create the confusion that would be required when the attack began. He pulled out a cell phone and punched in a number in Oran. He spoke to someone curtly in Arabic, snapped the lid closed, and walked off, full of self-confidence, to do his rounds. He knew that Mercedes would go and do her work in the dining room. After all, he thought, where could she go on board ship, and whom would she tell about him without fearing very severe consequences either in Chile or at her job on the ship?

The security man was mad at himself for letting Mercedes get the better of him. His evil little mind was running down the list of things he could have made her do for him. What a shame it was that she would be dead before tomorrow morning. Never mind, he told himself; there is still this afternoon. He silently thanked Allah for sending him this infidel woman for him to toy with. He was sure it was a reward for his past faithfulness and an encouragement for him to do his part in his mission to glorify Islam. The power that this little man derived from his desire to force Mercedes to comply with him was remarkable. The more degraded she was, the more he felt uplifted. The more pain he inflicted, the broader was his sadistic smile. Centuries of Arab male supremacy over their women still involved certain restrictions, but with this infidel woman there were no barriers.

Mercedes wondered how this monster could have found out so much about her personal life. Everything must have been carefully planned months in advance, and Diego was certainly involved. The miserable insect of a security man wasn't smart enough to have arranged it by himself. He might have been put aboard the ship to watch Niko, though. He might have seen her go into Niko's cabin, not because he was doing great detective work, but because he had staked out the Captain's quarters. Mercedes decided her tormentor was only a pawn, as was she, in the larger game of Islamist terrorism.

She had to warn Niko no matter what the personal cost. She simply couldn't ignore the fate of the cruise ship with its thousands of innocent people on board. But she had no evidence that this security man was a terrorist, only that he was an Arab, and a particularly obnoxious one at that. She had no way of collecting real evidence, but there were so many things that smacked of Al Qaeda linkages that she would have to tell Niko of her suspicions. After all, she had been right about the faux Chilean Chechens, and all she had to go on was their accent in Spanish. This time she hoped Niko's men would arrest this beast that had told her he was going to ride her like a camel. Getting him off her back was her number one priority, and she would do anything to accomplish this objective.

Niko was on the bridge when Mercedes called him.

"I'm sorry to bother you, Captain," she began. "But it's important. It's about the Lebanese security officer."

"What about him?"

"I think he's part of some kind of terrorist plot. I heard him speaking Arabic to someone. He said the word *Oran*. That's the only thing I understood. When he realized I had overheard him, he threatened me, even though I told him I didn't speak a word of Arabic."

"How did he threaten you?"

"He said he'd tell the company that you and I were having an affair. He said he could get us both fired. I don't believe he was watching me go into your cabin. I'm not important. He must have been watching *you*, and I just happened along. Why would a security officer be monitoring your comings and goings? He must be planning something that called for him to know your schedule and your habits."

"Thank you very much for bringing this to my attention. I'll look into the matter at once."

The Captain knew that Ivan was already suspicious of this man. Threatening to get them fired seemed lame to Niko. To bring charges like this against the captain of a ship, the man would have to have more than his own witness as evidence, and setting up a hearing would take time and be inconvenient for those involved. He had to be bluffing, and the threat was bogus to begin with. Why? Maybe Mercedes, being only a waitress, would think the threat credible. Or perhaps the man didn't need a foolproof story because he assumed the Captain wouldn't be able to testify, possibly because he would be dead. So it didn't matter what the threat was as long as it bought him enough time to pull off whatever it was that he was planning. Captain Niko didn't relish the idea of telling Ivan that he was having an affair with an employee. Perhaps he could just let him know that the man had been seen staking out his cabin.

Mercedes had not told Niko that this man held something else over her head, something that stretched all the way back to her family in Chile. She hoped that Niko would have the beast incarcerated before he could threaten her again. His treatment of her was indicative of the Islamist male's view of women in general and Western infidel women in particular. Mercedes had seen a secretly taped news program on television in which a Taliban man shot an Afghan woman in the head, ostensibly for some minor breach of dress etiquette, and this paragon of fundamentalist Islamic virtues struck her being capable of the same thing. His derogatory attitude towards her was so overt and so extreme that it seemed he had received amnesty from the godhead, and permission to do anything he wished. Sinking the ship, or taking it hostage, would vindicate this extremist's actions, and no amount of disgraceful behavior prior to that great and heroic activity would carry any weight with those who sponsored this kind of violence. He had wanted to make her life exactly worthless, which was his plan from the minute he met her. But now that she had temporarily thwarted his plan, she knew he would do everything possible to make her pay for her temerity. She prayed that the powers that be would be able to give this man what he deserved.

The powers that be were on the bridge at the time, and although they had doubts about the loyalty of the Lebanese security officer and his female colleague from Morocco, they had no hard evidence against them. Mercedes had not told them about the attempted rape. She hoped she would never have to tell Niko about that. If the man was arrested for terrorism, she would never have to speak about it at all.

Both Ivan and Niko knew intuitively that the man was involved in a terrorist plot, but since they couldn't prove it, they could do nothing more than keep him under close scrutiny. What they didn't know, however, was that their Islamist quarry had already been in touch with colluders in Oran.

CHAPTER SEVENTEEN

In mid-afternoon one of the group of fishing boats came abeam of Ali's vessel and called to the men on board. The captain told them he had just received a radio transmission from Oran, informing him that six of their brothers and sisters had been captured on the liner in possession of guns, and had been turned over to shore police at Gibraltar. He mentioned that there were still two operatives functioning on board, and he also reported to Ali that a group of American security people was active on board the *Controller of the Oceans*. Ali thanked the Algerian fishing captain for the information, and his vessel motored back to its previous position in the fleet.

Ali leaned back against the bulkhead and began to think. He had planned a two-pronged attack, but for security reasons he had intentionally not informed the two groups of each other's existence. Those on board the ship would be coordinated with those on board his fishing boat just before the liner reached the explosive net that awaited her in a watery ambush. Possibly two armed jihadists could take control of the bridge, or at least kill the captain if they had the element of surprise, he thought. In a sense not having anyone on board was a good thing, for if his booby trap worked the ship would surely go down anyway, and with none of the brotherhood alive on board, he and Al Jaza'ir would not have the problem of retrieving them. Part of The Detonator's fame was based on his reputation for escaping without leaving any of his men behind. Ali's vision of the *Scythe of Allah* unit called for warriors to fight the infidels, and he liked to recruit fighters. He left the important work of the recruitment of suicide bombers to other units of Islam's force.

Ali's escape plan for the fighters on board the ship called for the launching of the aftermost portside tender at the time of the first explosion in the bow. The tenders, used to ferry passengers ashore in places where the big ship could not get alongside the dock, were always kept fueled and ready to also act as lifeboats in an emergency. When the fighters of the Arab Brotherhood had finished their deadly work on the bridge, they were to set the ship's course on automatic pilot and rendezvous at the boat deck to make their escape. They were to head toward the fishing fleet just over the horizon to the west. If Al Jaza'ir's boat could find them in the ensuing maelstrom, he would pick them up. If not, they would be rescued by one of the boats in the fishing fleet. They would scuttle the tender, and no trace of it or them would ever be found. The insurgents would then make their way home from North Africa, receiving help as needed from certain safe houses along the way. Once at home they would pick up their mundane existences and await the next summons from the *Scythe of Allah*.

Having his people on the ship was an added assurance that she would be steered on the right course. It was not essential to Ali's plan, providing the tampering with the Sat/Nav was done correctly, and if the slight course change went undetected by the navigation officer on board. But to make the plan foolproof, Ali had planned for what he anticipated would be redundant human intervention. The mutineers had been instructed to kill the bridge officers, lock the entrance to the bridge, put the ship on automatic pilot, and head for the escape tender fifteen minutes before the ensuing explosion.

Ali estimated it would take fifteen minutes for the big ship to be brought to a complete standstill from its cruising speed. If, for any reason, no explosion occurred, Ali's cadre of terrorists would shoot everyone in sight, create as much mayhem as possible, and leave quickly. At least the casualties and the damage would serve as a warning to the infidels that none of their degenerate achievements were safe from the scythe of a disapproving Allah. His training as an engineer always made Ali conscious of the enormous costs the infidels were incurring to protect them from the just retribution of Islam. The loss to the unbelievers from the sinking of their nautical icon would be as nothing compared to the ongoing cost of the future security measures that they would be forced to take.

The failure of the first phase of his plan by the capture of the brothers on the cruise ship would merely instill a false sense of security on board the *Controller of the Oceans.* The crew would think they had averted an attack, and in this frame of mind they wouldn't be expecting phase two or the calamity that awaited them. Ships had been terrorized before, but sinking a vessel this size had never happened in times of peace. Ali's master plan, if successful, would result in the first incidence of a world-class ship being sunk by an enemy that had no Navy. That would be an accomplishment worthy of Allah and worthy of the Detonator. A victory of this magnitude would prove to the world that there could be no peace or tranquility until all people professed Islam, and all worshipped the One God, Allah. Ali was committed to his game plan, and even though his back-up tactic was compromised, his main plan was still viable. He remained optimistic as he sat in the fishing boat waiting for dark, and waiting for the burst of light that would dispel the dark, and announce that the giant ship was perishing. The others of his band took strength from his serenity while they cleaned the guns and made them ready.

At mid-morning David Feingold announced with a whoop of delight that he had solved the problem with the Sat/Nav. When he had calmed down a bit he explained that he had known for some time that the original factory-built unit had been tampered with, but he hadn't been able to figure out exactly what the tampering was meant to accomplish. He now had the answer.

"Well tell us, then! We're all ears," said Ivan.

"Someone has written a sub-routine in the satellite receiver so that any time the ship is within a short distance from the prefixed default, the Sat/Nav will guide the ship over a nearby point of latitude and longitude. It will do this regardless of the pre-set course being steered, or even a course steered manually by a helmsman. There's no signal to indicate this is happening, so nobody on board would know the course had been altered slightly. We're only talking about a small amount of distance, probably ten miles maximum. The only thing that's certain is that if we use the main Sat/Nav we're going to transit 27 degrees, 11 minutes, 18 seconds north latitude where it crosses 5 degrees, 30 minutes, 41 seconds east longitude on April 17th sometime tonight. I, for one, don't want to be on board at that moment," David said gravely.

Captain Constantine heard the ruckus and came over to see what the fuss was about.

"What do you recommend we do?" he asked, when he heard what David said.

"I'd use the stand-by Sat/Nav to steer with until tomorrow. If you like, you can run the main navigation system in parallel mode to the spare, so that you can tell how much of an error was inserted into the program. Once you've passed the default position it may be all right to start using the main system again, but I'd be careful on your return trip west, just in case the reciprocal kicks in."

"If I understand you, you're saying that if our course was close enough to steering the course backwards on our return voyage, the reciprocal course could also be affected?"

"Yes, Captain, that's a definite possibility. Whether you sail east or west on the same latitude, you're bound to cross the same longitude. I'm not an expert in the functioning of these devices, but just to be on the safe side I'd ask the manufacturer of the unit to replace it. After all it's their instrument, and your crew had nothing to do with the programming of it, therefore I think you should be supplied with a unit that works properly."

"Thank you Mr. Feingold. I'll contact the supplier at once."

Ivan began thinking aloud. "We're lucky that the waitress Mercedes reported the passengers with the peculiar accents. That tip led to the subsequent arrests of a total of six suspected terrorists, and may lead to others. The tampering of the Sat/Nav is another matter, and it makes me suspicious that we're facing a multi-pronged attack. It's just possible that we were intended to discover the people on board. They may be only a diversion to take our minds off the real danger. I don't think we were supposed to discover the funny business in the navigation system. That's far too subtle, too planned, and must be the work of a mastermind who thinks in the longer term."

"Assuming that is true," Captain Constantine said, "What do you think should be our response?"

"I'm still working on that." Ivan replied. "At the moment my feeling is that we're in the gun sights of a clever terrorist plotter. Trying to deal with his devious tactics is like playing three-dimensional chess. I'm not sure we've unraveled the whole scheme as yet."

"I think we should avoid the position where the Sat/Nav is trying to take us," said Niko. "I will use the spare navigation equipment and steer around the point to which we are being guided. Who cares what they are planning? Let's just not go to their party."

"That's one way to approach the problem," said Ivan.

"What else is there to do?" the Captain asked.

"Well, we could capture the rest of the terrorists instead of just avoiding their trap."

"Yes, but can we do it without jeopardizing the ship? My responsibility is to keep my vessel, crew, and passengers safe. This is not a warship."

"You're right, Captain, but we have an opportunity to show that terrorism doesn't pay. If we remove these modern day pirates from the seas, we may very well be saving many more lives than just those on board this ship."

"I grant you that, but is it my job? Should my company be expected to undergo such a risk? We have already invested a great deal of money and effort in security measures in order to defend against such attacks. Is it now to be our chore to go on the offensive and hunt down these villains?"

"No, that won't be necessary. But my government has committed huge resources to defend your ship. Without our help you wouldn't have known about the Sat/Nav and you might have sailed into very serious danger without any warning. Furthermore, you have my word that the U.S. will continue to assist you in every way possible to maintain the safety of your ship. If I understand you correctly, you're planning to change the course of the ship to avoid the default point that we've discovered."

"Of course, you didn't expect me to ignore your warning, did you?"

"No, but there are other steps that could be taken."

"Such as?" Captain Constantine inquired.

"Well, instead of just changing course you could halt the ship short of the danger point, and allow our Naval personnel to investigate the waters ahead," Ivan said. "I believe if you do it this way the pirates will come back to find out what happened, and when they do, we can capture them."

"Do you mean to imply that your Navy will sweep the waters before we pass through?"

"No, I mean that you will change course to avoid the hot spot, but you will delay doing it just long enough to make the rats curious enough to come out of hiding. Then *we* can trap *them*, instead of the other way round."

"Very well, Dr. Welland. I will communicate with our fleet captain in our headquarters and tell him what it is you wish me to do. If I receive his permission I will do what you ask, although it will take a lot more fuel to halt this ship, and then get it up to cruising speed again."

"Good, that seems fair to me. Now let's get Brooklyn up here with the satellite photos that were taken last night and this morning. Perhaps then we can do some additional planning."

Brooklyn answered Ivan's page without delay. She arrived with many photos that had been faxed to her on the ship by CIA analysts in Virginia. She spread them out in the order they had been taken. The technicians had isolated the area in the western Mediterranean Sea where Ivan had requested surveillance. The time period started just after dark and continued on with a photo for every ninety minutes of elapsed time. The resolution of the photos was quite good, considering they were taken from one hundred miles above in the total darkness of night.

Below each photograph were written the comments of the satellite photo analyst. These statements and explanations were meant to tell the layman what he was looking at when seeing the photos for the first time. Included in this information were the type of vessel and its speed. From studying these photos the CIA, Navy, and Coast Guard could observe any ship larger than a rowboat. This digital electronic and photographic equipment eliminated the possibility of large-scale naval surprise attacks. The Normandy invasion during World War II would have failed if the Germans had had this capability. It was also useful during the Cuban missile affair when Russian freighters had been discovered trying to deliver intercontinental missiles to Cuba. The eye in the sky technology had been honed to a fine point over the years and had brought a measure of security to the world that its populations didn't yet realize or appreciate.

With the photos spread out in order, Ivan and Niko examined them and read the analyst's interpretations. A series of little dots just to the south and slightly east of the proposed course to be sailed by the *Controller of the Oceans* represented the usual fleet of fishing boats from Mostaganem, Algeria. According to the analyst's notes, this was typical for the time of year. The fleet of boats would arrive in the area, set drift nets, and stay for several days until they had caught their limit. Then they would return to their home port and stay put for several days. Ivan and the Captain noticed that during the previous night one of the fishing boats had become separated from the rest of the fleet and had moved away to the northeast. The analyst from the CIA had noticed it, too. He couldn't be sure why this one boat had moved away from the fleet, but his comments indicated that it seemed to be setting a net. Perhaps it was looking for a better fishing ground. In any case the boat had returned to the fleet the next morning.

As far as Ivan could tell from the photo, the fishing boat had operated in the east west shipping lane used by large ships when transiting the Mediterranean Sea in and out of the Straits of Gibraltar. The lane included the proposed course of the cruise ship. The fishing boat had remained there throughout the night.

It was impossible to escape the conclusion that perhaps it had been setting a mine. They couldn't be sure, but it seemed as if the boat could have been using the fishing fleet as its cover. Or, of course, it could have just been doing a little poaching in the area in which fishing was prohibited. As long as the *Controller of the Oceans* was under threat of attack, its Captain had to assume the worst, and be prepared for it.

"It would be standard operating procedure for terrorists to try to lose themselves in a crowd," Ivan noted. "How would this tactic be any different, except that it's being done at sea?"

Captain Niko agreed. "We would never be able to tell electronically which fishing boat was the culprit if it were surrounded by other similar boats."

"Would we be able to tell non-electronically?" Ivan asked.

"We might be able to tell visually if we were close enough. The boat with no fish on board would ride higher on the water, as opposed to a boat loaded with a cargo of fish in its hold. If we could go aboard and search the boats we would soon find out which one had not been fishing."

"I don't think we'll be able to count on being given that opportunity," said Ivan. "I lean towards having the malefactor identify himself."

"How do you propose to arrange that?" asked the Captain incredulously.

"I'm not sure yet, but curiosity is great bait for a shark among fishes."

CHAPTER EIGHTEEN

The passengers had all returned from their explorations of historic Gibraltar. This night was to be one of the gala events of the cruise. The diners were to dress formally for a special dinner. Tuxedos for the men, and long, elegant dresses for the women were the uniforms of choice. The chatter in the dining room was at a noticeably higher pitch than usual, as the guests looked each other over. Commander Mercer and his dinner partner, Lieutenant O'Neal, were as striking a couple as any in the room for the first serving. The two officers were playing at being a married couple, which was difficult for them as both had avoided marriage for the past few years of their lives in order to pursue training opportunities that would help them rise in their careers.

"At least she didn't have to pretend to have children," the Commander thought. Children were conversational sore spots for Lieutenant O'Neal, as her parents were always nudging her to get married and make them some grandchildren. She usually begged off with the old cliché that she hadn't met the right guy yet. Actually there was a lot of truth in her story. She had dated off and on in high school and at Annapolis. The military men she met were high testosterone types, which automatically put her into a career competition. She had enough of that in her life without bringing it into her home. The assignments she had in the Navy had so far not provided her with access to an eligible pool of men who were not in the military, but who were confident enough in their own manhood to allow her to be herself. O'Neal hoped that future assignments would bring her into contact with more suitable candidates for marriage than she had yet met in the Navy Seals.

Mercer had his problems, too. He usually found his most successful dates to be with intellectual women, as they were more interesting. Like Ivan Welland, he was too intelligent to date women whose minds were only average. Unfortunately the female professoriate, his best hunting ground, was populated mostly by neurotics and political liberals who often made him waste his precious time while they tried to convert him to their way of thinking. The end of these relationships frequently came when the liberal professors became totally intolerant of his career choice, and began treating him as though he were a war mongering neo-Nazi when he didn't immediately agree that they were right and he was wrong. He had to wonder what kind of nonsense they were indoctrinating their students with, since they were more concerned with political correctness than with the facts themselves. Nurtured by the teat of liberty, they had seemingly grown up, formed their own pack, and returned to bite the mother that had fed them. He always wondered how we had managed to allow people like this to be in charge of the young minds of America.

Neither Mercer nor O'Neal was comfortable playing the self-importance game. In the military it was always clear who had the chevrons, bars, or stars. The civilians at their dinner table were involved in some not-too-subtle sniffing to arrive at some kind of less-than-perfect order of hierarchy. Fortunately there was a minister among the ten seated at the table, and when his occupation became public knowledge the others backed off the material success button a bit. The Seals were grateful that for some reason a man of the cloth could still have a dampening effect on the greedy, gluttonous and galling gathering with whom they were supposed to be enjoying dinner.

When the meal was over, the passengers from the first seating filed out to attend the first show of the live cabaret-style entertainment in the magnificent shipboard auditorium. Mercer and O'Neal filed out too, but they headed back to the bridge to receive their next assignments. Ivan and Niko had been putting the finishing touches on the plan to thwart the terrorist attack that they were now certain was in the offing.

"How was your dinner?" the Captain asked the Seals.

"It was a wonderful meal. Far better than the officer's mess on board our Navy ships, I can tell you," Mercer replied.

"Yes, Captain," Lieutenant O'Neal chimed in. "I totally agree with the Commander's opinion of the food. It was superb. Thank you so much for your hospitality."

"You are most welcome, my dear."

"Now let me show you what we've decided to do," said Ivan. "I want you all to feel free to speak your minds if you have any ideas to add, or if you'd like to take issue with our plan in any way."

"Yes, sir," said Mercer.

"There are three parts to the plan, and all of them require the assistance of the Seal team. The first job is to protect the officers on the bridge so they'll be able to maneuver the ship. The second is to launch the Seal boat so you can search for mines in the waters ahead of the *Controller of the Oceans* as we approach the default latitude and longitude. The third is to capture or destroy any boat containing terrorists that arrives to participate in, or gloat over, their murderous raid. Does anyone see it differently?"

"That seems to be it in broad strokes," said Mercer. "But can we get into the details now?"

"Certainly," Ivan replied. "Let's start with how we're going to protect the Captain and his merry band, shall we?"

"Captain Niko, can you tell me, please, where you and your bridge officers are positioned when the ship is under way?" Mercer inquired.

"I am seated in the chair in the center," the Captain said, "and the helmsman is just to my right. You have no doubt noticed that we no longer have steering wheels. These days steering a large vessel like this one is done with those little levers that resemble joysticks from a kid's video game. The actual steering is done by electronically-controlled hydraulics. The navigation officer is posted to the left, where you see the radar screens and the Sat/Nav equipment. The communications room is to starboard. That's where Dr. Welland's assistant, Ms.

Brooklyn, has been working. There is a junior officer roaming around keeping a visual eye out to sea. My cabin adjoins the bridge at the port far side, and that's about it."

"What happens when you're not on the bridge, Captain?" O'Neal asked.

"My first officer, who is also a fully-qualified captain, stands in for me. He has two assistants who alternate watches with him. Under normal conditions I have so many duties of a social nature that I am not personally able to be on the bridge as much as I'd like to be. I'm always there for docking and undocking maneuvers, however, and of course I can be paged or called anywhere on board the ship if I'm needed."

"Thank you, Captain," said the Commander. "Would you be kind enough to summon your chief security officer? I think he and I can work out the stationing of guards to protect the bridge. There is no need for you gentlemen to spend time on this matter."

"Is your boat ready to be launched?" Ivan asked Mercer.

"Yes, it just needs to be shoved out the door," he replied. "The Seal team is on full alert, and they've been briefed as to the nature of their mission. They'll be in the water in seconds, once I give the signal. They'll be in radio contact with me at all times. The team consists of the best-trained combat Special Forces that we have available. They're equipped with weapons such as RPGs, sharp shooter rifles, automatic weapons, handguns, and a .50 caliber machine gun. I wouldn't want to go up against them in anything less than a destroyer."

"I am sure you are right," said Niko.

Ivan grabbed the nautical chart that he and the Captain had been working on. The suspected point of contact was circled in red. "We don't want to approach this point on our course until the waters have been cleared and found to be safe. The Captain has decided to halt the ship just before we get to that position. Since it takes the ship such a long time to come to a halt, the enemy is bound to notice that we're stopping. It's during this time that the on-board attack should begin, if they still have enough manpower left to mount an attack."

"Isn't my ship going to be a sitting duck during this time?" the Captain asked.

"It would be if our enemy were a submarine," Ivan said, "but fortunately the terrorists are not that well equipped yet. Bear in mind that I've ordered air cover for the ship starting in about an hour, so that if there are any surface vessels in the area, we'll know it. The choppers are staged on Isla Alboran. They are fully-armed, night-attack helicopters and they've been briefed on our mission. They won't fire unless I order them to."

"I've seen what those babies can do," exclaimed the Seal team leader. "They carry the keys to hell. I wouldn't want to be on the wooden boat that provokes them."

"The owners of the cruise line are very grateful to the USA for all this assistance," said the Captain. "They have asked me to convey their appreciation to you and your government. They have left the handling of the ship in my hands. If I wish to stop the ship they will support that decision. That clears up all my questions of authority and responsibility, and I am fully committed to the plan that Dr. Welland and I have agreed upon. Gentlemen, and lady, let us make our final preparations, and may God be with us all."

It was a pleasant night at sea. A quarter moon hung in the sky, providing just a sliver of light pecking through the blanket of stars that covered the ship. Clouds came and went overhead, showing off an ever-changing kaleidoscope of the heavens to any observers looking upward. Those who looked down were treated to luminescent green splashes of color as the ship plowed its furrow through the plankton-laden sea. Occasionally one could see a school of bottle-nosed dolphins playing around the ship and daring it to outrun them. Those passengers not familiar with this facet of dolphin behavior were mightily impressed by the natural speed and gracefulness of these mammalian aquatic stars. Passengers who had chosen to watch this performance instead of the live show in the auditorium were not short changed. It was hard to know whether this last remaining species of Mediterranean dolphin was celebrating its fitness in having survived where its weaker relatives had failed, or whether they were just performing for the enjoyment of the audience on the decks of the *Controller of the Oceans.*

The boat that Ali had commandeered to carry the *Scythe of Allah* to the throats of the infidels was allowed to separate gradually from the fleet. Half the fun for a jihadist came from observing the cataclysmic results of his efforts. Ali knew that his men would appreciate having the opportunity to see the sinking of the newest icon of western nautical depravity. He too wanted to be close enough to hear and smell the explosions of his latest and biggest masterpiece of terror. He imagined that he, along with the rest of the world, would be watching the catastrophe on television for years to come. What a joy it would be for his men to also know that they had taken part in this mission. The martyrs on the 9/11 flights had worked their miracle in New York City. Ali would accomplish his feat on the floating metropolis in the Mediterranean, and if Allah permitted, he would gleefully watch the show over and over again as it was transmitted to the world by CNN and other major television networks.

Those full-time fishermen, who had only recently become part-time terrorists, were hoping that the plundering example provided by their piratical forebears would also lead them to some booty as well. From time immemorial the Arabs had been battlefield scavengers. Like vultures, Ali's crew had visions of a sea full of life-jacketed dead, or dying rich infidels, their corpses bedecked in watches and jewelry, just waiting to make a posthumous donation to the Algerian fishermen's benevolence fund. They could barely contain their impatience as they waited for the explosion that would bring them the chance to practice this age-old version of Arab entrepreneurialism. Lust for infidel blood, driven by Islamist fundamentalism, hid their hypocritical envy as they sought the same material wealth for themselves that they hated in Western culture.

* * * *

Brooklyn had been in contact with the admiral in charge of Naval Operations in the Mediterranean Sea. In response to her prodding, the admiral had unenthusiastically agreed to send a pocket aircraft carrier on a good will mission to Barcelona. The idea for this naval mission had been Ivan's, and to say that the admiral disliked receiving orders or suggestions from civilians about naval strategy, was putting it mildly. Nevertheless the helicopter carrier was proceeding southwest along the Spanish coast. The plan was for her to be nearby, but out of sight of the *Controller of the Oceans.* In this way they could quickly offer air support if it was needed, but by staying out of sight just over the horizon, the attackers would not be forewarned. Ivan felt strongly that this was the time to catch the Arab miscreants and be rid of them once and for all. It was not enough to avoid their trap; he wanted to capture them, too.

Every two hours Brooklyn had received the latest satellite photos, and had taken them to Ivan for him to study. The fishing fleet was still in the same position as it had been for the past three days. The boat that had wandered away from the fleet had returned to the anonymity of the crowd. Looking carefully at the picture taken from a hundred miles high, it seemed as if one boat was almost imperceptibly drifting away from the group. That boat was the one closest to the course of the *Controller of the Oceans,* and the direction of its drifting was bringing it slowly closer to the big ship. The three men on the bridge were monitoring the fishing boat's progress with suspicion.

"The currents and the winds do not account for drifting in this direction," Captain Niko pointed out. "If this boat were merely drifting, it would not be moving in our direction. I think it's safe to say that this vessel is up to something besides setting drift nets."

"Perhaps it's edging closer out of nervous anticipation," Ivan replied.

"That could very well be it," said Commander Mercer. "It reminds me of a runner trying to get as close as possible to the starting line before the gun goes off."

"I'll bring it to the attention of the admiral," Brooklyn said. "We can have a chopper standing by to intercept this fishing boat if it makes a run at us."

"Good, but let's make sure the vessel is in the attack mode before we unleash the chopper," Ivan said. "I'd rather not have an enormous diplomatic fiasco with the Algerian government. They'll claim we sank one of their peace-loving fishing boats unless we have absolutely certain proof."

"We'll have aerial photographs and witnesses, but it won't stop the Arab media from painting an entirely false picture of the event," Lieutenant O'Neal added.

"One of your Seals is a photographer isn't he?" Ivan asked.

"Yes, sir," replied Mercer.

"Whatever happens, have him take all the pictures he can," Ivan ordered him.

"Yes, sir. I'll see to it."

"From this point on I think we should all be armed," Ivan said. "Captain, are the weapons in your gun cabinet accounted for?"

"They are," Niko replied. "I've issued pistols to my chief of security and his assistant. These men will be posted in the engineering department and will be responsible for working with the chief engineer to keep the engine room secure. They will follow the ship's anti-terrorism protocols. It is of no use to have a secure bridge if the engine room is in enemy hands."

"Right you are, Captain," Ivan said. "Please issue yourself a weapon. You're bound to be a prime target as well. Whoever controls the captain controls the ship, by the way. We'll all be wearing bulletproof vests. Just so you don't feel undervalued, I brought one along for you, too." Ivan handed the stiff garment to the Captain.

It was agreed that when the ship was an hour away from intersecting the position of the suspected ambush, the Captain would slowly diminish the speed of the vessel until she came to a dead standstill, five miles from whatever trap had been set for them. At this point the Seals would launch their boat and investigate the water ahead up to the point of danger. They would use all the electronic equipment at their disposal; depth-sounding sonar, GPSS, and forward radar. If contact with something suspicious was made, the divers would go into the water and have a look. Once they discovered what they were looking for they would disarm the device, or if that were not immediately possible, they'd tell the Captain how to avoid it.

The men decided that if an onboard attack were made on the bridge and its personnel, its purpose would be to assure that the ship continued on to collide with whatever the terrorists had put in her way. The attackers, therefore, would need to begin their assault before the ship reached the trap, but probably not too soon before, lest they be overcome by the sheer number of crew on the ship. Now that the number of terrorists had been reduced by six, it was hoped that if any remained undiscovered, they would shelve their plan of attack.

That was a hope. Ivan did not deal with hopes very well. He wanted certainties, but life wasn't always as organized as he wished it were, so he prepared for the worst. If insurgents tried to gain unauthorized entrance to the bridge, he and his men would be ready for them.

As men do in the calm before a battle begins, Ivan thought of his family back in Washington, D.C. It was the middle of the night there, so Marina and baby Julia would be asleep in their beds. He and the others concerned with the safety of the ship would not see *their* beds that night. It was peculiar to think that the majority of the 3,000 people on board were totally unaware of the preparations being made to ensure their survival. If he had done his job properly, they would never even suspect that they had been in mortal danger while they were taking a vacation cruise. If, through some sort of failure on his part, the *Controller of the Oceans* was lost, it would be a larger disaster than the sinking of the Titanic, and he would be remembered as one of the two men who could have prevented the catastrophe and didn't. He had no doubt that Captain Nikolas Constantine felt exactly the same weight of responsibility.

The passengers on deck didn't expect the ship's motion to change until they approached the entrance to Barcelona's busy harbor. Some very few, whose senses were not dulled by alcohol and who had become attuned to the ship's motions and sounds at cruising speed, would be mildly surprised when the ship gradually slowed down. There was nothing more that could be done. There was no reason to advise the passengers that their lives were in peril. Why risk the ensuing panic that might occur from such an announcement?

The passengers might have a different opinion, and Ivan could imagine the comments of those who thought that since their lives were in danger they should have been informed of that little fact. Yes, this definitely had the potential for putting a strain on the complaint department, he thought. The average person had no idea how many terrorist plots and attempts had been thwarted since 9/11. They *did* know that there had not been any successful attacks since the twin towers fell. But to Ivan's great consternation the media, the unaware, and the political party in opposition managed to ignore that fact.

Responding to the covert operations of a mercilessly evil minority seeking to impose its will on a free society sometimes calls for stealthy action to prevent disasters like the present one. There would be plenty of time for transparency later, but first it was necessary to survive the attack. The people who put their lives on the line for the nation must not be sold out by revealing the game plan to the enemy before the conflict begins. History provides the opportunities for analyzing events, for judging in hindsight, and assigning blame or praise. Ivan believed that as long as we have death-dealing enemies, those we count on to defend us in times of emergencies need to be given the proper tools to work with, including the management of clandestine intelligence and the withholding of information valuable to the enemy.

CHAPTER NINETEEN

In the dining room Mercedes and her fellow servers were bussing the tables after the passengers from the second seating had filed out. As the staff did its work, ties were loosened and a general air of informality prevailed among those who had waited upon the rich and privileged. The cooks were cleaning up in the galley, and the dishwashers took over the prime focus. Huge piles of dishes were being passed into the enormous maw of the commercial steaming machine. Clean dishes and silverware were making an exit along the conveyor at the other end. Gloved workers were removing hot, sterilized dishes and stacking them on a table so the servers could cart them back out into the dining room to set up for breakfast. This daily task was a time of relative ease for the dining room staff. On the one hand they could be informal with each other as they went about their chores, and on the other hand they wanted to finish up the last remaining aspect of their jobs so they could enjoy some leisure time.

Mercedes, however, was in no rush for her work to be over. She didn't want to return to her room for fear that her tormenter would be skulking around in the corridor, waiting for her. She felt that she had been a victim her entire life, and she was sick of it. What was it about her that always got her involved with men who treated her badly? She had been abused so often she regarded it as almost normal. She was actually pleased when her abusers had a modicum of kindliness. It was all she felt she could hope for. She was always concerned about her son, her parents, and her bosses, but who, she wondered, was concerned about *her*?

She took her time doing her work. Her torturer knew her schedule, and had a passkey to her cabin. She felt trapped. She had no one to talk to about her situation. She couldn't report him to anyone on the ship for fear that both she and Niko would lose their jobs if their affair became public knowledge. She had no weapons, and even if she could kill him, the investigation that followed would be unthinkable. She could be prosecuted, convicted and executed if she were found guilty of murder. Her only hope of relief was that it might end soon.

She had no reason to believe that the threat of sexual abuse would be over soon, however, except for something intangible about the Lebanese man's attitude. He seemed to be under very heavy stress. The thought that he might be a terrorist engaged in a mission to attack the ship in some way was in the forefront of her mind. Maybe he was a suicide bomber. That might explain his behavior, which seemed to be part nervousness, part hate, and part fundamentalist fervor. Mercedes knew that Niko was suspicious of the man, and the fact that he wasn't under arrest meant that they didn't yet have the evidence they needed. Rape was not the crime they expected him to commit, but it was the crime she had to fear and avoid until they had sufficient proof of the murderous attack he was to be a part of.

Mercedes had to be back in the dining room by seven AM to serve breakfast. She was tired and wanted to get some sleep before she had to go to work again, but she had no intention of going to her cabin, where she might have to confront a lurking rapist. She decided to leave the dining room through the exit on the upper level, then head for the laundry room. She knew one of the women who worked there, and perhaps she'd let her spend the rest of the night curled up in a corner somewhere.

As she wended her way through the darkened corridors of the lower deck, she imagined that every shadow was the outline of the Lebanese security man waiting to pounce on her. She tried to tell herself that her fears were unfounded, but she still had the feeling that his evil eyes were following her from some hidden place as she scurried toward the laundry room. Every once in a while she would look over her shoulder to make sure he wasn't sneaking along behind her in the shadows.

She was relieved to see some light from the laundry room beckoning in the distance, and she picked up her pace. Just as she was rounding the last corner, somebody suddenly grabbed her from behind. She opened her mouth to scream, but a hand covered her lower face just under the nose, muffling her voice. She kicked and bit, but her assaulter had little difficulty getting her under control.

"Keep walking, bitch," said the familiar voice. "Don't give me any trouble or I'll shoot you in the head."

Mercedes felt the barrel of a gun pressing against the back of her neck. She instinctively raised her hand and bent forward to relieve the pain.

"Don't try anything, or you're dead," the Lebanese security officer hissed. "Keep going straight ahead, do you hear me? Just do exactly what I tell you, and you won't get hurt."

He removed his hand from her mouth so he could hold on to her arm and force her to continuing walking. He stayed behind her, nudging her occasionally with the barrel of the gun to indicate which way he wanted her to go.

"Is this the errand Diego wanted me to do?" she asked him, as soon as she was free to talk. She was hoping to distract him so she could figure out a way to make her escape.

"Yes, and you better not try anything or Diego will make sure your son and your parents will live to regret it."

"Where are you taking me?"

"Never mind that. Just keep marching."

The security officer decided to take the stairs to avoid an encounter with other people. After climbing up several flights of stairs he walked her horizontally toward the bow of the ship. By this time Mercedes knew he was taking her to the bridge, and she feared for the safety of Niko and his officers. What to do? How could she warn them without putting her family in jeopardy? She knew that Diego was merciless and would stop at nothing to make them pay if she refused to cooperate.

Finally they reached the bridge deck. The security guard poked the gun into her spine to move her along the corridor towards Captain Niko's cabin. He needed her to get the Captain to open the door, as his passkey wouldn't work in the locks of the bridge officer's doors. As they approached the Captain's cabin, the Moroccan female security guard stepped out into the corridor. She held a revolver in her hand, and exchanged a nodded greeting with her Lebanese co-conspirator.

The terrorist plan had been well conceived. They must have been hatching this plan for months. Mercedes despised her cad of a husband, who was willing to put so many lives in danger for what must have been just a few dollars.

"Knock on the door," the Lebanese man hissed, "and tell him you have brought him coffee."

Mercedes knocked, but there was no reply. It was unusual, for at this time of the night the Captain usually slept, leaving the ship in the control of his second-in-command. All the years at sea had earned Niko the privilege of being on the dayshift under normal conditions, and he preferred it that way, especially when they were expected to dock early the next morning.

Mercedes shrugged her shoulders to indicate that Captain Constantine was not there, and she didn't know where he was. She hoped they could go away and try another day, but that was not to be. She felt the pistol in her back again, guiding her to the entrance to the bridge. She knew that people were on the bridge, and very likely Niko was, too. She put her hand gently on the door handle and tried to turn it, but it was locked.

Her captors had no idea this was an unusual circumstance. They just presumed the door to the bridge was always locked. Mercedes couldn't think of anything she could do to warn those inside that things in the corridor were not normal.

"Knock," the Lebanese officer ordered, as he poked the gun hard against her spine.

She did as she was told.

"Who is it?" said the Captain's voice.

And then an idea came to her. It was only a small thing, but Niko might notice if she called him *Niko* instead of *Captain*. No employee was allowed to call the Captain by his first name in public. Mercedes could barely bring herself to do it even when they were alone.

"Niko, it is Mercedes. I have brought some coffee for you."
Besides not ordering coffee, he did notice that she called
him by his first name. He knew at once that something was
wrong. He signaled to the others, and pulled out his pistol.
Mercer dropped to his knees, weapon in hand. He was
positioned to the right of the door so that when it swung open
he would have a direct line of fire. He anticipated that staying
lower than eye level would give him a split second of focusing
time over someone expecting a standing target. O'Neal and two
other armed Seals crouched behind the long work counter.

"Don't shoot the waitress," Niko said in a clear, low voice.
"She is a hostage, and she has no part in this."

He put his hand on the door handle, took one last look
around the bridge to make sure everyone was in position and
ready, then turned the handle and pulled the door open just as
hard as he possibly could. The killers assumed they would have
the usual terrorist element of surprise on their side, and were not
expecting to be faced with armed, well-trained marksmen on the
other side of the door.

Mercedes had decided to drop to her knees as soon as the
door opened. She hoped she could do this before she was shot
in the back, but when Niko pulled the door handle with so much
force, she was pulled through the door at an elevation of about a
foot above the floor, landing on Niko's polished black shoes.

The Captain fell backward as a cacophony of automatic
weapons sounded over their heads. The male terrorist crumpled
dead in the doorway. His female companion was down in the
corridor. O'Neal looked outside and found no other terrorists.

The attackers had managed to get off several wild shots
before they went down, but the Seals called out that they were
all unhurt. Ivan, who had taken a position behind the metal
door, had fired only one shot through the open space between
the hinge and the doorframe. David Feingold and Brooklyn,
who were armed but were only to fire if the communications
office was breached, came out to see if everyone was all right.
They quickly saw that all those standing were fine.

Then they noticed that Mercedes, who was straddling the Captain, was stained with blood. Niko had taken a wild round in the shoulder from the security officer's weapon, and it was his blood that was on Mercedes' blouse.

The Assistant Captain, who had put the ship on automatic pilot just before the firefight broke out, was in the process of retaking manual command of the vessel's steering, and was continuing to slow the engines according to the plan Niko and he had agreed upon. As soon as he saw his wounded Captain on the floor, he picked up the phone and called the ship's doctor.

When the doctor arrived at the bridge he found a great deal more than he had bargained for when he accepted the position as ship's doctor for this cruise. There were three people down from bullet wounds. He quickly ascertained that one man was dead, and a woman in the hall was nearly dead, burbling blood from her mouth from internal wounds. Inside the bridge the Captain was sitting up, leaning against the counter. Mercedes was holding a towel against his wound to stanch the bleeding.

The doctor looked at the wound and quickly determined it wasn't life threatening. During the time it took to examine the Captain's shoulder, the female Moroccan terrorist expired. The doctor called his nurse and told her to bring two body bags up to the bridge at once. The Seals offered to help bag the bodies, an enterprise with which they had some prior experience.

"Doctor," said Niko, "you have thirty minutes to sew me up and get me back to my duties."

The doctor was an emergency trauma specialist who had served in the British Royal Marines. He had seen plenty of wounds and plenty of good men who had received them without complaint. He recognized Niko as being from that school.

"It's too bad you weren't shot in the chest," the doctor joked. "You'd be up on your feet and back at work already." He patted the bulletproof vest that Niko was wearing.

Niko stood up and took the towel from Mercedes. "I can hold this on the wound until I get to the surgery," he said. "You go to your cabin and change your clothes. Then come back with coffee, for real this time."

Ivan turned and spoke to the doctor softly. "I trust you'll agree with me that it's best to keep this gunfight to ourselves. If the passengers find out, you may have to prescribe tranquilizers for hundreds of people by tomorrow morning."

"And who are you?" the doctor inquired.

"I'm Ivan Welland, Security Advisor to the President."

"Then if I were to guess, I'd say your presence on board is not an accident."

"That's on a need-to-know basis, Doc, but I sure would appreciate it if you could get the Captain back here in a hurry. We may need him again soon."

Ivan looked altogether too innocent for the doctor to miss his meaning. Mercedes, meanwhile, she was very concerned about Niko. She also felt responsible for getting him shot. As she made her way to her cabin, she put another towel over her shoulders so no one would see the blood. She relived the fray in her mind, going over every detail, and wondering if she could have done things differently. She could have been killed, as she was not wearing a protective vest like Niko's.

She was glad that the fanatical Arab terrorist was dead. He deserved what he got. In many ways it had all turned out for the best. Her evil persecutor was gone forever. Her affair with Niko was still secret. Niko still had his job, and so did she. She had not had to tell Niko about what the despicable security man had tried to do to her. Her family was safe. Diego, might never receive his blood money, but he couldn't blame her for that. He would have lost it on wine, women, and gambling anyway.

When Mercedes reached her cabin she looked longingly at her bunk. Instead, she took a quick shower and went to the galley to rustle up some coffee for the brave men on the bridge.

The doctor injected Niko's shoulder with local anesthetic and sewed up the wound. It was more than a superficial scratch. There was an entry and an exit wound. The injury would leave a hollow depression when it healed, but the small amount of muscle that was missing would not be enough to permanently impair the function of the shoulder. The doctor warned the captain that the wound would hurt when the anesthetic wore off.

"Gunshot wounds are very subject to sepsis," the doctor told Niko. "Punctures are the wounds most likely to become infected, so I want you to take these antibiotics. Try not to use the shoulder and arm. Don't get it wet for a few days. Come back tomorrow, and I'll change the dressing and have a look. In five days I'll remove the stitches. Be sure you take the pills."

"Thank you, Doctor. I'll follow your instructions," Niko said, as he got up to leave. "Tell me, how do you happen to be so experienced with battle wounds?"

"I joined the British forces in Iraq as a trauma surgeon," the doctor said. "I have a question for you, too. How did so many armed people happen to be on the bridge when the terrorists tried to burst in? You must have known they were coming."

"These days, more than ever before, we follow the Boy Scout motto, *Be Prepared*," Niko said. "Can you deal with the corpses until I can arrange for disposal of the bodies?"

"Indeed. Would you like me to do a little amateur autopsy on the cadavers? Maybe we can learn something of interest."

"Why not?" the Captain said thoughtfully. "But right now I must get back to the bridge. Thank you taking care of me."

"He's a good man," Ivan said, when the doctor left. "He got you back on active duty in jig time. How are you feeling?"

"Actually, I don't feel too bad. He patched me up and injected me full of painkillers and penicillin. If I'm shot again tonight I'll be ahead of the game," Niko smiled.

Just then Brooklyn appeared with some printouts.

"Here's the latest satellite photo, sir. The fishing boat is moving towards our course again. I've advised the Navy."

"I believe you were right all along, Dr. Welland. This fishing boat is probably just waiting to pick up the pieces. *Our* pieces," said the Captain.

"I take no pleasure in being right," Ivan answered, "unless we escape safely and bring the villains to justice.."

"I'm trying to get the FBI crime lab interested in taking the bodies of the terrorists off our hands," Brooklyn said. "I imagine their forensic experts ought to be able to do some matching of fingerprints and DNA to see if our dead friends are linked to any other incidents of international terror."

"Good thinking," Ivan said. "Now that we're all a part of Homeland Security, we can only hope that the CIA and the Bureau will exchange information for a change. Comparing their DNA to the DNA samples of prisoners and dead jihadists could tell us something about which families are members of these Al-Qaeda cells. It might also reveal the whereabouts of the leaders of the Arab Brotherhood, so we can cut off some of the tentacles that have been spreading all over the Middle East."

"The Bureau is sending their top Arabic interrogators to Gibraltar to see what they can learn from the prisoners that we dropped off there," Brooklyn told them.

"That's good too," said Ivan. "Make sure they let us in on it if they find out anything useful. Is there any other news from Washington? Does anyone miss us?"

"Only one person so far."

"Oh, who's that?"

"The President," Brooklyn said.

"What? Did he really call?" Ivan asked.

"Yup. I told him you were out fighting the bad guys. He said he felt more secure already, now that he knew that."

Mercedes was pushing her coffee trolley up the corridor to the bridge, and she was stunned to find no bodies and no mess. She had been wondering how she was going to get the coffee into the room with the corpses strewn in the entranceway. When she knocked on the door everything inside went still, and revolvers appeared in several hands simultaneously.

"Who is it?" Niko asked.

"It is Mercedes with the coffee you ordered."

Mercer went to the door so the Captain would not have to get out of his seat. He looked outside in both directions, and then admitted her. He still had his gun in his hand.

"Are we going to have more shooting?" Mercedes asked, looking at the officer's pistol.

"I hope not, little lady," the Commander said in his best John Wayne voice.

No one but Ivan got the joke, but everyone on the bridge did get coffee. Mercedes served her Captain first.

"You should serve my guests first, Mercedes," the Captain pointed out.

"I only serve you first when you have been shot," she said, and everyone laughed good-naturedly.

Mercedes had been anxious about Niko, and wanted to have a close look at him. She decided he looked quite well for a wounded man, but perhaps the drugs were sustaining him. She served coffee to everyone who wanted a cup.

"How did that awful mess get cleaned up so fast?" she asked the Assistant Captain as he took his cup of coffee. "I was dreading being asked to clean it up."

"The nurse took the bodies down to the doctor's surgery, and then I had housekeeping come and clean up the rest," the officer said. "You know you don't have to do everything on the ship yourself, Mercedes."

"No, sir."

Captain Niko was pleased that his subordinate officers were following his orders to the letter. The great ship was now down below half speed. In forty minutes they would come to a dead halt. Just time enough to drink the coffee, eat a piece of cake that the chef had sent along, and for Mercedes to clear away the cups and plates. The radar showed no ships or obstructions ahead. Ivan stepped out onto the starboard observation deck that led out from the side of the bridge. He could see nothing but sky and sea, although he vaguely thought he heard a helicopter engine whirring in the distance.

The men chatted amiably. There was an undercurrent of nervousness among them that all the officers were trying to cover up. Each of them worried. None of them complained. No minds present were exempt from *what ifs*, and *supposings*. Mercer and O'Neal announced they were going to get into their wetsuits so they would be ready to launch the Seals' boat immediately after the ship was at a standstill. Wishes for good luck and good hunting were exchanged, and the Seal officers left the bridge. Those left behind all hoped the Seals would be safe, and keep the *Controller of the Oceans* safe, too.

Mercedes returned her cart to the galley, and was intending to go to her cabin to sleep, as she was scheduled for the early breakfast shift. On the way she thought perhaps she would step out on the crew's deck to get a little air. She leaned against the rail and looked over the side at the dolphins.

She had the impression that they were disappointed that the ship had discontinued their race. At its present speed it was no trick for the sea mammals to keep up with the ship. She imagined what might be going on in the minds of these animals. They probably thought the ship was a huge fish which had slowed to feed. Perhaps, she thought idly, they should do some fishing on their own. As she considered the playful frolickers, she was surprised and strangely disappointed when suddenly the whole school disappeared.

Her mind turned from thoughts of her mammalian relatives to thoughts of her own plight. It was very likely that she had narrowly escaped death. She was certainly glad to be alive and breathing the fresh, clean sea air as she looked up at the sky and down at the sea. What did it mean to be alive? She had felt like dying two hours before when she had almost been forced by the security guard to do despicable things. The quality of her life, however, was evidently secondary to the preservation of it, for here she was. Was dumb survival the raison d'être of her life? To what extent was freedom the most significant part of being alive? The Muslims seemed to feel the primary purpose of life was submission to a God who wanted adherence to his rules, even to the giving of one's life or the taking of someone else's life, in order to assure devoted obedience.

Mercedes was beginning to understand that only a free person can really feel devotion. In order to properly follow, you must be free not to follow, or the choice means nothing. All her life she had been a victim because she had not truly exercised her free will. She had allowed others to control her so often that it had become her mode of life. The worst of it was that she had accepted dominance, and believing there was no alternative, had even begun to like it. The sparing of her life gave Mercedes an opportunity to see things as they really were, along with the incentive to change. She would no longer bend to the will of a fear-driven religion, or bend to obey the wishes of men. That part of her life had died when she was allowed to live.

She had resolved to make changes in her life, and was about to go to her cabin when she became conscious of the fact that the ship was hardly moving any more. Although she had been on the bridge a few times she had, of course, not been privy to the strategic planning that had been discussed there. She was puzzled but not concerned. There had been no sign among the officers on the bridge that the engine room personnel had been taken hostage or killed. Niko had returned to his post, wound and all, and had resumed command. She interpreted that to mean that things were under control, but that the officers were being careful just in case there was more danger ahead.

It was very still on the bow of the ship, with the engines hardly audible and with the vessel in irons. She was enjoying the light, balmy breeze coming off the continent of Africa to starboard. Her body was tired, but her mind was restless. She knew she would toss and turn in her bunk before falling asleep, so she thought she might as well remain on deck.

She began to think about Captain Niko. She contrasted his patient, kindly character with that of her husband. There was really no comparison. Diego was a treacherous tyrant, a lecherous lout, and a sorry swine of a man. Niko, on the other hand, was honorable, thoughtful of others, and fair-minded. He led by example and was well liked by all who served under his leadership. Niko's only flaw was his inability to resist the women who threw themselves at him. But she had the feeling that he was sated now with women of easy virtue, and was ready to change his life.

At that moment, alone with her thoughts, she decided to divorce Diego. She'd never find a decent man as long as she was married to him. Why stay married to him? Was it to satisfy some regulation of a religion that in its attitude to divorce was easily as cruel to women as was Islam? Staying with Diego was only a hypocritical show of cultural cowardice. It didn't do anything for their son either, as Diego was the worst possible example of what a father should be. Separating a drunken, gambling, abusive, and financially unsupportive father from his son would be a blessing in the long run for the boy, no matter what his innocent childish loyalty might be now.

She was only sixteen when she had impetuously married Diego. Should she be made to pay for that mistake forever? If Diego made even the slightest move to bring disgrace on her family she would sue him for child support, slander, defamation of character, or whatever charges she could find to bring against him. He was afraid of the law, and couldn't afford a lawyer anyway. She would bet anything that the coward would leave her alone rather than pay her child support. Yes, she would make an end to this disastrous marriage as soon as possible.

Her thoughts focused on Niko again. She looked out to sea and reflected on how much of his life must have been spent doing what she was doing now, staring out into the emptiness at the distant horizon. The little she knew of his personal life bespoke an unhappy marriage, divorce, separation from his children, and other lonely experiences. She imagined his trysts, assigning them little importance, as sex without love is banal. That was something she knew all about. It was at the core of her pointless suffering as a helpless victim.

Mercedes believed that if she could get Niko to talk about it, he would realize that he was being victimized, too. Perhaps he already knew that his women were using him to flatter their egos, and maybe he was ready now to stop this unproductive behavior. Perhaps they could work on it together. Half dreaming, she was startled into alertness by the sight of a small boat coming into view along the port side of the ship and proceeding directly ahead off the bow.

As soon as the *Controller of the Oceans* had come to a standstill, the loading door opened and the Seal team pushed their boat out into the Mediterranean. The team, in their black wet suits, sat in the boat as it dropped a few feet down into the water. The ship's door closed after them. The Seals looked up at the white hull of the ship, which from sea level looked as formidable as the White Cliffs of Dover. The ship accentuated the comparative small size of their boat. Yet in spite of its size, the little boat was responsible for seeing to it that the monster remained intact.

Mercer turned the key and the muffled engine started up. The boat was nearly silent at slow speeds. He steered it along the port side of the ship, heading towards the bow. They looked up, but were unable to see anyone on board. None but the most serious revelers and gamblers were still awake. But the boat, being so close to the ship, was hidden from the view of those who might be on the upper decks looking down at the water.

As far as Mercer could tell, no one on board had seen the launching of the Seals' boat. Only Mercedes on the bow, and Niko and his officers knew there was a small boat out there in the darkness. The *Controller of the Oceans* was equipped with huge searchlights, but Ivan and the Captain were loath to use them, particularly while the ship was standing still. It was difficult enough to keep the huge ship's position a secret under the best of conditions, as international regulations demanded that all ships have running lights and stay within recognized shipping lanes. The cruise liner was white as snow, as long as the Empire State Building lying on its side, and as hard to hide as an elephant in a bathroom. Ivan and Niko had done their best to dim the lights and keep radio silence, but there was no way for the modern Barbary Pirates not to know that the juiciest prey in the world was in their pond. Their radar had not shown any obstacles ahead or beneath the ship, so they were compelled to search the waters with divers.

Mercedes watched in awe as the unlit boat moved slowly ahead of the ocean liner until it disappeared from sight. The bottlenose dolphins saw it, though, and just before Mercedes lost sight of the Seals' boat she could see them surrounding it as though it were a long-lost friend or a newborn calf spawned by the larger ship. It was as if they had grown impatient with the mother ship, and were glad at last to be moving again, and to have company along the way. A mile or two later, when the divers went over the side, the mammals were joyfully beside themselves, happily cavorting with the Seals. The divers, for their part, could have done without this attention, but they were not given the option, as now they were in the dolphins' playpen.

Mercer had devised a grid pattern to superimpose over a blow-up of the nautical chart of the area, and Pugni had steered the course up to the exact position of the suspected danger. He had noticed a strong, east-moving current. They had used the boat as a centerline and divided the team into two parts – one worked the left side of the boat, and the other the right.

The dolphins did not have a game plan and came at the divers like so many torpedoes from all directions, just turning away in the nick of time before smashing into them. Mercer had to smile at the playful nature of these animals, although they made it hard for him to read the delicate electronic sensing devices that he was using to help him in his search for foreign objects in the water.

The divers' search moved further away from the big ship as little by little the Seals progressed in their work. Mercedes could no longer see any sign of the boat from her position on the bow of the ship. The divers were using large, waterproof searchlights to peer into the sea as they moved ahead bit by bit. Boats floating overhead could not see the lights under the water.

Ivan, Niko, and the crew on the bridge waited to hear from the Seals if it was safe to proceed. According to the GPSS on the boat the Seals had passed Lat. 27 degrees N., and Long. 5 degrees E, and still had not discovered anything unusual. Mercer ordered his frogmen back into the boat. His team couldn't swim ahead of the ship all the way to Barcelona.

Ivan was pacing back and forth on the bridge, his long legs striding from one side of the bridge to the other. His mind was grappling with Mercer's lack of findings. Had he imagined the whole external plot against the ship? Perhaps they had thwarted the terrorists by capturing or killing all that were on board, and that was the end of the affair. That would be nice if it were true, but it didn't account for the Sat/Nav equipment that had been tampered with. Why would one go to the considerable length of reprogramming the navigational equipment? No, he felt certain that something out there was set to explode. Perhaps the mine, or whatever it was, had moved off station. What could cause that? Was it placed in the wrong location? Then it hit him.

"Captain, do you think the currents could have shifted the mine?"

"Well the currents are strong here, but they are irregular. The cold water from the Atlantic Ocean comes in with the tide and sinks under the warm Mediterranean seawater on its way out through the Straits of Gibraltar. It's possible that the mine dragged its anchor due to the current, but how can we know?"

Just then there came a terrible roar, and a geyser of upwelling water shot high into the air. It was as if a twenty-inch battleship shell had landed in the sea ahead of them, out there near where the Seals were diving.

Captain Constantine grabbed his night binoculars and looked ahead. He was immensely relieved to see the Seals' boat speeding back towards the ship. Seconds later there was another explosion, then another, then another, and another…

CHAPTER TWENTY

When he heard the blasts, Al Jaza'ir slapped the diesel engine into gear and revved up the motor. He headed toward the sound of the explosions, coaxing as much speed out of the vessel as he could.

Ali was staring in the direction of the noise, looking baffled. Where was the smoke and fire? The normal detonations of his IED devices on land were different from those at sea. Underwater demolition was another thing altogether. He missed the attending fires, and the debris scattered everywhere.

He had heard the sound of many heavy explosions, so he had to assume that the *Controller of the Oceans* had run into his net of death. What else could have made such explosions? No other vessel had a deep enough draft to make contact with his ingenious, custom-made underwater bombs. Perhaps the big ship had sunk under the sea so quickly from multiple hull piercings that the anticipated smoke and fire was extinguished before it even had a chance to start.

In any case he would have to see for himself, therefore he permitted his greed-driven but loyal crew to continue on to the scene of the perceived disaster. All eyes were focused on the distance. Finally they could see the superstructure of a huge ship looming up from the sea as they approached. Ali realized at once that the *Controller of the Oceans* had not been visibly damaged. Perhaps it was disabled? It appeared to be dead in the water. He was mentally reviewing the details of his plan to see what could have gone wrong. He decided that the members of the SOA on board the ship must have taken charge of her and forced her to stop for some reason, but what reason? Why had the ship not been damaged? That was impossible. What had set off the explosions, then? At the end of his determined musings, Ali decided they must go to the aid of those brothers on board the cruise liner. Perhaps they could scuttle the ship, sink her, and take their brother Muslims off the ship before it went down.

The younger jihadists on board the boat were heartsick to see the *Controller of the Oceans* still afloat. They had expected to have a picnic just picking up the spoils that floated off the ship, and perhaps shooting a few half-drowned infidel passengers for target practice.

Ali saw that it was necessary to buck up their morale, so he outlined his alternative plan to board the ship and scuttle her. He went inside the small cabin and directed Al Jaza'ir to head directly for the cruise liner. He got out some plans and photos of the ship that had appeared in the newspapers and pored over them. He was glad he had thought to clip the articles out of the paper. He knew that the combatant who could innovate under pressure had an advantage.

He sat in his boat, staring at the unharmed ocean liner in the middle distance. He felt as though he were taking a pop quiz for terrorists. He couldn't understand what had set off the explosions before the ship ran into them, but that was already in the past, and right then he had to concern himself with what they were going to do next.

He forced himself to focus on the present situation. One of his problems was that he had used all the plastic explosives in his net. He had not wanted to have any left on board the fishing boat in case they were inspected later, or in case they were fired upon. The idea was to blow up the enemy, not to make it possible for *them* to blow up *his* boat, so he had used every ounce of plastic he had brought with him. But since fabricating bombs at this point was out of the question, how could they now sink this water-borne infidel cathouse?

Ali had been unimpressed by previous terrorist cruise ship attacks in which a small boat loaded with gunmen sails close to a cruise ship and gets off a few rounds before it heads off to hide. Attacks like those were an embarrassment to a world-class terrorist like the Detonator. The worst was the incident off

Somalia in the Indian Ocean, where a few self-deluded and self-appointed anti-American terrorists took on a destroyer of the U.S. Navy with a rocket-propelled grenade launcher. In a matter of minutes some brave but dumb Muslims were dead, and others taken into custody. That was definitely not Ali's idea of an attack on America.

His leathery, olive-skinned face showed deep concern for his men and their mission. He was not above turning around, escaping, and fighting on another day. He decided to take his lead from Allah, who patiently waited until the infidels were placed at his feet.

Suddenly he noticed some bee-like dark spots buzzing in from the north. Choppers from the carrier took off the moment the satellite revealed that the fishing boat had sped up and was heading for the ship. In a few minutes Ali knew they would blow his fishing boat out of the water if he didn't do something. He ordered the crew to arm themselves. He positioned men with RPGs on either side of the fantail. The others huddled inside the small cabin out of view of the Americans. He told Al Jaza'ir to head for the ship as fast as his boat could take them.

"The Americans won't fire missiles at us if we're alongside the ship," Ali explained. "The helicopters won't take a chance on hitting the ship or its passengers. They may think this boat is loaded with plastic explosives, too, in view of the earlier blasts. We will not disabuse them of this idea. As soon as we can get aboard and take some hostages it won't matter whether we have explosives or not. We will trade our way out of here."

The Algerian at the helm did as he was told. The fishing boat, helped along by the winds, made it just in time and nestled against the windward side of the *Controller of the Oceans* before the first chopper could fire on it.

"Now we have a stalemate," Ali said to his comrades. "We must turn it into a victory. Al Jaza'ir, see if you can get the captain of this floating brothel on the radio."

Mercer and his team had scrambled frantically out of the water and back into their boat at the sound of the first explosion. They had not yet reached Ali's net, and were still perhaps a half mile from the blast site. Lieutenant Pugni had spun the boat around on its axis and was heading back toward the ship before the plume of erupted water had fallen back into the sea.

As the boat sped away, Mercer observed the succeeding explosions and the eruptions they caused. He noticed that they seemed to be occurring in a straight line, at a distance of about a hundred feet from each other, as if they were connected together in sequence. There were so many explosions, and so many geysers in the air that the Seals could only watch in fascination.

Had they not been so focused on the explosions behind them they might have noticed the fishing boat closing in on the *Controller of the Oceans* from its starboard quarter, but by the time they turned their attention to the front, the big ship was between them and the other boat, and they could not see it making its approach. Nor had they been seen. The Seals did notice the two Marine attack helicopters hovering near the stern, and wondered what it was that seemed to be the focus of their attention. The Seals came along the port side of the ship, totally unaware of the drama on the starboard side of the vessel.

"Let's get the Captain on the radio and see what's going on," Mercer said to Pugni. "We need to know if they want us to go back to the site of the explosions and see what caused them, or if they want us to bring the boat back on board."

Pugni couldn't get through to the Captain because Niko was busy listening to threats and receiving demands from Ali.

"Send the helicopters away, or we will blow up your ship," Ali was saying.

Ivan, standing next to the Captain, heard the demand and whispered, "He's bluffing. If he were intending to pull a suicide mission, he would have done it already."

Welland wanted to be directly in charge of the negotiations. Command of the Seals and the Marine helicopters were under his purview, but he realized that command of the civilian ship at sea was naturally in the hands of the Captain. He hoped that Niko had developed some confidence in him and his men by this time. He had tried carefully to bring him into the decision process every step of the way. He had no right to seize the ship, or commit it to any actions without the consent of its Captain. On the other hand, he was the man in charge of an ongoing hostage situation involving two thousand or more American passengers and the U.S. Navy in international waters.

"Captain," he said finally, "I'd like to handle this situation. I promise not to exceed my authority and to obtain your consent before involving your ship in any action. I will fully disclose my plans before I do anything. Do you agree?"

"We are partners," Niko answered. "I have tried my best to do my part. I trust you to do yours, so I'm handing the hostage negotiations to you. But I cannot relinquish my responsibility for the safety of my ship and its human cargo."

"Agreed," Ivan replied. "I think it best if I impersonate you during the radio communications with the terrorists. In this way we can buy some time if I tell the terrorist leader that we have to check various things with the Navy before we can agree to his demands. And by the way, do you have any ideas about how to handle this situation?"

"If I were sure that the terrorist boat had no explosives on board," Niko said, "I'd just sail away and leave him behind. His boat can only do 12 or 15 knots at top speed. This ship cruises at 30 knots, so we could just run away from him."

"That would certainly be the simplest thing to do, but I see three problems. First, he may not have heavy-duty explosives on board, but he might have the RPGs that terrorists seem to have no trouble obtaining, so your ship would almost certainly suffer some damage and casualties between the time you start and the time you get up to speed. Second, we don't know yet what caused the detonations, or if there are more up ahead that could possibly sink this ship. And third, if we run away we don't catch the scoundrels."

"Well, what do you have in mind, then?"

"The terrorists evidently don't know that the Seals are in their boat just on the other side of the ship. If they had known this, they would never have dared to come so close to your ship. Likewise if the Seals had seen the terrorist's fishing boat they would have put themselves between us and the enemy, and either attacked them or called in the helicopters to do it."

"How are they going to do that?" Niko inquired.

"It would only be fair if we sank their boat in the same way as they planned to sink yours."

"What do you mean, Dr. Welland?"

"I mean from underneath the water with explosives. I'm going to order Commander Mercer and a party of Seals to swim under the *Controller of the Oceans* and place a small remote-controlled bomb on the leeward side of the hull of their boat below the waterline. The remainder of the Seals will stay with their boat. When they hear the explosion they'll circle behind this ship and put the final touches on the fishing boat, and its crew, too, if need be. If we do this correctly we shouldn't even scratch the paint on your new ship."

"I see," the Captain said admiringly.

Ivan took it to mean that the Captain approved. "Now I must speak with that terrorist," he said, taking the microphone.

"This is the Captain of the S.S. *Controller of the Oceans*" Ivan said. "I have decided, for the sake of the lives of my passengers and crew, to accept your condition that we send the helicopters away. But you understand that I don't command the U.S. Navy. I will have to contact them and request that they recall their aircraft. This will take a few minutes. I will call you back as soon as I have an understanding with them."

"Don't take too long," Ali replied. "I'm not a patient man, and neither is my God."

As soon as he clicked off, Ivan grabbed the other radio mike that was tuned to a secret frequency shared with the Seals' boat. "Commander, come in please."

"Mercer here."

"This is Welland. Please listen carefully. While you were out exploding those mines, the fishing boat that we've been watching for two days closed in on us. She is at this moment cheek to cheek with us on the starboard side. The chief terrorist got us on the radio and claims his boat is loaded with plastic explosives. He's threatening to blow us up if we don't obey his orders. The choppers showed up from the carrier when they observed the fishing boat heading straight for us. Unfortunately they were too close to us, and the choppers didn't open fire on the boat because they were afraid they might damage the ship. So I need you to dive under the ship, place an explosive charge on the windward side of their hull, big enough to sink her before they can fire at us. I'm sure the terrorist was bluffing about his boat being loaded with plastic explosives. If he had intended a suicide mission, he would have done it when he first arrived. How long will it take you to rig such an explosive device and place it where it will do the most good?"

"Not long, perhaps ten minutes. We're all still in our dive suits, so we're ready to go as soon as the CPO can rig us up."

"Excellent. I'll stall off the terrorists until you give me the word that you're ready. By the way, they don't know you're there. So what you'll do is this: you and the other divers will swim under the hull of the ship and place the explosive devices. After you've done that, you'll swim back to the other side again, where you'll be shielded from the explosion. The Seals remaining with the boat should float down to the stern of the ship, and when they hear the explosions they should come to the starboard side, prepared to suppress any remaining terrorist fighters. Are you clear on your mission? I didn't think you'd mind, so I promised Captain Constantine that you can do this without putting a scratch on his new ship."

"Roger that."

"Welland out."

"Brooklyn," he called, "Get me the admiral on that carrier."

In a couple of minutes Ivan found himself connected to Rear Admiral Smith. "Admiral, can you have your pilots pull back out of sight of this fishing boat for now? We've got a bomb threat situation underway here and the choppers are making our Arab friends nervous. The Seal team we've got on board is handling the situation. I'll contact you when it's safe for your aircraft to stand down. I'd appreciate it if you could recall the choppers now."

"Will do," he replied.

Next, Ivan called Ali.

"Is this the fishing boat captain of the boat alongside the *Controller of the Ocean?*" Ivan asked.

"Yes, of course. Who else did you expect it to be?"

"The helicopters are being recalled. It may take a couple of minutes for the message to get through, but just hang in there and don't do anything foolish."

"I'm not in the habit of doing foolish things," Ali snarled.

"Now that I've sent the helicopters away, I don't suppose I can send you away too?"

"Very funny, Captain. I'm glad you can still joke at a time like this. Now I would like to come aboard your ship."

"I'm sorry, but unless you have a ticket, that will not be possible," Ivan said.

"We will see in a few minutes how the funny Captain goes down with his ship if you don't give me respect."

"Very well, with the utmost respect and admiration I can tell you that we do not dock in the dark in the middle of the ocean. Setting up the gangway takes time, and since you didn't supply us with sufficient notice of your visit, all the equipment, stairs, and railings are stowed safely away while we are at sea. It will take time to rig all that up."

"Then, Captain, you'd better hurry up and do it."

"I'll see to it right away Sheikh," Ivan said.

"How did you know I was a Sheikh?"

"You are obviously used to receiving respect, so I assumed you're an important man, that's all. What is your name, then?"

When Ivan received no answer he turned to Captain Niko and said, "You heard the most respectable Sheikh. Have your men prepare to lower the gangway. Tell them to work slowly, very slowly, but show some progress so the Sheikh doesn't get too antsy. Meanwhile Mercer can go about his business."

CHAPTER TWENTY-ONE

Mercer quickly formed a huddle with his men and relayed to them the information he had received from Welland. He divided them into two groups – the water team and the boat team. He would head the diver's team, and Pugni would be in charge of the boat. The divers would dive under the *Controller of the Oceans* and find the fishing boat. They would place their charges in the center of the keel, so when the explosives were detonated they would break the spine of the boat as well as blow a big hole in the hull.

Ivan had instructed Mercer to shape the charges to explode away from the cruise ship, so he could keep his promise to Niko that he would not damage the hull of the liner. Mercer pictured the fishing boat being blown in half, with the two ends quickly filling with water and sinking. The blast was to be Pugni's signal to come around the stern of the big ship, ready to shoot it out with any terrorists who might still be able to fire a gun.

The diving team consisted of Mercer, O'Neal, and the CPO. The Chief was the demolition expert, and he set to work preparing the charges. The Commander and the Lieutenant put their arms back in the tank harnesses, checked their regulator gauges, and strapped their weapons around their thighs. The Chief handed each of them a charge, and they helped him into his tank harness. Flippers went on last. They sat on the gunnels of the boat, with their masks adjusted over their faces. It was a routine they had all done in Seal training school. They looked at Mercer for his order, and when given, the three leaned backwards and slipped into the sea.

Pugni's crew checked the guns to make sure they were ready to fire. He told the boat crew that they should plan to pick up the dive team first, and then the survivors of the blast, if

there were any. He told the men that they could use the extra
manpower on board in the event they had to take or subdue
prisoners. He had his men push the boat along the side of the
big ship in the direction of the stern. They were in the lee of the
ship and the sea was calm as they slipped along. He would start
the engine only after he heard the explosion, so as not to tip off
the enemy that there was another vessel in the water. When the
Seals' boat reached the stern, Pugni looked at his watch and
gave a hand signal to his men to wait in silence.

O'Neal and the Chief followed Mercer by holding onto fine
strong pieces of line that were made fast to his oxygen tank and
streamed off his back for ten feet. These were necessary
because it was night and they didn't want to get separated from
each other. They could not use their underwater lights, as the
men on the terrorist vessel might see them. Mercer swam down
under the hull of the *Controller of the Oceans,* keeping contact
with the hull with the back of one hand. The biggest challenge
of the mission was to locate the fishing boat in the dark from
under the water. The giant ship was over a thousand feet long,
and although it was resting alongside, the fishing boat was only
sixty feet long, and Mercer didn't know whether it was
amidships, forward, or aft of the cruise ship. His guess was that
it was not anywhere near the bow, as boarding gangways were
generally located a bit aft of amidships. Mercer led his team
towards the center of the ship.

He would have to go to the surface for a quick look to
make sure they were going the right way. It was critical that he
not be spotted by any of the men on the fishing boat. This was
a time when he could have used a dolphin diversion, but for
some reason there were not any around. Stealthily he poked his
face out of the water. He could see the dark form of the fishing
boat against the white hull of the cruise ship. It was perhaps
two or three hundred feet further aft. He swam underwater
along the chine of the ship leading his tethered teammates
towards their target. Mercer no longer needed to surface. They
could work in the dark as they had practiced many times during
exercises. The greatest risk was that one of them might be

trapped between the ship and the fishing boat and be crushed. The steady breeze coming off the continent of Africa created a chop that slapped against the liner's windward side, bouncing the fishing boat into its steadier consort. A diver's nightmare is being caught between two bobbing boats.

Ali was speaking English on the radio, and his crewmen were admiringly listening to him harangue the Captain. He was prodding him to hurry up and get the gangway set up. He was accusing Captain Constantine of stalling, and threatening dire consequences if he didn't move faster. The crew might have better used their time than nervously sitting around waiting for the gate to a pirate's dream to descend, but even those loyal to Islam are prey to the seven deadly sins. While they were calculating how much loot they could take off the ship before it sank, the Seals under their boat were planting the means for them to reap their heavenly reward first.

Ivan, high above on the bridge of the cruise liner, was continuing to irritate the terrorist leader with his quick-witted banter, and his slow-moving progress with the gangway. In between lame excuses and delayed responses, Ivan was ordering his people to make a number of preparations in advance of the anticipated explosion of the fishing boat.

"Brooklyn, you and Damian should write a short speech for the Captain to deliver over the intercom to the passengers to explain what has been going on. Be careful to reassure them that all is in order now, and that we'll be continuing our voyage as planned in a very short time."

"Okay boss," Brooklyn said.

"Captain, please have the doctor stand by to treat injuries, and to receive more corpses if things go that way. Also, have your searchlights directed down into the water so we can see what we are doing the second the explosion occurs. When we are clear of these pirates we will still have to proceed as though there are mines in our path. I suggest that we send the Seal boat ahead of us for a few miles and let them finish checking the waters ahead of us. I don't believe they ever reached the longitude and latitude default before the explosions occurred.

Why the blasts happened prematurely is still a point of interest for me, but a fortuitous one for us. Let me know if you concur." "I will do as you ask," the Captain answered respectfully. "My dear Sheikh, you must be patient with us. You've seen how we obeyed your command to dismiss the helicopters. We are operating in good faith here, I can assure you."

Neither Ivan nor Ali believed that. Ali's men wanted to fire a rocket propelled grenade at the ship to make a point, as they loved to shoot those things anyway. Ivan was waiting to hear from Mercer that the explosive charges were set so that he could give the order to remove the ship from the clutches of the pirates, and the Sheikh from his Sheikhdom.

Ali was a good tactician, but he was being forced to act precipitously. His original plan had not turned out as expected. He had no idea that the voice he was hearing on the radio was not the Captain's at all, but belonged to the very man that had thwarted his scheme for the destruction of the *Controller of the Oceans* from the beginning. In like fashion, Ivan didn't suspect that he was speaking personally to the most revered bomber of Islam. The man known to the inner sanctum of Al-Qaeda as the Detonator was obscure to American intelligence sources.

Ivan Welland, the brains behind the raid of the caliphs in Mecca, was unknown in Islam, but feared anonymously by reputation. He had influenced the President to hire perhaps the most renowned scientist in the field of genetic research to set up a data bank containing DNA samples from proven terrorists, dead or alive. This information was being used to identify links between terror cells throughout Islam, and had resulted in many arrests, and the foiling of a number of plots. Now he was the President's National Security Advisor, and had his history been known in the Islamic world, he would have been the target of the mother of all fatwahs.

Fate had conspired to put these two brilliant men into direct contact with each other, but had failed to advise the participants of their dubious fortune. It was an unscheduled battle of Titans. Ali, trapped at sea by the American attack helicopters, had done what any fighter does when he has an opponent with a longer reach: he moved inside. Ivan, unable to strike a leveraged blow because of the proximity of his opponents, prepared to launch an uppercut, as prescribed in the boxing texts.

Mercedes had to cross back and forth on the deck several times to see what was going on. Except for the Seals, she had been the closest one to the explosions. She had thrown herself down on the foredeck and had remained there as one after the other of Ali's plastic explosives detonated. When the maelstrom ended she had stood up and watched the Seal boat speeding back to the ship. Then she had witnessed the fishing boat heading for the *Controller of the Oceans*. She had seen the helicopters approach the fishing boat, and she had noticed the way its occupants had tucked the boat in against the sides of the ship so they would not be fired upon by the choppers. She had witnessed the Navy Seals slide beneath the water and disappear from view. She did not need script directions to tell her what was going to happen and which side of the ship she should be on to see the next act of the drama. But one part of it took her completely by surprise. She was astonished when she saw the gangway being made ready to take the fishermen aboard.

She leaned out over the rail as far as she could so she could see more clearly. When she did so, she was spotted by one of the terrorists who took aim at her with his rifle and fired. Mercedes felt a sharp sting in her left upper arm, and she was knocked backwards to the deck. She sat up, leaned back against the railing, and felt blood oozing out onto her clean shirt. She knew she was not hurt too badly, as her first thought was of her second shirt of the night being made bloody, but this time it was *her* blood. She held her hand over the wound and felt the warm, wet blood.

Down on the fishing boat Amin, Ali's son, was reaching up to grab the gangway apparatus that was being lowered very slowly and was now just out of his reach. The rest of the crew were standing, guns in hand, breathing hard with excitement in the cabin, waiting to run up the gangway as soon as Amin called to them that it was ready. Under the hull the plastic explosives had been made fast to the bottom of the fishing boat. Mercer and his two cohorts had retreated back under the keel of the ship. They had to put some distance between themselves and the explosion that was coming so as to avoid being concussed. As soon as they were in position, Mercer contacted Ivan.

"Everything is ready down here. We await your order to fire," Mercer said.

"You may fire now," Ivan answered with relief. He had run out of stalling tactics, and the enemy was only inches away from boarding the ship.

The force of the blast and its accompanying tumultuous thump knocked Mercedes down again. Amin, standing on his tiptoes on the roof of the cabin reaching upward, was launched straight up in the air like a rocket. When he came down he was on the gangway as he had intended to be, but he had sustained several broken bones from falling and smashing against the aluminum gangway. He was unconscious, but he was the lucky one. The men in the cabin had been injured to differing degrees by the force of the explosion.

The boat was nearly severed in two, and was sinking fast when Pugni and his Seals careened around the stern of the big ship and bore down on the bodies of the terrorists which were floating free in the flotsam of the remains of the fishing boat. The searchlights on the liner came on and lit the area. Mercer and his team reappeared from beneath the hull of the ship, but this time astern of the sinking fishing boat, which enabled them to be picked up by Pugni in the mount and dismount style used by the Seals to retrieve their swimmers from the water. The Seals' boat then dealt with the terrorist casualties.

The maimed dead bodies of Al Jaza'ir, his son, Muhammad the boat owner, and the two divers were retrieved before their boat sank. They had been killed instantly. Sheikh Ali bin Yemeni had somehow managed to survive, but he had sustained massive injuries and his continued survival was by no means assured. The *Controller of the Oceans* had managed to escape without damage as Ivan had promised her Captain.

In the annals of terrorism conflicts, this one would go down as a great victory for the United States. Ivan, whose boyhood ambition was to be an admiral when he grew up, was relieved to have in a small way followed in the footsteps of Nelson, Dewey, Farragut, and Jones. If he were a writer of fiction like Forester, this little battle would have been worthy of one of the episodes in the life of a modern Horatio Hornblower.

Ivan received the news on the bridge radio from Mercer on board the Seal boat. He immediately had Brooklyn connect him with the admiral on board the carrier that was waiting to receive instructions and a status report from the liner.

"Admiral? This is Welland."

"Yes, Dr. Welland, this is Admiral Smith. What do you have to report?"

"The terrorist boat has been sunk by your capable Navy Seals team. We have some casualties. Oops, let me clarify that. The casualties are *theirs*, not ours. Do you have a trauma doctor on board? Can you take the wounded prisoners off our hands?"

"I'll send a Medi-Vac chopper over to pick up the human detritus. How many are we talking about?"

"We've got four in need of body bags, and two not far from it," Ivan said, disapproving of the admiral's choice of words to describe human remains, even terrorist remains.

"Okay. Have the Seals put them in their boat and pull away from the ship so our helicopter can approach in safety. We'll transfer the merchandise without landing."

"Roger that. Thanks. Welland out."

Ivan called Mercer to relay the admiral's instructions. Then he turned to Niko. "We might as well lower the gangway the rest of the way so we can remove the body that's on it."

"No worries," said the Captain. "It is already taken care of. You probably didn't realize that our gangway is hydraulically controlled. It cycles on, or off. It is either all the way out or all the way in and it has only one speed."

"I didn't know that."

"That's what I thought, so I took care of it for you."

"How did you manage to slow down the process and stall long enough to allow the Seals to do their job?"

"We just switched it on once, and kept pulling the power plug, and pushing it in again to lower the stairs inch by inch. We did it just enough to make them think we were obeying them."

"Congratulations Captain, and thank you. That maneuver may have saved many lives, and possibly your ship as well."

"You are too kind," said Niko trying to be humble. "At sea we must learn to improvise. Now if you don't mind I'll call the doctor, and tell him he can go to bed."

Down in his surgery the British doctor was surprised to see a patient walk in at that hour of the night. Normally he would not be there, either. He had been roused from his sleep and told to be prepared to receive wounded and dead in his clinic. None had come. He had just about given up on the idea that he would be needed, when Mercedes entered his office. She was bleeding from a wound that was almost precisely the same as the one the Captain had sustained earlier. He was working on cleaning her wound, and was about to start suturing it when the phone rang.

"Hello, Doctor's office." he said.

"Doctor, this is the Captain speaking. You may go back to bed now. I'm glad to say that we have no casualties that need your services."

"*You* may have no casualties Captain, but *I* have one."

"What?"

"I have a young lady in a waitress uniform with a gunshot wound," the doctor said.

"What is her name?"

"Her badge reads Mercedes León from Chile."

"I'll be right there," said the Captain. "Don't let her die!"

"What a strange thing for the Captain to say," the doctor blurted out to Mercedes as he returned to stitch her up.

"What did he say?" Mercedes asked.

"He said, *Don't let her die. I'll be right there.* Did I say anything about dying?" the doctor asked Mercedes.

"Not that I heard," said Mercedes.

The doctor went on sewing. Just as he cut the thread the door to the surgery burst open and Captain Niko flew into the room. He ran to Mercedes and enfolded her with his good arm. "My God, what happened to you? How did you get shot?" He didn't wait for an answer, but began kissing her forehead gently, then her cheek.

The doctor was amazed by the degree of solicitous concern he was showing for a crew member. Was he this concerned for the health of *every* member of his crew? If so, what a captain this was! What was happening on the ship? Two shootings in one day, on a cruise liner – that had to be some sort of record. And the call he had received instructing him to be ready to take in casualties and bodies, what was *that* all about? Multiple explosions, helicopters, small arms fire, and then the only casualty is a waitress. What kind of battle was this? Certainly not a food fight, thought the doctor.

When Niko's fears for Mercedes' life were finally allayed, he said, "How did you, of all people, manage to get shot?"

"I decided to get a little air after I served coffee to you and the officers. I was on deck up by the bow, and I witnessed everything. The explosions, the two small boats, the divers, the sinking of the fishing boat, everything. I looked over the rail to see what was going on, and someone on the fishing boat shot up at me. That's all I know."

The doctor finished dressing Mercedes' wound, giving her a penicillin shot and some pain pills. A lot of questions still remained in his mind about what was taking place on board this ship. Listening to Mercedes' explanation informed him much more than most of the crew and all of the passengers. Evidently the *Controller of the Oceans* had repelled at least two attacks by terrorists, which explained to some extent why the ship had been at a dead stop for the past hour or so, and it also accounted for the explosions. A full explanation was not forthcoming at this time, he gathered, so he released his patient and told her to get some sleep.

"I'll see you to your cabin, Mercedes," said Niko. "Thank you, Doctor."

The Captain followed Mercedes to the door of her cabin. He hardly ever went to the crew's quarters. He felt his presence there would be seen as spying on the crew in their private non-working times, so he didn't do it.

When he saw Mercedes' Spartan little cabin, Niko felt guilty for living in such elegant surroundings at sea while she was consigned to such a small space.

"You must envy me my wound so much that you decided to get one too," he said jokingly, stroking her arm gently. "I'm glad you're all right," he added, looking at her with love in his eyes. "I wish I could stay here with you for a while, but I must return to the bridge. We might not be done with these wretched terrorists yet."

Mercedes smiled at him and stretched out on her bunk. Niko could see that the doctor's sedative was taking effect. He kissed her tenderly, and quietly left her room.

"See you tomorrow my darling," he whispered, and turned off the light.

Back on the bridge, Ivan reported to Niko that the wounded prisoners had just been loaded aboard the helicopter. Mercer and his team would go ahead of the ship and continue to make sure that no mines remained undetonated. Both Niko and Ivan hoped that this whole nasty business was now at an end. They decided to shine the searchlights ahead to light the area as they slowly followed the Seals. Their presence could no longer be a secret to any living thing for miles around.

"You're going to have a lot of explaining to do, Captain," Ivan chuckled, indicating with a nod of his head the passengers who were now gathering at the railings on every deck, craning their necks to see what had caused the loud explosion that had disturbed their peaceful slumber at such an ungodly hour.

CHAPTER TWENTY-TWO

The exhausted Seals moved slowly ahead, carefully searching the waters as before. Unlike the earlier tour that was accompanied by a rollicking school of dolphins, this trip along the plotted course of the *Controller of the Oceans* was devoid of any living thing, as far as Mercer and his team could see. Lieutenant Pugni piloted the boat, keeping it exactly on course. They were using every available light to peer into the dark waters. They swam in two teams, working on either side of the Seal boat at a width slightly more than the beam of the ship. One swimmer on top of the water looking down, and one at a depth equal to the draft of the ship looking up, guaranteed that a ship the size of the liner would not encounter any mines.

The team had just about reached the default point on the Sat/Nav when they encountered thousands of strange floating lumps of matter. The last time they had moved along their grid they hadn't come this far because the explosions had gone off, and they were driven back to seek safety. Gingerly they now approached the lumps and examined them. They turned out to be chunks of fish. They cautiously checked the larger pieces, looking for booby traps. Perhaps these were the equivalent of roadside IEDs put there in the way of the ship.

On closer inspection Mercer decided the chunks of flesh did not come from fish, but from dolphins. They could not be booby trapped because they were at various depths. Some were floating on top of the water, while others were sinking slowly at random depths. Mercer studied the pieces and decided that these chunks of flesh and bones must have resulted from the blasts that had gone off just a little while before. The school of dolphins must have swum into the trap that had been set for the cruise ship.

But how could this be? It was hard to associate this behavior with mammals that reportedly have built-in sonar. Why would they swim into anything, let alone a number of mines? Mercer had heard fishermen complain that large fish like sharks, whales and porpoises often swam into their nets and got tangled up. In their efforts to untangle themselves they tore fishing gear to pieces and made themselves very unpopular with the fishermen.

That must be it, Mercer thought. The explosives had been hung on fishing net, and when the first dolphin hit the net and the first bomb went off, the noise must have confused their sonar. Instead of avoiding the danger, the entire school must have plowed into the net, setting off all the explosive devices. Mercer related their action to the beached whale pods that for no apparent reason occasionally run themselves onto beaches to die. After all, dolphins are just small whales, so this was the most logical explanation for the strange phenomenon.

The Seals continued on for a half mile beyond the default latitude and found nothing but clear water ahead. Commander Mercer ordered his teams back into the boat. He radioed the bridge and told them it was all clear, and that the Seal team would return ASAP. Pugni needed no encouragement to put the throttle down and take the tired crew back to the ship for some well-earned rest. Once the Seals and their boat had been lifted back aboard, the *Controller of the Oceans* began to move forward, gaining speed minute by minute. Mercer dismissed his crew with a short "well done" speech, and headed to the bridge.

Ivan was profuse in his praise and compliments, but he was a professor, after all. He saw that Mercer was not comfortable with flowery compliments, so he backed off a bit.

"How were you able to set off those explosions, and not be blown to smithereens?"

"We didn't set off any explosions except the one under the fishing boat," Mercer replied.

"All right, Commander, then tell me what did?"

"I don't know for sure, but I have a theory."

"Okay, what's your theory?" said Ivan a bit impatiently.

"We discovered a lot of chunks of fish flesh just now. The explosions must have killed some large aquatic mammals. We were being led along by a school of playful dolphins that were making it difficult for us to read our gauges because they were constantly swooping close to us.

"Swooping?" said Ivan. "Can dolphins swoop?"

"Plunging, then," Mercer replied. "You know, diving and playing around, the way dolphins do. So anyway, my theory is that they set off the explosions. I think the explosive devices were hung on an anchored fishing net. The first dolphin accidentally swam into the net, setting off the first bomb. The noise from the bomb exploding disoriented the sonar responses of the other dolphins and they swam into the net, which set off the rest of the bombs."

"You mean to tell me that we traveled thousands of miles, hauling around tons of material, enlisting the help of several of the Navies of the world, using the latest electronic technologies, and the brains and bravery of our best manpower, and after all that it was the *dolphins* that saved our lives and foiled the plans of a very intelligent, determined enemy?"

"Yes, sir, I believe that's what happened," said Mercer.

"If that's how it happened, then it has the ring of divine intervention about it," said Ivan.

"I thought so too, sir. Especially when the dolphins in this area are an endangered species and need all the family members they can get. It's a sort of biological version of the Biblical view that greater mammalian love hath no species than this, that it give up its life for its friends."

Years later, having had sufficient time to reflect on the matter, Ivan still believed that all the laud, honors, and promotions that had been given to him, to Commander Mercer and to Captain Constantine might more properly have been granted to those spirited guardians who allow us to nourish the illusion that we have cruise control.

As for Captain Niko Constantine, he spent no time at all thinking about past glory. He had saved his money and bought a small house in the port of Piraeus when he retired. From his window he could watch the busy port traffic come and go while he drank ouzo or coffee without a care in the world. It would take a little getting used to, this new life of his, but Niko didn't worry about such things. He had been given a generous salary increase and other benefits to compensate him for the additional duties that came along with his new command.

"Niko, we're home!" came his wife's familiar voice. The front door slammed shut, and another little voice called out for her daddy.

Niko jumped up from his chair by the window and ran to greet Mercedes and their four-year-old daughter, Sophia.

"Look, Papa! Look what I made in nursery school!"

Sophia thrust her chef d'oeuvre into her father's face while he lifted her over his head and twirled her around. Mercedes smiled as the two of them laughed in delight. Her husband was as handsome as ever, and still amazingly strong and vital for a man of his age.

Niko lowered his little girl to the ground, and turned to face Mercedes.

"I'll get the groceries from the car," he said, giving his wife a long and lingering kiss.

"Ew, *gross!*" cried Sophia.

"Don't look, then," Niko advised her.

Just then Juan came into the house, carrying several bags of groceries.

"Don't worry, Dad. I've got them."

"You're home early!" Niko observed. "What happened? Did they expel you?"

"No, school got out at three today. There's some kind of a teachers' conference going on," he said from the kitchen.

Mercedes smiled to herself when she heard the adolescent crack in her son's voice. He was becoming a man, and she was proud of him. He was already ten times the man that Diego had been, if you could call him a man in any sense of the word. He had been tried and convicted for conspiracy to blow up the *Controller of the Oceans,* and had been given twenty years to life. Mercedes hoped he would rot in jail. Her parents had both died shortly after her marriage to Niko – probably largely due to the stress that Diego had put them under with all his threats and demands for money. Juan, thank God, barely even remembered him any more. He considered Niko to be his father now, for Niko had adopted him after marrying Mercedes when he retired from his post as Captain of the *Controller of the Oceans.*

As Niko and Juan and Sophia laughed and talked in the kitchen, Mercedes wandered over to the window in the hall and scanned the ocean.

"So this is happiness," she thought.

It was beautiful and quiet, just like the sea. She had had glimpses of it sometimes on board the *Controller of the Oceans,* but she never believed it would fall within her grasp. She felt her throat tighten as she counted her blessings and gave thanks for the family she loved so much.

"Look," Niko said, coming up behind her and putting his arm around her shoulder. "Look out there. See them?"

Mercedes followed the direction of his hand as he pointed out to sea. Two dolphins broke the water and dove back down again, just as two more came up for air. One by one the whole school appeared, cavorting and jumping and diving for the sheer joy of being alive.

Niko drew her close to him and gave her a long, romantic kiss. Juan peeked through the kitchen door.

"Whoops, time for a walk," he called to Sophia. "No, don't come this way. We'll go out the back door. Dad and Mom are tired and they want to take a nap. They're old, you know, and they have to take a nap every afternoon."

"*Every* afternoon?" Sophia repeated, her eyes widening with astonishment. "I don't want to get old, then."

"Everybody gets old eventually," Juan told her. "If they're lucky," he added philosophically.

"Well, who's making them take a nap? They don't have a mom, so why do they have to take a *nap?*"

"Come on, Sophia, let's go to the playground."

"I'm glad *I* don't have to take a nap."

Juan took his half-sister by the hand and guided her out the back door.

Niko scooped up Mercedes and carried her deftly into the bedroom, while Sophia's piping little voice trailed off into the distance.

In their condo in Washington D.C., Ivan and Marina awoke to the hungry cries of their brand new identical twin sons, Lincoln and Jefferson, who, along with their sister Julia, were ready to greet the new day.

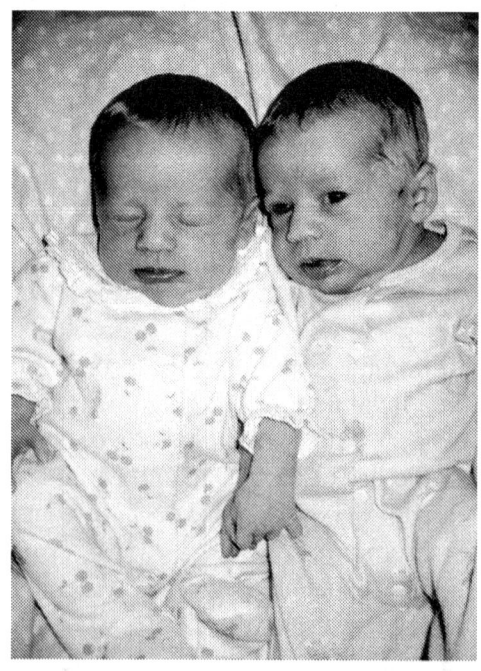

Lincoln and Jefferson Welland

AIDAN DE VRIES

Council of Caliphs

If you enjoyed reading *Cruise Control,* you will also like the prequel, *Council of Caliphs,* by the same author. Brand new first editions are available at www.erserandpond.com, or you may send a check or money order for $24.95 (please add $1.50 sales tax plus $8.00 for postage and handling) to Erser and Pond Ltd, 1096 Queen Street, Suite 225, Halifax, Nova Scotia B3H 2R9, Canada. Checks and money orders should be made out to Erser and Pond Ltd.

www.ingramcontent.com/pod-product-compliance
Lightning Source LLC
Chambersburg PA
CBHW071137260626
47162CB00003B/816

* 9 7 8 0 9 7 8 1 7 6 1 1 2 *